FAST AND LOOSE

NIGEL TRANTER was born in Glasgow on 23rd November 1909 and educated at George Heriot's School in Edinburgh. After leaving school he trained as an accountant, but took up writing full-time in 1936, a career only partly interrupted by service in the army during the Second World War.

Almost his entire literary output is concerned with Scotland's history. His non-fiction, from his first book—*The Fortalices and Early Mansions of Southern Scotland* (1935)—deals principally with his life-long interest in Scottish architecture. He also wrote over eighty novels, many of them drawn from his unparalleled knowledge of Scottish history. Notable among these are *The Gilded Fleece* (1942), *The Queen's Grace* (1953), *Balefire* (1958), *The Bruce Trilogy* (1969–71) and *The Wallace* (1975). Two of his novels, *The Freebooters* (1950) and *The Stone* (1958), are concerned with the Stone of Destiny, a subject of great interest to Tranter, who was involved in negotiating the return of the Stone after its theft from Westminster Abbey in 1950.

Nigel Tranter died in January 2000.

Other B&W titles by Nigel Tranter

THE STONE
THE QUEEN'S GRACE
BRIDAL PATH
THE GILDED FLEECE
ISLAND TWILIGHT
HARSH HERITAGE
THE FREEBOOTERS
TINKER'S PRIDE
BALEFIRE
THE FLOCKMASTERS
KETTLE OF FISH
FOOTBRIDGE TO ENCHANTMENT

FAST AND LOOSE

NIGEL TRANTER

B&W PUBLISHING

Copyright © Nigel Tranter
First published 1951
This edition published 1994
by B&W Publishing
Edinburgh
Reprinted 2000
ISBN 1 873631 29 4

British Library Cataloguing in Publication Data:
A catalogue record for this book is available from
the British Library

Cover illustration:
detail from *Wilds of Assynt* by D. Y. Cameron
By kind permission of Perth Museum & Art Gallery

Printed by WS Bookwell

I

"MONEY!" the young man said bitterly, disdainfully. "Gold—is that all that you can think on? Sordid metal—the base traffic of slaves and Englishry! Are you master of this vessel, sir, or a huckstering Jew!" And he stamped a tarnished-buckled foot on the seamed timbers of the deck.

At his side, the man dressed in priestly black intoned sternly—albeit with a pleasing Highland lilt to his voice. "They shall set up to themselves images, of gold and silver, and shall fall down and worship them! *Amor sceleratus habendi!*"

The third man, much older than the previous speakers, drew a great ham-like hand over lips and scraggy beard, and spat expertly over the side, to leeward, out of the corner of his mouth. "Aye, sirs, I am master o' the *Florabel*, and nae mair a Jew than your Honour or his Reverence, here. But"—he grinned sardonically—"nae mair am I a Samaritan, see you!" And he spat again, with his fascinating accuracy. "Even a shipmaster maun live."

"Scoffer! Heretic! Prostituter of the Word!" the priest declared, turning a pair of lively brown eyes heavenwards—though they took in his companion on the way up.

That young man frowned. "But I told you, fellow," he insisted. "You shall have your holds full of cattle, at Ardcoll, to pay for our passages. You shall have hides, and tallow, and wool . . ."

"And the pick of the queans of twenty glens, whatever," the cleric put in, helpfully.

". . . and *uisge-beatha*. Who knows, my father might even have a little money. Your miserable gold!"

"Aye. I'ph'mmm. May be, your Honour," the mariner conceded. "But, look you, a wheen placks in the pouch is worth a power o' Hieland stots in the heather! Aye. A poor ship-master canna sail on promises. . . ."

1

"Sirrah—do you doubt my word?" his would-be passenger cried, hotly. "Were you mistaking my name?" He drew himself up to his full height—that was just an inch or two less than his reverend companion unfortunately, but still topped a sinewy six feet. "I am Colin Og mhic Colin MacColl, Younger of Ardcoll!" That was as good as a trumpet-blast as he said it.

And the priest's right hand was clapped automatically to the region of his hip-bone, where, beneath his black cassock, something solid and graspworthy seemed to hang. "Eat meat, Son of Colin!" he urged, simply.

"Eh . . . ?" The seaman's jaw fell, he gulped, sought expectoral relief, thought better of it, and swallowed.

"Now—our passages!"

But the sailor only shook his grizzled head wordlessly.

They stared, both the young men. But the ecclesiastic did more than stare. "Fellow!" he exclaimed. "Is it you, a Dumbarton shipmaster, has not heard the name of Colin MacColl of Ardcoll, An Colin Mor!"

The older man tugged at his beard. "Aye, masters, I have. 'Deed, I have. And if you had all the placks and bawbees and Golden Ryals in Scotland, I wouldna gie you passage to Eynart Bay, much less to Ardcoll. Wi' all respect to your Honours, I would not—as sure as my name is Wat Gibson!"

"Why not, man? What ails you?" the young man with the difficult name demanded.

"Need you speir that?" Captain Gibson cried. "Speir of any shipmaster on the Clyde, and he'll tell you. Devil the one will put his bowsprit north o' Barra Head. And wi' fair reason! Na, na, my masters—you're no' sailing wi' Wat Gibson."

"But, damnation, man—you are the only master sailing out of Dumbarton, or Glasgow itself, for north of Inveraray, within the month! If we do not sail with you, we do not sail at all."

"That may be, sir." Gibson opened his lips to a gap-toothed grin. "Unless ye get a Queen's ship to take your Honours!"

"Reprobate! Watch your words!" the priest warned, to his companion's black frown. "An Colin Mor's arm is long!"

The mariner glanced comfortably behind him, at the

villainous-looking cluster of rascals near the deckhouse, that helped to make up his crew. And he laughed. "No' so lang as reach aboard the *Florabel*!" he said. "Na, na, your Reverence— nor to any port the *Florabel's* like to make, frae Clyde to the Campbell country."

"Be not too sure, fellow . . ." the priest began, when the young man in the somewhat tarnished finery waved a silencing hand.

"Take us as far as the Oban, then, sirrah. It is half-roads, at least."

"An' your Honours wi' nae siller? What aboot my holdful o' stots? An' the wool an' hides? Or is it MacCailean Mor that's going to pay your passages?"

It was the young men's turn to spit—both of them. They spat with unanimity and vigour, if with less precision than the more experienced mariner—and, shame upon them, they spat on the deckboards.

"Do not name that name in my presence!" Colin Og cried.

"May he rot in hell everlastingly!" the cleric suggested, and crossed himself.

The shipmaster looked from one to the other, and puffed out his cheeks. "Aye. I'ph'mmm," he said. "The Campbells and the MacColls are unfriends, are they . . . ?"

"The Campbells and all good men are unfriends!" he was corrected stiffly. "They are the spawn of Satan, and the scum of hell." There was entire conviction there, and authority too, coming from the Church. "Name stealers!"

"D'ye tell me that, now!" Captain Gibson nodded. "An' me wi' a cargo o' musketoons an' ball for MacCailean . . . for the Duke o' Argyll himself!"

The two so authoritative suppliants exchanged glances. "Say you so?" Colin Og said. "For Inveraray?"

"Na, na. For the Oban, in Lorne. Ye maun be lang away frae the Hielands if ye dinna ken that Duke Archibald Campbell canna thole Inverara. . . ."

"We have been furth the country," he was told, with dignity. "Rome and Versailles and London, and the like."

3

"An' you wi' never a plack or a groat between ye?"

"Creature—do you question An Colin Og!"

"We were robbed," the same Colin Og informed, quickly. "Robbed. By . . . by the last rascally shipmaster, from Bristol. A race of thieves and rogues."

The other shrugged at that. "You'll hae things that ye could sell? Baggage?"

"No."

Sorrowfully the priest sighed. "The accursed ruffians took all. All is gone. *Aurum omnes, victa jam pietate, colunt!*"

Captain Gibson grinned. "Then it looks like ye hae a lang walk ahead o' ye, my masters. Ye'll no' sail in the *Florabel* to Ardcoll nor yet to Lorne." He chuckled suddenly, and his grin changed to a leer. "Forbye ye *work* your passage! I'm short-handed. Join my bonny lads, here"—and he jerked his head backwards—"an' I'll sail ye to the Oban."

"Work!" The word, exploding from two pairs of lips simultaneously, was drowned in a hoot of ribald mirth from the watching seaman. Eyes blazing, Colin Og MacColl took a pace forward, hand on his sword.

"By God—would you insult a Highland gentleman!"

If the priest was behind a little, he was nowise behindhand. "Carrion!" he cried. "Your tongue shall slit for that word, to a Son of Colin!"

Precipitately the shipmaster retreated. And only a little less promptly the group at his back moved forward, solidly. Captain and crew joined forces. Before the menacing line of fully a dozen scowling seamen—or perhaps it was before the evil glint of cold steel from more than one suddenly evident knife—the two Highlandmen paused. After all, they were not dressed for this sort of thing, and the clothes that they stood up in, being their all, must be guarded from unnecessary rents and tears.

MacColl dropped his hand from his sword-hilt, and his companion raised his to his crucifix. For a long moment there was silence, save for the screaming of the gulls around the bare masts above them.

Then Colin Og nodded his black-ringletted head briefly.

"Your word will be remembered, cur's-get!" he declared. "MacColl does not forget," and swinging about on his somewhat worn-down heel, he strode for the side.

His companion lifted his right hand, thumb turned down. "Curse, consume, and confound you, each and every!" he mentioned. "Rack, roast, and rot you, brand, blast and burn you, one and all!" His magnificent and mellifluous voice savoured the words lovingly. "May worms eat you, living and dead, may pangs pierce and prostrate you, and may your unshriven souls squirm eternally on the hot hob of hell!" And completing his remarks with a telling snap of the fingers of that upraised hand, that cracked like a whiplash, he turned and followed his master.

At the steep gangplank that slanted down, from the deck to the wooden quayside, Colin Og MacColl jerked his head at the dark-avised, lean and watchful man who stood there, apart from the other seamen, and the large cleric at his heels in his turn drooped his left eyelid, and at the same time raised his right eyebrow and swivelled his glance forward, a complicated gesture the undoubted eloquence of which the still-faced sailor received with complete absence of expression.

Long-strided, in velvet coat and fluttering cassock, the Highlandmen stalked regally down to the quay.

Up and along the narrow cobbled wynds of Dumbarton, beneath its towering castle-hung rock, the two men strode, one always just half a pace in front of the other. Young Colin of Ardcoll kept the crown of the tenuous causeway, as was his right—and it was worth keeping, with the stinking swills of the gutters a trap for the less sure-footed or the less determined, on either side; whoever had to step therein, it was not going to be Colin mhic Colin, nor for that matter, Father Tormaid his foster-brother. Elbows out, they marched up Dumbarton's vennels as though they owned them, as though their bellies were full, and if Colin Og had to shoulder a drunken sailor or a stumbling packman out of his way, or elbow a stodgy burgher into a more appropriate position, it was all done without ill-will and with a calm assurance that precluded any unseemly argument. And when it was one of the opposite sex who had to be passed, it was done with a gallant flourish that seldom if ever forced the lady actually into the mire—with even an arm-circling assistance if she was young. Indeed, once, when a clumsy oaf of a fisherman, pushed where he belonged, cannoned into a little child and sat her down howling in the gutter, Young Ardcoll stopped, picked her up, wiped her eyes with the skirts of his already rather stained blue velvet coat, and patted her tow-head before proceeding on his way. And again, when passing a window out of which a comely young woman leaned in converse with a fellow below, he doffed his broad-brimmed and feathered hat with a sweep and grace that made quite immaterial the fact that the feather was broken and the crown gashed, and wished her the top of a fine morning. Father Tormaid added a blessing and an appreciatively upraised eyebrow. He was good with his eyebrows was Tormaid.

Up past the Cross, amongst a huddle of dismal and dilapidated hovels, the walkers abruptly turned left-handed down a dark and ill-smelling lane, hurrying now with less of dignity and assurance to their gait—as well they might, for the stench was overpowering in this close where the clean winds of the Firth did not penetrate. And in at a black low-lintelled doorway in a low-browed house they dived, with the haste of frowning distaste, down half a dozen broken steps, into the noisome gloom of what was no more than a semi-subterranean den.

"Faugh!" Colin Og snorted. "A badger's earth would be sweeter than this!" He peered into the dim recesses of the place. "A tankard of ale, woman, for Mary-Mother's sake!"

"Can ye pey noo, then?" a shrill voice demanded.

"*Dhia*—this again! A plague on . . ."

But he was overborne by Father Tormaid's great bellow. "Satan scorch you—enough! Fetch ale, slut—or fetch your misbegotten spouse from whatever deepmost sink he may be stewing in. Raise not your screeching Lowland tongue at the son of An Colin Mor!"

6

"Och, Guid sakes—Mr. MacColl should pey for his yill like ither folks . . ."

"Woman!" the priest roared, so that the very walls of that kennel seemed to shake. "Virago! I told you—dare not to name An Colin Og with a beggarly Mister! Like any miserable Southron lairdling! Colin mhic Colin he is, and Colin mhic Colin, or Colin Og, you will name him! Now, go!"

In the further obscurity, the barely-seen woman shuffled, muttering, away into still deeper cave-like fastnesses beyond. On a rude bench beside one of the running walls, the hunched figure of a man hawked, and spat on the foul earthen floor, and was silent.

Colin barked a short laugh, part-amused, part-rueful. "You are a terror for the niceties, Tormaid *avic*!" he said. "And much profit it like to work us. This minute, I'd blithely exchange my namely state for a solid meal and a pouchful of Golden Ryals!"

"Och, Colin boy—never say it." His companion shook his short-cropped head, and his deep voice was entirely gentle, affectionate. "More likely you are to line your stomach, undowered, as the son of An Colin Mor than as a nameless clansman out of the heather."

"But not to win a passage to Ardcoll, it seems!"

"That you shall have, too, brother—never fear. There are more ways of killing a cat than choking it with cream, see you."

"More ways, may be—but less comfortable!"

The young cleric chuckled. "Man, Colin—what you need is faith!"

Shaking his handsome dark head, the other held his empty stomach. "What I need is food," he corrected. "And it is a far cry to Ardcoll!"

"Not so far as it was . . ." his companion began, when a chattering from the innermost premises of that warren heralded their host. The priest's upraised voice positively belled. "Come you, Macdonald—would you let your she-devil baulk Young Ardcoll of a cupful of ale!"

"Och, sirs, sirs—I would not, no." A stooping obsequious figure came limping forward, an elderly man of ragged and unkempt appearance, who spoke anxiously in the soft Gaelic. "Your pardon, Colin mhic Colin. It is the wife, here—she does not understand. Just a woman of the Lowlands she is, with no knowledge to her. I have the jar here. . . ." And in English, of a sort. "Quiet, woman! Is it Highland gentlemen would be refused the drink in a Highland gentleman's house!"

"Your sentiments do you honour, sir," Colin Og approved, gravely. "But if I might make the suggestion—as one Highland gentleman to another, of course—just the crumb of a bannock would help down the ale and complete the perfection of your hospitality!"

"Och, ochan—the pity of it!" the tavern-keeper bewailed. "And me with naught but the crust of old bread in the house. Hard times they are, for honest men. Here's nothing to be putting before gentlemen the like of yourselves."

"Lord o' Mercy—is that the way of it? My sympathy with you, Macdonald, and you in the crutch of sorrow." Colin MacColl sighed, and shook his head. "I fear it must be the crust of bread, then, whatever."

"An honoured man you are this day, Macdonald, that the Heir of An Colin Mor should deign to break your crust with you," Father Tormaid mentioned. "Myself, I am not a proud man either, and will share the bite likewise, in the name of good-fellowship."

The honoured man blinked watery eyes, gulped, and sighed. He put down his stone ale-jar on the littered table, wiped a pair of beechen cups with his sleeve, pushed them over, and turned to limp whence he had come, shooing his scolding wife before him as he would a clucking hen, and with no enthusiasm upon him.

"The great pity that this is the only Highlandman to be keeping a tavern in Dumbarton," the priest lamented. "A crust, Lord help us . . . and a mouthful of cask-rinsings! And in this pigsty!"

"Faith, Tormaid—faith!"

Nevertheless, the two Highland gentlemen ate the hunk of stale bread and emptied the nogs of staler beer, with little sign of reluctance; indeed, the necessary gentlemanly restraint with which these inadequate viands required to be dealt was a severe trial—as was the non-indulgence in crumb-picking thereafter.

The last drops were being drained from the ale-jar, under the wistful regard of their host, when a lessening of the feeble light that percolated through the open doorway from the narrow wynd without, turned their heads. A man, stooping, was entering therein.

"Angus Obanach Macdougall," the tavern-keeper announced; evidently, out of long practice, he could see in the dark.

"Good," Colin Og declared. "Macdougall—come you here, man. You serve a damned grasping churl of a master!"

"That is so, sir—was I not after telling you the same, last night?" the newcomer said, slow-voiced. He was the dark-faced silent sailor from the *Florabel's* gangplank. "Och, just a miserly Sassunach, he is, with no understanding to him."

"So we saw. Did you hear the cur suggest that we should *work* for our passage?"

"I did so, Colin mhic Colin, and me misbelieving my ears. Black-affronted, I was. His bowels should be tied round his neck to be choking him, for that same!" The Gaelic is a picturesque language, meet for real eloquence.

"Exactly. We are all at one on that, Macdougall," Colin Og agreed. "And his crew? An ill-favoured lot, it seemed."

"Yes, then. For the most of them, that is true, yes. Two voyages I have been on the *Florabel*, and the little black fellow here my best friend!" And the seaman touched the horn-handled dirk stuck prominently into his belt, caressingly. "But there are the two other Highlandmen in it, the cook and another— Islesmen both, out of Skye, but sort of half-honest of their kind." He cast a glance towards the tavern-keeper. "Macdonalds."

"Beggars cannot be the choosers," MacColl observed, judiciously, when he was interrupted by Father Tormaid.

"The cook, say you? That, now, is interesting." And patting his stomach, he belched hollowly.

9

"M'mmm. So. Five Highlandmen . . ." Colin Og pondered. "And the creature said that he was short-handed?"

"He is, yes," the Macdougall from Oban agreed. "Five men short he is, or more."

"And are there no Highlandmen in this Dumbarton, to sail a ship north for a breath of the heather and the tangle?"

"Not a Campbell ship!" It was the innkeeper, Macdonald, who answered that. "There are a wheen Buchanans and Lamonts about the place, but they will not be sailing on Argyll's business."

"So! My bonnet off to them," Young Ardcoll acceded. "But if they were to be given the whisper, privately, mark you, that this ship would be sailing a lot farther north than Argyll, and that there would be rich pickings in it for good clansmen—how then?"

"It could be that some might be changing their minds, An Colin Og."

"It could be, and it *shall* be! See you to it, Macdonald. When do you sail, Macdougall?"

"Tomorrow's morn, at first of day, with the tide."

"Then you have not long, Man o' the House, to get your Buchanans and Lamonts. Go, you!"

"But, sir—it is not . . ."

"But nothing!" the priest roared abruptly. "But not, at the Son of Colin. Begone!"

"Five men only, it is required. These you will get." That was Young Ardcoll, and entirely authoritative, as he turned his wide shoulder on the Macdonald. "Now, Macdougall—how are you going to be getting us aboard your vessel tonight, unseen?"

The still-faced sailor stared unwinking for a long moment. "Is that the way of it, then?" he said, at length.

"It is," MacColl agreed. "If we may not travel in the poop, we will travel in the belly."

"Is it An Colin Og will be stowed amongst the cargo, like any gangrel-body, then?"

"So be it Colin Og is not insulted with base talk about

work, he cares not where his person may be stowed!" the MacColl answered, with dignity. "You tell me that the *Florabel* is the only bottom sailing north of Kintyre within the month. Colin Og sails with her, then—yellow gold or none!"

"Surely," Father Tormaid agreed. "*Rem acu tetigisti!* The position in a nutshell."

The man Macdougall shrugged. "As you say, gentlemen—though for myself, I mislike it. By darkening this night, there will be scarce a man on board, and not one sober, I'll wager. That is the way of it, last night on shore."

"And Master Gibson?'

"Drunk as a log, by sundown, whatever."

"Excellent. Then, let us say, an hour after dark, we will be down at the quay, hiding amongst the fishing-gear. If you will give us a sign when all is clear, Macdougall—perhaps a whistle. . . ."

"No need in it, Colin Og. Come you aboard singing and shouting and lifting the lid off hell itself, and there will be none to question it. Others will be doing that same, all the night. Myself, I will be waiting for you, and leading you below. It will be easy, just . . ." The seaman paused, for a moment. ". . . but it will not be seemly nor suitable, for the son of An Colin Mor, whatever!"

MacColl half rose from his bench. "Creature—*whatever* the son of An Colin Mor does is seemly and suitable! I tell you that . . ." He stopped, and subsided again, with a hint of a smile playing about his mobile lips. "Moreover, the suitability and the seemliness will appear later, I promise you!" he ended easily. "Now—off with you. Expect us tonight, an hour after the dark."

"And see you, Macdougall—let our priest's-hole amongst Argyll's muskets be suitably nigh to your Skyeman cook's galley," the cleric shouted after him. "Man does not live by faith alone!"

Colin Og MacColl rose to his feet. "Let us out of this before the stench chokes us, Tormaid."

"Readily, Colin *avic*. But whence?"

"We might make trial as to whether the ladies of Dumbarton are as hospitable in their pantries as they are in their bedchambers! Come, you!"

That April night, with a chill drizzle drifting in off the Firth and the western sea, two roistering, reeling plaid-happed figures presented themselves singing at the gangway of the deserted-seeming *Florabel*, tripping over a recumbent seaman on the darkened quay as they approached. From behind them, across the black water that reflected the lights of the riverside taverns, a suitable echo of their singing came hearteningly, with faint shouting and shrieking and skirling as added weight.

At the head of the gangplank, the man Macdougall, materializing out of the gloom from behind the deckhouse, met them, and led them forward, unspeaking. Singing still, they followed—and when Tormaid Urramach sang, it was singing indeed. On their way, they passed two silent motionless figures standing beside the foremast. Colin Og ceased his carolling for a moment, to touch the Macdougall's arm.

"These?" he whispered. "Are they safe?"

"A Buchanan and a Graham," the seaman informed. "Macdonald the Tavern sent them. Two more there will be, he says, before we sail."

"Good, then."

Macdougall halted, and turned. "Down here, now—and watch the heads of you!"

They were conducted, silent now, down a companionway where the smell of cooking, though stale and sour, was as balm to their souls, down past the sounds of unseen snorers and mutterers, where other smells were evident, and farther down still, into the very bowels of the ship, where the only smell was that of bilge-water, foul and stomach-turning. They were ushered, under the faint light of a hanging-lantern far above, stooping and squeezing, through a narrow hatchway in a bulkhead, into complete darkness. Bumping into and tripping over solid objects, they came to a speedy halt.

"A light, for Mary-Mother's sake!" the priest complained,

rubbing elbow and hip.

"No light," their guide returned, grimly. "You are better wanting it, and your cargo kegs of Campbell gunpowder! But here, at your feet, is a pile of old sailcloth, that will make you a fair couch. Lie you there, and if you must stretch your legs and relieve yourselves, through the hatch and down into the bilge with you. But carefully, see you."

"Careful we will be, Macdougall, while there is call for care!" Colin Og assured him, stooping to feel over and around the heap of sailcloth.

"And the galley?" Father Tormaid asked. "Your cook's *sanctum sanctorium*? I thought that I smelled the whiff of it, on our descent into this nethermost pit?"

"Right above, it is. Above the lazaretto. I will be fetching you your victuals each night . . ."

"It is night now, Man of the Sea—a good time to be starting the system," the priest suggested, promptly. "Practice, they say, does be making perfection."

"I will be seeing what is in it," the sailor allowed. "Poor fare, for the son of An Colin Mor. . . ."

The Son of Colin licked his lips, and swallowed painfully. "Angus Obanach Macdougall—let myself be the judge of that!" he pleaded. "And quickly. Besides, viands, like women, may but gain by the darkness!"

As the seaman edged back through the bulkhead, Father Tormaid spoke a last word. "How long, man, till we make the Sound of Kerrera?"

"Four days or five, if the winds be not contrary, Father. But . . ."

"Let the Sound of Kerrera wait its turn," Colin Og declared. "I am more interested in when we sight the Ross of Mull. When you bring us that word, Macdougall, we will see what is suitable and seemly. Now—victuals, in the Name of Mercy!"

The two young men sank down on the unseen couch of sailcloth, as the sailor's bare feet padded up the ladder outside. "This, I think, is not going to be the least comfortable voyage of our travels, brother," Colin Og observed. "But I swear we

13

will be worshippers of the sun ere we see Ben More of Mull!"

"I believe you, Colin *avic*," Tormaid chuckled. "It must be *numen lumen*, even if it is not *astra castra*!"

"And what may that signify, mouther of gibberish?"

"God be our light, who has replaced the stars by the cook's galley!" the priest intoned.

"Amen to that, then," the Heir of the MacColls concurred, with fervent and entirely pious sincerity.

II

IT was pallid early morning on the first day of May, when
Angus Macdougall came hand-under-hand down his ladder
into the dark and fetid gut of the *Florabel*, to acquaint the
dozing troglodytes therein that the Ross of Mull was looming
distant on the port bow. It was four days exactly since the
vessel's blear-eyed crew had coaxed her out of Dumbarton
Harbour and beat her down the long reaches of the island-
dotted Firth of Clyde, in the face of the prevailing south-
westerly wind of that seaboard—a wind which, of course, had
eventually turned to their advantage when, at last, rounding
the long Mull of Kintyre, the *Florabel* had swung her bowsprit
north towards the narrow seas of the Hebrides. Since then, if
they had not literally run before that unfailing breeze, it was
only because their barque was not exactly built for running.
Rising and falling to the long westerly swell of the Atlantic,
dipping and rolling in the cross-seas from the innumerable
islands and peninsulas and promontories of that terrible
coastline, keeping good sea-room between herself and the
treacherous foaming skerries that reached far out from every
land-mass, the *Florabel* had waddled heavily northwards. Four
days and nights of uneventful sailing, for the ship's company;
four days and nights of darkness, of stench, of heaving and
swaying, of the groaning of timbers and the wash and gurgle
of bilge-water, of trying inactivity and adequate if uninspiring
feeding, for the stowaways. Four days—or eternity.

There was no hesitation, no somnolent reluctance, about
the MacColls' reception of the news, expected as it was. There
had been ample time for plan-making. Like Jonah, in a similar
situation, they had had enough. Colin Og's questions and
instructions were brisk and definite. A man of action, he now
entered into his own. Who was sailing the ship just now, he
wanted to know? Where was the master—asleep in his cabin?

How many of the crew were on deck? How were the other Highlandmen placed?

Macdougall could answer all. It being two bells of the morning watch, the boatswain was on the poop, and Master Gibson snug in his hammock. All but five of the crew were below, asleep—and of the five, two were Highlandmen. The cook slept in his own galley, and the men that Macdonald the Tavern had found for them slung their hammocks in the fo'c'sle.

The Sassunach members of the crew on deck—where were they?

One at the wheel, one lookout in the bows, and one in the waist.

Good, said Colin Og, his questioning finished. Tell the Highlandmen on deck to wait there, watching the watch, and fetch the others down here from the fo'c'sle, and the cook likewise. And let them have a lantern in it, in the Name of Mercy, gunpowder or none!

So, in a few minutes, they were gathered at the foot of the companionway, the two Skyemen, a Lamont, a Buchanan, Macdougall, and the MacColls, the latter blinking and screwing up their eyes to even the pale smoky illumination of a ship's lantern that the cook carried. Colin Og wasted no time on preliminaries; what he had to say was brief, clear, and peremptory, and was accepted as such—orders to be obeyed. No man questioned the right of Colin mhic Colin to give his orders, nor questioned the orders themselves. There was no need. Only one query he asked of them—whether any of them preferred the assistance of some part of the Campbell's cargo here in the hold, to reliance on their own personal methods; a question to which the Highlanders gave a unanimous negative. Leaving Donald Glas the cook at the bulkhead to the hold, with his lamp and his instructions, Colin signed the others upwards.

Directly above, outside the lazaretto from whence the sound of multiple snoring issued to join the creaking of ship's timbers, the hatch was closed quietly, a bar slid into its socket, and the

Lamont left on guard. Mounting higher, the remaining five men came out on to the wet deck and into the wan light of early morning. Shielding their eyes against the seeming glare of it, the two stowaways waited awhile till their sight should return. The Buchanan and the second Skyeman, at a nod from Macdougall, slipped away aft.

Gradually the MacColls' eyes accustomed themselves to the half-light. They were facing the bows, northwards, and against the grey pallor of the cloud-hung sky, land loomed blackly. All around them, except due west where the ocean stretched unfettered into lingering night, in a seemingly unbroken line dark mountains made a distant jagged frieze to dark water streaked with the dirty white of combers. But to the north-west, on their port bow, the upheaved ramparts of the land sank and dwindled to a long low belt, jet against the banked and lowering rain clouds.

"The Ross of Mull," Macdougall whispered, pointing. "Running for the mouth of the Firth of Lorne we are, with Colonsay astern."

Peering from under a shading hand, Colin Og nodded. "It is a blessed sight," he conceded, ". . . though devilish painful on the eyes."

"*Miserere mei*—I am as blind as a bat!" the priest complained at his ear. He was breathing deeply of the chill salt-laden morning breeze. "But praise be to God for a breath of fresh air—even Campbell air!"

His foster-brother turned to look aft, cautiously, over the hatchway roofing. "Can we make the poop, unseen?" he demanded.

"If you are bending low and following me round under the starboard gunwale, where there is shadow in it . . ." Macdougall said. "Is Father Tormaid ready?"

Stooping almost double, Colin Og and the priest crept behind the seaman to the bulwarks on their right. There, with the young day lightening the east, the gunwale cast a girdle, not so much of shadow—there was insufficient light for that—as of sheer gloom. Under its cover the two MacColls moved, crouching, aft, while Angus Macdougall, straightening up, strolled idly along in front of them. Whether thus he was able materially to screen them is debatable, but owing to the intrusion of the deckhouse, the masts and their cordage, and sundry other gear, their route would be only intermittently visible from the poop. And of the two figures thereon, one, obviously the boatswain, officer of the watch, paced steadily from side to side of the ship, his perambulations, judged by his attitude, more concerned with keeping warm than with any keen scrutiny of scene or course, while the helmsman, behind him, hunched over his wheel, seemed to be sunk in a coma suitable to the hour. No eagle eye, from the poop, was scanning the *Florabel's* decks—or scanning anything, indeed; with Colonsay safely passed half an hour back, the vessel had ample sea-room for the remainder of the watch.

The progress of the three men aft, then, was accomplished entirely without incident—unless the necessity to step over a body outstretched in the mainchains could be called an incident. The grinning Graham, who crouched nearby, took up his position at the rear of the little procession, immediately behind the large person of the priest, who, his cassock kilted up above his knees, cast a frowning glance at him; Father Tormaid, with his height as well as his cloth to consider, conceived this situation to be distinctly undignified, especially from the back view.

They reached the poop steps, and under the sheltering over-hang the two long-legged MacColls resumed the upright with sighs of relief. Apart from the manifold incessant sounds of a ship at sea, the gurgle and slap of waters, the creak of timbers, the whine and strumming of wind in sails and rigging, the *Florabel* proceeded quietly on her way.

Colin Og looked at Tormaid, eyebrows raised, then at Macdougall, and nodded. The seaman raised a hand in acknowl-edgment, and turning, padded across the deck to the port side. A moment or two later, there sounded a notable splash, and then a voice uplifted in Highland English, to look, to look at that, in the name of Mary and all the saints!

18

A gruff voice from the poop answered. And nodding the second time, Colin touched his foster-brother's arm and climbed the poop steps three at a time.

"Creature! Offspring of Bastards," he said, in a pleasant and easy manner, "turn you, and your hands empty!"

The boatswain, leaning over the port poop rail, whipped round—to find a musketoon levelled unwavering within a yard of his ample stomach. Goggling, he gulped for breath and words, found none, and so stood, his mouth open.

Colin Og jerked his head, said a word in the Gaelic, and the cheerful Graham stepped forward and relieved the boatswain of the heavy pistol that he carried at his waist. With knowing hands he continued his search, unbidden.

Young Ardcoll glanced behind him to where the trembling helmsman stood beside his wheel, a clerical arm barring his chest and the glinting point of a delicately-wrought dagger at his throat, and nodded.

"You observe the situation, fellow?" he asked the boatswain conversationally. "The *Florabel* is changing course, a little. You are a man of some experience of the sea, I take it. Do you prefer to go on sailing this ship, or to go overboard on a course of your own? The choice is yours."

The other looked desperately fore and aft, and saw nothing to reassure him. Macdougall was coming up the poop steps, a *sgian dubh* in his hand; a new figure stood in the bows as look-out, and of the non-Highland crew, not a man was to be seen. He licked his bearded lips, and nodded, unspeaking.

"Wise man," Colin Og commended. "Cherish you your wisdom!" To the Graham, he spoke, taking the pistol from him. "His belt off, and tie his hands. Macdougall—you can steer this ship? Take you the wheel, then. Mull has an ill coast to it, westward, I'm told, and the Torran Rocks are namely. See to it that we have room and to spare." He saw the boatswain's hands buckled behind his back, and then, stepping over to Father Tormaid's side, raised an unerring hand and brought down the butt of the heavy pistol full on the crown of

19

the helmsman's head. "To relieve you of a burden, brother," he mentioned, as the seaman slumped unconscious in the priest's arms. "No time for persuading such."

Tormaid nodded as, letting the fellow slide to the deck, he put away his exquisite little dirk. "No doubt but you are right, Colin *avic*," he agreed.

"Over the side with him?" the Graham questioned, hopefully.

The priest raised his great voice in stern reproof. "Indeed, no! Would you murder an unconscious man—even a Sassunach? Below with him, and lock him up. If the creature has to meet his Maker, let him do so decently, with his eyes open!"

Colin Og smiled. "He will thank you, no doubt, Man of God!" he observed. Then he waved such trivialities aside. "Wait you here, and help our boatswain keep a good course, Tormaid. I have a word to say to Master Gibson." He beckoned with an imperious hand to the Skyeman standing below in the main-chains. "Lead me to the master's cabin," he commanded.

The *Florabel's* prow was swinging westwards as he strode down the poop steps, whistling *An Colin Mor's Wedding*, tunefully.

Under the poop, leaving the Graham outside the adjoining officers' quarters, the borrowed musketoon in hand, Colin Og MacColl threw open the door of the master's cabin, stalked within, and with a single upwards slash of his dirk severed the supporting cords of the captain's hammock. With a crash Master Gibson fell to the deck, his slumbers rudely terminated. Before he could even begin to disentangle himself, before he could formulate a single appropriate word, any such reactions were stillborn by the considerable pressure of judiciously-placed if down-at-heel footwear at the root of his neck.

"Quiet, you!" he was told, a shade redundantly. "Or sleep everlastingly!"

A rattling noise from the other's throat might have indicated some appreciation of the situation.

"You will not talk," the younger man went on, even-voiced. "You did your talking in Dumbarton port, the other day, you will recollect. Now, it is the Son of Colin's turn to talk. This, for your information. Item: you are no longer master of this ship. Item: this ship is no longer sailing to the Oban, and Campbell-defiled Lorne. Item: the cargo is no longer consigned to the creature Argyll. Clan Colin has better use for it, and the worth of it as shown in the ship's papers will be duly entered against Clan Colin's account with Clan Dairmid. Item: the said cargo includes some scores of kegs of gunpowder. A man, this minute, stands with a lantern and a train of powder to those kegs. Also, one of them will be rolled to directly under this cabin. You understand? Nod your head, man—do not talk! Was I not telling you your time for talking was done!" That was a long speech for that man.

Wat Gibson's rolling eyes had to serve in lieu of head-nodding.

Colin Og resumed. "You will not stir from this cabin. You will not speak nor sign to a living soul. A guard is at your door, and he will be the happy man if you will but do something foolish. I owe you a slit tongue, you will mind. Probably it would be wiser to make it a slit throat, and be done with it!"

The said throat heaved noticeably beneath the restraining boot.

"Take you heed, then." The young man removed his foot, and stepped to the door. "Graham," he said, carefully in English, and quiet-voiced—he did not whisper; the son of An Colin Mor would not whisper—and pointed backwards, within. "Tie it up in its hammock. Securely. And do not be sticking your *sgian dubh* in it before it is necessary. Mine it is, see you, and . . ."

At that moment the door of the cabin opposite opened, and a heavy man came lurching out, sleepy-eyed. He paused, blinking, at what he saw. And while the words were still unformed on his lips, MacColl acted. Like one of his own Ardcoll wildcats he sprang, and the explosive upwards drive of the dirk, still in

21

his right hand, took the fellow directly under the chin. But it was a backhanded blow, with the hilt of the dagger, of course, since unfortunately a Highland gentleman was precluded from using his clean steel on an unarmed opponent. And all in the same movement, as the man staggered backwards, his head jerking up, Colin Og's long left leg shot behind him, behind his knees, and he toppled. His attacker's rush carried them both onwards, MacColl on his feet, by a miracle of nimbleness, and his victim almost horizontal. Through the doorway back into the cabin they hurtled, but as the falling man crashed to the deck, Colin somehow disengaged himself, and by quite a feat of agility not only halted his forward impetus but forced himself backwards. A hand behind him, grabbing the edge of the door, he slammed it shut and ended up with his back against its panels, knees slightly bent, facing into the cabin, his knife glittering in his hand.

But his vigilance was unnecessary. The *Florabel* carried only two mates, and the one who was not twitching at his feet was turning over in his hammock, peering owlishly. An alarmed man, he struggled urgently as the intruder launched himself at him, but hammocks are not the easiest contrivances to get out of promptly, and while he was still kicking and swaying convulsively, Colin Og had him. Knocking him down into his blanket with a left-fisted blow, MacColl had his right hand upraised to strike, when, swiftly thinking better of it, he took a single step backwards, flung his dirk into his other hand, and whipped out his long slender-bladed Ferrara. Even as the other yelped his fear, Colin lunged—and the sword skewered neatly through the network of the hammock directly above the mate's chest, adequately pinioning him within. And with a mighty heave up and over, using the sword-hilt as a fulcrum, the hammock was completely turned turtle, and there the unfortunate mariner hung, like a trussed fowl, suspended face downwards in his own bedding, cold steel across his breast and an iron arm across his back. All in a tithe of the time that it takes to tell.

"The first word out of your mouth will be the last,

whatever . . ." Colin was mentioning, when the cabin door that he had slammed opened, and the man Graham peered in, anxiously.

"Is it yourself needing a bit hand, Colin mhic Colin?" he wondered.

The roar with which that was answered was startling—and hardly in keeping with its maker's previous insistence on silence. "Out, you!" he cried. "Begone! Think you An Colin Og cannot deal with a parcel of miserable Sassunachs!" As the door closed discreetly, MacColl leaned farther forward, and catching the hilt with his dirk hand, swung round the sword full cycle, so that the wretch in the hammock was once again face uppermost, and now as tightly wrapped in his cradle as a grub in its cocoon. And with a last vehement thrust, he drove the whole thing forward, so that the point of his sword bit deeply into the timbering of the bulkhead behind—bit and held. And there, sword and bedding and man remained, still suspended by the ropes, but attached to the walling like an insect on a pin.

Colin Og turned to the first victim, now stirring on the deckboards. Slashing down with his dirk the two remaining hammocks hanging there—presumably the man's own, and the boatswain's—he picked up one, draped it over the groaning seaman, and rolled him over and over in it. Then, taking the other coil of cordage, he wrapped it round and round the swaddled sufferer, and tied its supporting ropes securely. A casual glance round the cabin revealed sundry objects hanging from pegs. Two were heavy cutlasses. Stepping over, the Highlandman unsheathed one, tested its point with his forefinger, and stooping, lifted up the recumbent mate's feet, hoisted them as high as they would go, with an eruptive jerk, and drove the cutlass unerringly between them, through the ropework and into the *Florabel's* stout timber side. Then, drawing the second hanging cutlass from its sheath, he moved back to the other trembling unfortunate, gauged the matter with a raised eyebrow, and with a vigorous thrust, replaced his darling rapier by this clumsier weapon—suitably enough, for service as a staple.

23

And thus, leaving one mummified mate standing on his head, and the other hanging like a picture on a wall, Colin Og MacColl stalked out of their cabin without a further glance, his naked Andrea Ferrara aswing in his hand. He had scarcely a glance, either, for the Graham, conscientiously if urgently busy at his trussing, in the master's quarters opposite.

There remained only the crew—a mere bagatelle. The Son of Colin strolled forrard, his blade describing pleasing designs in the brightening light of morning. He noted that the black outline of the Ross of Mull was now well on the starboard bow, with the open sea wide before them, and turned to nod a congratulatory head to the tight-lipped boatswain in acknowledgment of his helpful navigation. Father Tormaid raised a hand in something between a blessing and a suitably nautical salute.

Down their old companionway, forrard of the fore-chains, he found the Lamont still on guard outside the lazaretto, from inside the barred door of which echoed quite a deal of banging and shouting. Colin gestured downwards, with his thumb, towards the deeper fastnesses.

"A keg of powder from the Man of Skye, friend," he requested. "Myself, I will discover if he has another lantern in his galley, there."

By the time that the Lamont came panting up the ladder clutching the barrel to him, the door was trembling under blows from within, and Colin Og MacColl had acquired a lighted lantern from the cook's galley.

"Out with the bung," he was instructed, and drawing the inevitable *sgian dubh*, he worked the stopper loose.

MacColl tipped the keg over and a stream of black powder poured out. When quite a little heap was spilled, he righted the cask, and glancing at his companion, reached out his hand, and tore quite a considerable segment off the surprised Lamont's ragged shirt.

"Heed it not, friend," he was advised, easily. "You will have your pick of the shirts on board, presently!" He twisted the

24

stuff into a rope, and tucked one end of it well into the bung-hole, leaving a long tail of it hanging outside. Slopping some of the oil from the lantern into the palm of his hand, he smeared it on the cloth. "Now," he ordered, "Unbar that door."

The Lamont hesitated. "Will I be after fetching two-three of the others, then, Colin Og?" he suggested.

"Why?" That was a bark.

The other did not pursue his proposal. He stepped to the door, and slid the bar, that held it fast, out of its socket. The fist-beating on the other side held it shut, still, for it opened inwards. Colin Og took a pace forward, raised his foot, and pushed with sudden violence. The door flew open, to the accompaniment of cries of pain and the thudding of bodies. The scene within was reminiscent of a stage inferno. The lazaretto, dark save for the smoky light of a single lantern, was at a somewhat lower level than its entrance, and down the few steps thereto more than one man obviously had been hurled by the effect of the MacColl's footwork, knocking over certain of their fellows in their fall. The effect of struggling bodies and writhing limbs in that black hole, with the half-naked crouching figures surrounding—crouching because the deck-head was so low that no man could stand upright—made a telling picture, to which the foul stench that arose therefrom materially contributed. Father Tormaid should have been there, to do justice to it. In the accommodation for her crew the *Florabel* scorned unessentials. The man who spoke was concerned with effects, but his own effects only. Taking the two paces to the top of the steps, he drew a breath of the fetid air, gulped, and spat. "Animals!" he cried. "Stinking scum! Hell's-broth! I, Colin mhic Colin of Ardcoll, now command this ship. I sail her to Ardcoll. You may help me sail her there. Or you may rot here in your kennel, till I am finished with the ship and you. Or you may go straight to hell, here and now. The choice is yours. What is it to be?" There was silence for a few moments, apart from the scuffling sound of tumbled men getting to their feet. The seamen stared at each other, and then at the arrogant figure above them. Then a muttering grew, and swelled. Colin Og did not allow it to continue. "Your choice?" he rapped. "The ship is mine, and all on it!" A shower of questions and demands rose from that dark place, not all politely couched. The man in the doorway cut them short with a vicious downward slash of his sword, more telling than any words.

"Curs!" he shouted. "Would you question An Colin Og? Choose now, or . . . !"

He stopped. A stir amongst the men at the foot of the steps drew his eye. Quick as thought he acted. Throwing up his rapier, he caught the hilt in a different grip, a backhanded grip and in the selfsame movement, launched it fiercely downwards. Like a javelin the slender blade streaked from his hand, and took a crouching man clean through the right shoulder. With a scream of agony, the fellow staggered, and a knife dropped from his nerveless hand with a clatter. A shuddering sort of sigh went up from his companions, eight or nine of them, as they pressed backwards.

Colin Og stood to one side, and pointed, behind him this time. Clear in the early light that slanted down from the companion-hatch, the powder-barrel stood, and the Lamont with the lantern beside it. Colin spoke. "You know what that is?" he declared. "Gunpowder. The ship is filled with it. That cloth lighted, the keg run down these steps, and the door barred, and you will leave this hell for the next, apace! Choose, you! Do you sail the ship under my orders?"

There was silence, save for the whimpering of the wounded man, scrabbling with his fingers at the transfixing steel. Then, from a big hulking fellow, unhappy in the foreground, came a surly "Aye." It was taken up around him, a mumbled chorus of reluctant assent. Only the casualty failed to add his quota. He had sunk to his knees, at the foot of the steps.

The MacColl stared at the scene, distastefully, almost as though he regretted that the cleansing properties of a keg of gunpowder were not after all to be utilized. Another man, one of his mates, stooped over the sufferer, his hand out to the sword-hilt. But with a barked word, MacColl stopped him.

"Back!" he said. "Keep your filthy hands from Colin Og's sword! That steel is mine, and clean. No ship's scum will touch it. Bring him up here."

The seamen stared, doubtfully.

"Bring him, I say!"

The man who had stooped to the sword stooped again. A companion assisted, and together they part pushed, part hoisted the swooning wretch, the rapier projecting from just beneath his collarbone, up the few steps. At the top, Colin Og stared at the trio for a moment, then leaning forward, grasped the hilt, put up a foot to the other's middle, and thrust mightily. With a yell the sufferer fell backwards, dragging his two fellows part-way down the steps with him. The owner of the sword eyed it fastidiously.

"Soiled steel," he observed. "But a clean wound. Better than the creature's deserts. Not many such as he have felt Colin Og's steel!" He wiped the weapon on what remained of the Lamont's shirt. "Had you oafs worked that blade out, you would have been the death of him. Pour some *uisge beatha* into the wound, and he will suffer less than he ought. Now . . ." He glanced over them. "Which is your leader—your spokesman?"

There was a shifting and a murmuring amongst the throng below, and two or three pointed to the fainting man beneath the steps.

"Ah. Unfortunate," Colin said. "You will have to select another, then." He waited, while the men shuffled. Frowning, he pointed. "You! You will serve. Come here."

A middle-aged stocky fellow came reluctantly up.

"You carry a *sgian dubh*—a dirk?"

The man reached behind him, drew an ugly sheath-knife from the waist of his breeches, and held it out.

MacColl ignored it, but jerked his head in the direction of the Lamont, who stepped over and received it.

"Take him to the poop," he was directed, in the Gaelic. "Tell Father Tormaid that he is for the cannon's-mouth. And send down one of your fellow scoundrels, here." And he took the lantern.

When the Lamont and his charge were gone, Colin Og spoke, but hardly as though he was addressing that company. "In case the thought was coming to any of you that you might be braver men aloft than down here, only the two of you will be allowed on deck at one time. The rest will be here, with the powder-barrel. You will remember that. Now, two of you—come up. You will do—and you."

The pair of mariners came slow-footed.

"Knives?"

One man shook his head. The other produced an evil dagger of Oriental design.

The sword-tip gestured, and the sailor dropped the weapon. Colin Og put his foot on it, and jerked his head. "Aloft," he said. Hand on the door, he spoke over his shoulder at the others. "Remember—the keg is here at the door, with a gillie and a flame." And slamming it shut, he pushed the door-bar into position.

"Man of Skye!" he shouted down the companionway, to their old refuge below. "Breakfast, in the names of all Saints!"

His hunger temporarily checked, Colin Og leaned back against the poop-rail in the smile of a slant of watery sunlight, and watched the sandy beaches and green machairs of Iona drop away on their starboard quarter, and the terraced rocks of Ulva rise like giants' steps ahead. If the stocky creature in front had been in a position to move his thick body—which he was not—then Colin could have seen, far in front, beyond the flat Treshnish Isles, in the clear rain-washed air, the towering mountains of Rhum, even a hint of the jagged teeth of Skye. But the obstructive fellow was unable to move. He was the crew's spokesman, and lashed to the muzzle of the *Florabel's* only cannon, an admirable position where, as well as fulfilling other useful purposes, he could act as an excellent and much-concerned lookout against the reefs and skerries of that rock-strewn sea; for, of course, should the ship unfortunately strike any such, it was quite probable that in the flurry of sinking nobody would have time to untie him. Colin Og himself was not inclined to move. He was very content with the view that he had—Skye could wait. In fact, he was very content altogether. The Hebrides and the hills of home and Marsala of Eynart were before him, his stomach was full, the white gulls were keeping pace with the dipping mastheads, the sun was shining, and all was well with the world. He gave his Maker thanks for it all—subconsciously, if not in so many words. Colin mhic Colin was that sort of man.

But if An Colin Mor's son was thus suitably and humbly grateful for all his Creator's mercies, his foster-brother was still more so. From the other side of the cannon-bound individual, the great rich voice of Father Tormaid rose into the clear air in tuneful, joyful praise. "*Gloria in Excelsis Deo . . .*" he sang, as he poured out his heart to the morning.

III

IT was a night and nearly two whole days later, with the sinking sun painting all the naked peaks of Ross in a pattern of ochre and inky black, and staining all the floor of shimmering waters to burnished gold, before the *Florabel* sighted another sail in that western sea.

It was the individual at the cannon's mouth who saw it first; after all, he had nothing else to do. He saw it sail out of a belt of purple shadow under the loom of the land, into the shining plain of light, and he cried out his news—for undoubtedly he was glad of the diversion, any diversion; he had been tied up there for forty hours, and time hung heavily.

All eyes followed his direction. She was a long, low curious-looking craft, antiquated in design but far from insignificant on that account. With no great spread of sail to her double masts, she seemed to be getting along at a good pace, nevertheless. No man on board failed to recognize her for what she was.

It was the boatswain who voiced that recognition, agitatedly. He was an agitated man, was the boatswain, and had been for the last forty hours. "She's a galley!" he cried. "One o' thae damnation piratin' Hielan' . . ." He stopped short, swallowing his words, with an agonized glance right and left at his companions. "She's . . . she's a galley," he ended up.

Colin Og MacColl took the telescope, which was now as prominent an item of Father Tormaid's equipment as was his crucifix, and levelled it on the stranger. "A double-bank galley of, I'd say, three score oars," he announced. "Four—no, six cannon. No banner, nor markings."

"A MacNeil?" Angus Macdougall at the wheel suggested. "An ill breed . . ."

"Silence!" Tormaid cried. "Was not An Colin Mor's own mother a daughter of MacNeil himself!"

His foster-brother shook his head. "It is a thought far north from Barra for MacNeil. Bold he would have to be, with Clan Donald jealous of their waters. Clanranald, it could be, after making a call on the Mackenzies."

"It wouldna' be the . . . ?" The boatswain licked hesitant lips. "Your Honours—might it no' be . . . ?" His courage failed him, there.

Colin Og glanced at him. "Yes, Sassunach?" he wondered, easily.

But the other shook his head, dumbly.

The priest chuckled. "We shall soon know, I'm thinking. MacNeil, MacDonald, or the Devil himself, he is for coming this way, if my eyes serve me."

Colin Og nodded. "He has put about, yes. He is for exchanging the courtesies, as is but suitable between gentlemen."

Indeed, it was apparent to all that the galley had altered course, and now was approaching them on a tack that would bring her across the *Florabel's* bows before long. The boatswain's alarm was not to be contained.

"We'll hae to luff quick, Masters," he exclaimed. "We can sail a wheen points closer into the wind. If we're to outsail her, wi' yon accursed oars, we'll need clap on every stitch o' canvas. Wi' the airt the wind's in . . ."

"Peace, man—peace!" Colin interrupted. "What's this talk of outsailing him? If he would be greeting us, would you reject his civility?"

"Civility! Goad—it's cannon-balls he'll greet us wi'!" the shipman groaned. "Och, sirs, I ken thae piratin' deevils . . ."

The flash and boom of a cannon from the approaching craft abruptly substantiated the boatswain's qualms. The shot fell far short, throwing up a scintillating column from the golden sea, but its purport and authority were effective enough.

"Look ye, now!" The navigator clasped and unclasped his bound hands behind his back. "Did I no' tell you. Port your helm, man, or it'll be all by wi' us!" That was to Angus Macdougall, steering, anxious-eyed himself.

"Not so," the MacColl declared. "Would you have An Colin

31

Og turn tail on any man! If he's for a word with us, we will go meet him, as is only mannerly." He shrugged. "Besides, we could not outsail him, with all his oars, in this heavy tub, save direct before the wind."

"*Dictum sapienti sat est.*" Father Tormaid agreed. "There speaks wisdom, ruffians."

"He'll blaw us oot o' the watter wi' his culverins, an' us full o' gunpowder!" That was a wail.

"Then we will give him the less target," Colin announced. "Farther over with your helm, Macdougall. And quiet you, shiplouse—your whining wearies me."

So, head on, the two vessels approached each other, the *Florabel* making good speed with the south-west breeze astern, the galley urged on in the wind's face by her sixty long oars. There was no more gunfire. Colin Og, as an afterthought, ordered the temporary release of the man cluttering up the muzzle of their own single 9-pounder demi-culverin. For an exchange of maritime courtesies, undoubtedly it looked better that way.

Rapidly the distance between the ships lessened. In the full glare of the setting sun the low raking galley made a strangely archaic yet menacing picture, the rhythmic sweep of her serried oars churning up gilded quicksilver on either side of her. Colin Og eyed those oars thoughtfully.

"How quickly does this craft answer to her helm, Macdougall?" he enquired, presently.

"And the wind with her, as now, quick enough."

"As well so, perhaps. The helmsman of a galley, I take it, with the pull of three-score oars to handle, may be less nimble." MacColl laughed. "The porcupine, see you, if he was un-mannerly, might have his quills rubbed the wrong way!"

Macdougall stared, but Tormaid suddenly hooted and slapped the long thigh beneath his cassock. "Rich!" he cried. "Oh, excellent! Could you do it, man—run down yonder craft's side, and shear off a score of oars, like corn beneath a sickle?"

The helmsman rubbed his chin. "I could be trying, whatever—and him letting me!"

32

Colin Og turned to the boatswain. "You understand? You will be ready to give whatever uncouth orders are necessary for the trimming of the sails, to bear down quickly alongside our friend of the oars."

"Mercy on us—he'll hae us exploded wi' thae cannons, first or last, if we close wi' him . . ."

"Then you will at least go to meet your Maker in better company than you usually keep, craven," he was assured, easily. "Besides, such lessons in manners may not prove necessary. He may be a Highland gentleman."

While the other digested his own impressions of Highland gentlemen, the priest spoke. "The pity, Colin *avic*, that we have no flag, no ensign, to show. With the black eagle of An Colin Mor at our masthead, due respect would be shown us."

"M'mmmm." An Colin Mor's son accepted, doubtfully. "Saving for a Mackenzie, or a MacQuarrie, or a MacNichol, or even a lesser Macdonald—upstarts all!" He sighed. "But it would be a comfort, I grant you, to see my father's black eagle fluttering above. . . ."

He got no further. His foster-brother's phenomenal lung-power saw to that. "Mother o' Grace—look yonder!"

Father Tormaid's outstretched hand pointed to the galley's stern, where a great banner had just broken and was streaming out behind in the evening breeze. And, by a trick of the wind, plain for all to see, was vividly emblazoned thereon a black crouching eagle on a field of gold.

"Well, now!" Colin Og said.

A groan escaped from the lips of the boatswain, who had seen that flag before.

With manners-teaching no longer on the programme, the *Florabel* shortened sail, put up, and stood into the wind, waiting. Very submissive she looked. The galley seemed to find her suspiciously so. At about four cable's lengths, she circled the almost stationary ship, warily, her swivel-culverins on fo'c'sle and poop never leaving their target.

Colin Og lounged back against the rail, Tormaid's telescope

to his eye. "They keep confoundedly low," he complained.

"There is a parapet around all of her, and they peep from behind it like novices in a nunnery! I can see no faces . . . but I think that I can see feathers lifting from a bonnet, there—three feathers!"

"Three!" Tormaid cried. "Then it must be Himself—An Colin Mor! Here is a welcome, indeed. Your own father come to bring you home!"

"Three feathers under that banner must bespeak Ardcoll himself, yes," Colin Og agreed. "This is better than your fatted calf for the returned prodigal, Tormaid!" He grinned. "But, I think, a small bit of a surprise for my good parent would be well conceived. Come you, brother," and he hurried for the poop steps, and down, the priest following. At the foot, he turned, and shouted back to the boatswain. "Shipman—act you as though you were master, for your sins! I need not warn you to do as yonder galley tells you. Untie his hands, Macdougall—it will look the kindlier!"

So, within the doorway beneath the poop, the two MacColls waited. From above, a commentary on the situation was called down to them by the Graham, relayed from Angus Macdougall at the helm. The galley was coming up astern. She was no more than a couple of cable's lengths off. She was hailing them, now. . . .

From over the water a high and challenging cry came to them, asking in the Gaelic what ship was that, and whither bound.

After translation by the Macdougall, the boatswain lifted up a somewhat tremulous voice to reply that she was the *Florabel*, one hundred and forty tons, out of Dumbarton on coastwise trade, with passengers for Eorsary.

A few moments' consideration of this, and the word came back to them, forceful and clear, and only a little interrupted by the screaming gulls that escorted both craft, to the effect that, in the name of the noble and mighty Colin mhic Colin mhic Cormac, Lord of Ardcoll, Ardtarff, Eorsary, and Calinish, of the Hundred Glens and all the Islands of the Sea, high chief

34

of all the MacColls and their kindred septs, the vessel *Florabel*, now in ward of the said Colin, was required to heave to, to lower a boat, and to prepare to receive a boarding-party, under pain of immediate destruction.

"Calinish is new!" Colin Og commented. "Macleod's territory."

"MacColl's now, then—God's will being done!"

"M'mmm. I wonder, now . . ."

Orders from above indicated that the authoritative instructions were being expeditiously and expediently carried out. The *Florabel's* only boat was lowered, manned, and pulled away astern to the waiting galley. There was some shouting, to do with the shortening of sail, and miscellaneous upraised voices competed with Graham and the seabirds. Then suddenly, there lifted above the other sounds the skirl of the bagpipes, high, vigorous, dominant, lifted and maintained.

The two men under the poop looked at each other, gleaming-eyed. Colin Og swallowed, unashamedly. It was the first time that either of them had heard that sound in three long years.

The piping drew nearer. Apparently the musicians—there obviously were two of them—were now in the *Florabel's* boat. The tune they played was a rousing one. The toes of the boots of both the waiting men tapped out its rhythm, of their own accord.

First up, over the side, came two fierce-looking and hairy creatures, naked save for the philabeg, or short kilt, unshod, with dirks in their hands and unsheathed broadswords under their oxters. They were joined by a saturnine man, long and lanky and stooping, with a great beak of a nose, and one side of his face horribly disfigured by an ancient wound, his person adequately covered at least in doublet and tight-fitting trews, if in stained and somewhat ragged tartan. His bonnet was adorned with a single feather. At sight of him, each of the watchers in the doorway drew a quick involuntary breath. Behind this sinister-seeming individual, a succession of discordant wails and groans, puncturing the more regular piping effects, seemed to indicate that at least one of the musicians was endeavouring to play his way up—no minor feat, on a swinging ship's ladder. Red in the face, but blowing spasmodically still, this stalwart came into view, and, stalking in front of his fellows, proceeded forthwith to strut up and down the deck, what time his colleague in harmony climbed up to join him, followed by two more swordsmen as villainous as the first. This augmented assembly appeared to be not in the least interested in the *Florabel*, her crew, or her acting master— who stood unhappily near the poop-steps—but peered back over the side whence they had come with every appearance of concern. Even the eyes of the perambulating and perspiring pipers were turned thitherwards. Inevitably, so were those of everybody else on board.

After a due and suitable interval the tips of three eagle's feathers appeared above the bulwarks. For a moment they seemed to hesitate there, and then, abruptly, there was a convulsion, and a man came vaulting lithely into view, in a swirl of limbs and vivid tartan. The stooping scar-faced personage raised a harsh and penetrating voice, and a claw-like hand, at which the two instrumentalists ceased their blowing, while their bagpipes choked and expired into comparative quiet.

"Make way for the Son of Colin!" he cried, in English. "Let all men uncover!" and he swept off his bonnet with a flourish.

Actually, apart from one of the pipers, there was no man in sight in a position to obey this last injunction—all were hatless. All, that is, save for the man who stepped out of the doorway beneath the poop, at that moment, Colin Og MacColl—and he kept his ostrich-feathered beaver firmly on his dark head. He paced forward half a dozen strides, and stood staring at the newcomer.

And undoubtedly, he was something worth the staring at. Indeed, except for the clothing and the style of his hair, Colin Og might almost have been staring into a mirror—almost, but not quite. The man bore him an uncanny likeness, though only the most unobservant beholder, after a second glance, would have mistaken the two. The young man opposite—and he *was* a young man—though similarly built, was just a little more stocky, his features, though identically moulded, were in total just a trifle heavier, hard as it would have been to say exactly where. His eyes, too, were paler, grey-green where Colin's Og's were purely brown, and their expression more intense, if perhaps the merest hint less lively. Altogether, the one was a slightly less chiselled edition of the other—but with fully as heroic an air and as proud a mien. And he suffered nothing on account of his garb. Dressed in the full magnificence of the philamore, or great kilt and plaid, in a brilliant scarlet and black tartan, with a silver-buttoned doublet of the same blue-green sett as the scar-faced man, great jewelled brooches on bonnet and shoulder, a striking sporran of badgerskin, and a handsome armoury of tremendous broadsword, elaborately-handled dirks, and silver-mounted pistols, he was altogether a notable and eye-catching figure. There was nothing shabby, tattered, or down-at-heel about this swack fellow.

He was staring now, as Colin Og was staring—and others, too. Indeed, the pair of them were the target for all eyes—and not without reason. It was Colin Og who first found words.

"Cormac!" he said. "Well, now—here is a surprise, 'fore God!"

The newcomer twice opened his mouth to speak, twice thought better of it, glanced swiftly at his stooping and grim-faced companion, and then barked a short laugh. "Colin *avic*!" he cried, his voice rising in seeming confidence—though his green eyes still were busy. "Coll, of my heart! My father's son! The wanderer, himself. Welcome home, brother." And stepping forward, he held out his hand.

Colin Og took it, but without any corresponding flourish. His brow was furrowing. "Cormac—our father?" he demanded. "He is . . . he is not . . . ?"

His brother shrugged, and shook his handsome head, in one. "He is not dead, no. But he is not the man he was, at all—a sick and failing man, Colin, to my sorrow. Changed sad days they are, indeed. . . ."

"Changed, yes. You wear three feathers in your bonnet

today, Cormac? How is that?"

The other's eyes flickered, before he laughed again. "That is just for the honour of the clan, whatever. You would not have Colin's wolves leaderless?"

"Three feathers are the mark of the chief, of An Colin Mor himself, brother."

"They could be the mark of his deputy, Captain of Clan Colin, see you, Colin mhic Colin." That was the strangely grating and high-pitched voice of the man with the scar.

Young Ardcoll did not so much as glance in the speaker's direction. "I am listening, Cormac *avic*!" he said.

"Och, Iain Cam refers to a device, just. It was necessary, see you. Lochgarve was old getting, with little heart for the clan's advancement. Myself, now—I was able to give more heart to the business."

"And Clan Colin has prospered exceedingly," the man Iain Cam declared, pointedly.

"And no courier bringing me my moneys for a twelve-month!" That, from Colin, was as pointed.

Cormac MacColl shook his head. "Do you tell me that, Colin! Bad, that is—bad! My sorrow—the thieves and robbers there are about! Slain and robbed they must have been . . . by the accursed Campbells, no doubt."

The brothers' eyes met, brown and green, and neither dropped. "It could be," Colin acceded, even-voiced, and paused significantly. "And Lochgarve—the Captain?" he went on. "What of him? Three years ago, he was a man in his prime . . . and my friend! He is well?"

This time, the other's eyes did not flicker, either. "Unfortunately, he died. A pity, it was."

"I see." Colin Og's mobile lips were very stiff. "God rest his soul!"

"Amen to that!" Cormac sounded fervent.

The wry-faced Iain Cam started to laugh, thought better of it, and changed it to a choking cough.

From Colin's back came a deep voice. "Three years ago, Wry Iain of the Cairn was an outcast of this clan, and no man

walked in his company, by order of An Colin Mor!" That was
Father Tormaid, his eyes on the scarred face.

Iain Cam of the Cairn thrust his hawk-face forward. "You
will watch your words, you . . ."

Cormac MacColl interrupted. "What—does that cock still
crow! They have not cut your comb, then, with your . . . your
tonsure, Tormaid!" He grinned. "All of a priest, now, eh—
Tormaid, the Man of Peace!"

"There are swords and swords, Cormac mhic Colin," the
cleric answered, readily. "Some here would find that I can use
them all! Even a man of peace may have his armoury."

"You tell me so?" The other threw up his head and laughed.
"Knowing my Tormaid, I believe you! Good it is to hear your
dove-like roar, Reverence!" He turned back to Colin Og, and
slapped his shoulder with an accession of heartiness. "But this
is no talk for brothers new met after two years—or is it three?
I misremember. Colin *avic*, it does me good to see you—it
does indeed."

His twin brother laughed, as suddenly. "You were an able
liar always, Cormac! I never could rival you. Myself, I am
glad too, to be with you. I have been away overlong—much
overlong, it seems." Something seemed to have released the
string of his emotion, for he chuckled genially. "I take it kindly
that you came all this way to meet me, brother!"

Cormac smiled appreciatively. "Saint Ninian must have been
at my helm . . . or perhaps one of Tormaid's fine Italian saints!
We have been down in the Torridon country—I was getting
grievously short of galley-slaves. There is woeful lack of
shipping in these seas, these days."

"Ah! I wonder why?"

"There you have me!" Cormac grinned. "Strange, it is. Trade
must be failing. Yours is the first Southron we have seen this
voyage. Out of Dumbarton, I hear?"

"That is so."

"Good. And her cargo? What have we got?"

"Her cargo, my good Cormac, is mine!"

The other's brows shot up. "Yours?"

"Yes. I accepted it, in the name of An Colin Mor, two days back."

Cormac's voice had an edge to it. "But . . . the master said that he was on coastwise trade? He did not . . ."

"That poor craven is master of nothing—not even his white-livered self! *I* am master of this ship. The man who *was* master is below, in chains."

His brother looked about him for the not very evident crew. "And your men?" he demanded.

"They lurk and linger," he was told, easily. "Perhaps they are afraid of your bagpipes! But they served."

"Say you so! Then they will serve a little longer." He turned. "Iain Cam—see you to it. Turn her about, and make for Coigach Point and the Sound of Kilninian. We will go ahead in the *Iolair*. Do you require more men?"

"I think not, Ardcoll. I can deal with . . ."

"Ardcoll!" Colin Og snapped. "*Ardcoll*, did the fellow say?"

"Och, just a slip of the tongue, Colin *avic*," Cormac assured cheerfully. "He has the slippery tongue, has Iainie—like the sword of him! Come—we will over to the galley, and be back at Ardcoll long before this lumbering tub."

"Look you, brother," the other said quietly. "I told you, did I not, that I was master of this ship? She is mine, and I will bring her to Ardcoll in my own time. You may sail with her if you will, and with pleasure—as a passenger. But I do not need the assistance of your ill-favoured bullyrook here . . . and if you are in haste for Ardcoll, take him with you!"

"*Iosa Criosd!* I'll take that from no man!" the scar-faced Iain cried, stepping forward, his hand on his broadsword. But Cormac MacColl's imperious arm barred his way.

"Quiet, you," he said. "Colin's sons are speaking!" He looked at his brother, one eyebrow raised. "You are a thought hasty in your judgment, it might be? But that is no uncommon fault in our family, eh? Look, *avic*—your men are few, and timid, and mine are many, and wearying for a ploy. We will not argue whose prize this ship is . . ."

"We will not!" Colin Og agreed. "We will not argue, at all,

here and now. Do you sail as my passenger, or return to your own ship?"

Cormac's voice quivered a little. "Softly, brother! I have five score armed men, within the crook of my finger."

"Bravely tailed you are, fine fellow." Colin nodded. "But, for your own ear—myself, I am well tailed, too, with five score barrels of gunpowder in my hold this minute, and a sour lad with a lantern standing by! This ship sails my way—or not at all! Choose, you."

Eye met eye again. Cormac stared, and bit his lip. Overhead the gulls still wheeled and screamed. Then, abruptly, he swung on his brogan heel. "I will be waiting for you at Ardcoll," he said, shortly. "Come, the rest of you!"

Iain Cam, the wry-faced, looked very wry indeed, frowned darkly, hesitated, and then rose to his duty. "Make way for Cormac mhic Colin, Captain of Clan Colin!" he cried—though the said gallant figure of a man already had a muscular leg over the side. And with a darted glare at Colin Og. "Way for Ardcoll!" That was a shout, as he strode to follow his leader.

And the pipers blew.

Expressionless, Colin watched them go. Tormaid at his side was less restrained.

IV

UP in the dipping bows, leaning against the taut and strumming cordage, Colin Og stared ahead into the wan heart of the northern night, where the aurora borealis was flickering fitfully over the dark waters. Though there were stars winking above and behind, no stars gleamed in front there, out of the chill pallor that was neither light nor darkness, but only the stark emanation of that frozen infinity beyond the far rim of the sea.

In the graven lines of the man's face was reflected, perhaps, something of the starkness, the ache, of that terrible emptiness. Well might it. Always, in strange lands and foreign cities, that pallid north had meant home to him, drawing him, magnetic indeed. But now, it seemed, his homecoming was to be vastly different from his daydreams and anticipations. The evening's events left no doubt as to that. Alone in the bows he considered it all, and no man—even Tormaid his foster-brother—sought to invade his solitude.

Three years ago he, elder twin son and heir of An Colin Mor, Chief of Clan Colin had left his father's house of Ardcoll and the mountains and valleys of the Eorsary peninsula, to travel reluctantly south, in deference to the imperious wishes of his most potent maternal grandmother, daughter of a Sassunach earl. She, the Lady Clementina, with strangely mistaken ideas but a bottomless purse, had insisted out of her abysmal ignorance that one at least of her daughter's sons should not grow up a complete barbarian like his father, but be subjected for some period of his youth to the civilizing influences of the South. The MacColl, with the mannerliness of his race and a wholesome respect for the fruit of broad English acres—if scarcely for the owners thereof—had given his chiefly word; but he had managed to postpone its fulfilment until a small matter of the hanging of a King's ship captain

42

from the battlements of his castle of Duncolin had precipitated sundry exchanges culminating in the royal suggestion that his son and heir might profitably honour his Court by a prolonged visit, like the heirs of certain other Highland chiefs of magisterial habits. This demand for a hostage, which looked like being enforced—with the deplorable and hated Archibald of Argyll as King's representative—seemed to provide an obvious occasion for a Highland gentleman to redeem his promise to an irascible mother-in-law as well as to a fractious monarch. So, in his twentieth year, An Colin Mor, Colin the Great, despatched An Colin Og, Colin the Younger, in the care of a captain and troop of King's dragoons and of his foster-brother Tormaid the Postulant, on the long, long road to London and his further education.

It had not all worked out quite as any of them had intended, either chief, mother-in-law, or king—as frequently happens to the most suitable arrangements of even such as these. It had been the year of Our Lord seventeen hundred and one, and within six months, Dutch William had fallen from his horse on the way to Hampton Court, broken a collarbone, and curiously enough died of it, and the redoubtable Lady Clementina Horncastle had taken a fit whilst belabouring one of her coachmen with his own whip, and thereafter become a bedridden paralytic. Young Colin MacColl, finding Queen Anne uninterested in hostages, or anything else in particular save short-lived babies, also found himself hurriedly consigned by his grandmother's embarrassed Whig nephew, the Earl of Horncastle, to Rome, where another and less distinguished nephew was some sort of Papal secretary. This had developed into anything but the Grand Tour that the suggestion of such a programme conjures up, Lord Horncastle being of a distinctly economical frame of mind. Indeed, before he had got further than Paris, Young Ardcoll was despatching urgent messages home to his father for the means of sustenance suitable for the heir of so illustrious a chief as An Colin Mor. He had been somewhat disappointed in the results, since unfortunately the Laird of Ardcoll, Ardtarff, Eorsary, etcetera, though lord of the hundred glens and all the islands of the sea, had never been similarly richly endowed with ready money.

In Rome, thanks to Tormaid's abilities with pen as well as tongue, the Papal official had put up with them a little less grudgingly than at first seemed likely. Moreover, Colin's undeniable efficiency with either rapier or broadsword was more than once put to excellent use by the Church Militant. By such means, aided by a certain native ingenuity, the parsimonious doles from Lord Horncastle, and the infrequent contributions from far Ardcoll, they managed to subsist for some twenty months at the Hub of Civilization. When, however, not only had there been no courier from Eorsary for more than half a year, and their reluctant protector was promoted and sent as legate to somewhere outlandish in the Americas, but cryptic word arrived from London that this remittance would be the last, that the Lady Clementina had died and had had the good sense, in a moment of lucidity, to suitably adjust her will before she did so—then, all things considered, the call of the bens and the glens had begun to be urgent. With a Knighthood of the Holy Manger conferred on one, and a priesthood conferred on the other, Mother Church had seen them hurriedly and probably thankfully off her premises.

It had been a long road home, for gentlemen of scruples and empty pouches. Tormaid's cloth had on the whole been a help, but more than respect for the Church had been required to bring two otherwise unendowed and hearty-eating young men across the breadth of Europe and the narrow seas. In decency, a veil should be drawn over that journey. Painful details would advantage none.

And now, Colin Og was faced with a homecoming other than that he had expected. His proud father, it seemed, was a sick and ailing man—must be, for this evening's events to have been possible, at all. His younger brother—younger by only an hour or two, admittedly—was cock of the walk, and calling himself Captain of the Clan, while his old friend Duncan MacColl of Lochgarve, who as chiefest cadet of MacColl had been Captain of Clan Colin as his right, was not only demoted but dead. And, perhaps most significant of all, this crooked and wry-faced Iain of the Cairn, whom for his misdeeds his father previously would not permit to set foot on clan territory on pain of hanging, now flaunted it brazenly as brother Cormac's lieutenant.

All this added up to a disturbing total, at which the man in the bows did not attempt to blink. It seemed that he might be going to have to pay even dearer than he had anticipated for his grandmother's unfortunate misconceptions on the benefits of education.

Only the one purely metaphorical bright patch gleamed in the wan northern sky ahead—Marsala Macleod of Eynart. Marsala would be nearly twenty-one, now . . . and he was a lot braver man than when last he had seen her.

It was high noon next day before the *Florabel*, leaving the Summer Isles astern and rounding the cape of Rhu Coigach, came in sight, across the wide Bay of Eynart, of the long promontory of Eorsary. Almost like an island it lay, fifteen and more miles of it, thrusting out into the Minch, in a series of soaring peaks, plunging valleys, and dizzy cliffs, a harsh-seeming and frowning land softened by the green machairs and the yellow beading of sandy beaches. Slashed with the light and shadow of the midday sun, the blue mountains still streaked with white in their northernmost corries, the deep brown of rolling heather moors, the sombre skirts of the climbing pine forest, and the prevailing gleam of sparkling water, it made a colourful picture for the cloud-shadows to sail over. Colin Og and Tormaid the Priest stared at it long and misty-eyed, before they trusted themselves to words.

Standing in towards that upheaved and far from welcoming coastline, their apprehensive navigator, the boatswain, once again grew vocally alarmed, till an almost invisible breach in the rampart of cliff and rock was pointed out to him, midway down the peninsula. On closer approach—very close approach indeed—this was seen to be the curiously concealed entrance to a narrow sea-loch that wound away inland between towering

45

scree-lined hillsides. Shaking an unhappy head to match the rest of his quaking person, the boatswain piloted the cautious *Florabel* within these grim portals, under minimum canvas. Undoubtedly, the Fionnghall, the fair sea-rovers from Norway who once had conquered this seaboard, would not have found Loch Coll so very different to one of their native fiords.

After a narrow mile of unchancy wind currents but apparently consistently deep water, the loch took a sudden turn to the east and opened out. The change was immediate and astonishing. Instead of a constricted lane between dark walls of stone and gravel and raw earth, there was an open and pleasant sheet of water within a wide and green valley, a fair and fertile basin of the hills, backed to north and east by tall mountains but enclosed to south and west by only low and gently sloping grassy braes, over which white croft houses were scattered, each beside its patch of tilth. And, at the far end of the loch, on a spur of rock that jutted arrogantly into the saffron-weed-fringed water, rose the sheer curtain walls and square keep of a tall tower, An Colin Mor's castle of Duncolin. Stern and proud it stood, dominating all save the still more dominant mountains, and below it, amongst a huddle of lesser craft, the raking galley lay at anchor.

From the poop Colin Og considered his home, eager-eyed. It was all as he knew it—nothing seemed to be changed. The church tower still was not repaired. The cattle pens still were full. The dye-house still steamed and the tannery still smoked. The drying nets still festooned the shore, and the eagle banner the castle flagstaff. Yes—and more than the eagle banner; the *Florabel's* tack revealed another decoration to the castle. Projecting from the northern parapet was a boom, from which dangled three dark objects that swayed in the breeze. Always it had been Clan Colin's duty and pride to see that its chief's castle walls did not go unfurnished with hanging men—on the north side only, of course, northerly winds being rare. It seemed that in some respects at least, brother Cormac was not unmindful of tradition. Though one dangler had in the past normally been considered adequate. . . .

The boatswain was, of course, worrying about his soundings, and the vessel's draught. The MacColls assured him that there was deep water right up to the castle walls. Under scant sail, the *Florabel* crept in.

It was Tormaid who voiced the doubt that too much normality could be unsuitable. "I see no crowds to welcome the Son of Colin," he mentioned. "I hear no cannon fired to bring you to your father's hall. I observe no boats sailing to meet the young chief. Clan Colin, I think, requires awakening."

His foster-brother nodded. "The thought occurred to myself." He glanced behind him. "In our quiet way, we will do what we may . . . for sloth is an ill thing. Macdougall—call the gunner. That toy—is it loaded?"

"It is, yes. Will we have the ball out, Colin mhic Colin?"

"Not so. A cannon without a ball is like an empty promise—a sheer deceit. Let the ball be. Creature—you are gunner? How true is your aim, with this? Good. Then take you me that figurehead off yonder galley."

"Excellent," said the cleric. "Most apt."

So, in a minute or so, the 9lb demi-culverin thundered, shattering the midday somnolence of the guardian hills, wakening a thousand echoes, and arousing a multitude of screaming gulls from every roof and rock and skerry. The shot was no bad one, for a start, missing the *Iolair's* bows by only a foot or two, and plunging into the clutter of small boats beyond, one of which it sank, throwing up a prodigious column of water.

"Man, man," Tormaid chided, as Macdougall and the gunner reloaded, "if you cannot be hitting a stationary target, with the wind astern in calm water at a stone's throw, the saints be praised there's been no battle in it!"

"Just a hint to the right, and you are there," Colin Og encouraged.

The second shot hit the figurehead fair and square, demolishing it entirely, with some small amount of rigging and the like—which was small loss, the thing being in only doubtful taste, and a capture, almost certainly, from some uncouth Irish princeling.

Now they did not have to complain of lack of attention. With the reverberating reports, men, women, and children materialized from all quarters like rabbits from their burrows. Shouting, skirling, and the barking of a hundred dogs echoed across the water to augment the screeching of the gulls. At the windows and on the parapet-walk of the castle, gesticulating figures appeared. Colin was content. The *Florabel*, with her way almost lost on her, drifted in under the castle walls, and dropped anchor half a cable's length from her late target.

And glancing up, in passing, at the three pendant figures that twirled and dangled in the breeze from the boom above, the two MacColls' mouths tightened. One was, as it were, overripe fruit that had hung there for some time, obviously, and the blackened face was unrecognizable. But the other two were newly bloomed, noticeably fresh, and though the features were understandably contorted, they were yet quite identifiable. And Colin Og and his foster-brother knew both of them. One was an elderly greybeard, Martin the Teacher, who had tutored them as boys. The second was young Alastair of Glenoran, companion of Colin Og's youth. These two looked barely stiff.

It was something of an innovation for MacColl notables to be decorating An Colin Mor's private gallows.

By the time that Colin Og had a boat lowered, and was being rowed to the castle jetty, a more suitable welcome committee had gathered to receive him. Cormac was there, with Iain Cam and two or three others, none of whom watched the newcomers' arrival with any noteworthy kindling of eye. Behind them, numerous faces peered from corners and apertures. As the boat's prow touched the landing steps under the frowning walls, it was Cormac MacColl who spoke.

"Brother," he said, "the reason for your unseemly cannonade escapes me!" His voice was level, but only just.

"Since no fireworks display signalled my homecoming, I was forced to provide my own," Colin told him. "Your haste to reach Ardcoll has been singularly barren of result, Cormac *avic.*"

"Once again, your judgment may prove hasty!"

"That awaits your proving." Colin jumped ashore, and came up the slippery weed-grown steps. "This is scarcely the traditional welcome for Colin's Heir!" he declared.

Iain Cam began, "Colin's Heir may not . . ." But Cormac cut him short with a quick flick of the hand.

"All things in their place," he said. "With our father a sick man, it would be unsuitable to have any noisy festivity. He would not wish to be disturbed. . . ."

"My father must be a changed man, surely!" he was interrupted.

"I fear that you are right, in that," the other acceded. He lifted his glance across the sparkling water. "I fear, too, that your gunner has done damage to my ship!"

"The creature did only what I ordered." It was Colin's turn to glance up, high above them, to where the gallows-fruit swayed and spun amongst the squabbling gulls. "I see friends of mine where I had not expected to see any of the name of MacColl . . . even such as this Wry-face, here!"

"An Colin Mor still has a long arm . . . even in sickness!" his brother answered, briefly.

"But a short memory, it seems!" That was Tormaid, at Colin's shoulder. "These men, unless my eyes fail me, had served him well . . . unlike some who appear to be thriving!" And his eye ran over the group opposite.

"Hold your tongue, puppy!" a fat gross man, mountainous in his plaid, growled.

"It is a wise priest that saves his breath for his benedictions," Cormac observed, with his own smile. "But, come—here is no place for talk, wise or foolish. Inside with us, in the name of Mercy."

"Duncolin's door stands wide!" the fat man intoned, and turned to lead the way within.

"Wide it must have stood, indeed, these past months!" Colin Og agreed, significantly. "But I will be glad to see the inside of it, nevertheless, brother."

"We will close it, then, behind us," Cormac said, and his

excellent teeth showed in something wider than a smile.

Up the worn stone steps of the winding turnpike stairway the men climbed, rawhide brogans and down-at-heel buckled shoes. On the first-floor landing, the fat seneschal led them into a large chamber, stone vaulted and stone paved, with deep window embrasures in the ten-foot thickness of the walls, and an enormous open fireplace, heraldically carved, on which a mountain of peats smouldered. The walls were decked with an assortment of hangings, tartan, tapestry, tattered banners, and reed-matting, the flagstones strewn with skins of deer and sheep, and a great table ran almost the length of the floor. This was the hall and principal apartment of the castle. Its aspect had not changed noticeably in the exiles' three years' absence nor, for that matter, in the three centuries previous.

Cormac waved his hand towards the table. "Food, brother, and *uisge beatha*, and even some red Portingall wine that a passing shipmaster was kind enough to bestow on us. Fill your bellies, and you will be the better company!"

"May be. But first, I will see my father."

His brother stroked a not insignificant chin. "He is resting," he said. "But I will go up, to see that he is ready to see you . . ."

"You will not!" Colin snapped. "In this house, no man stands between me and my father!" and wheeling round, he stalked out of the hall to the farther stairs.

The others exchanged glances, and turned to follow on, making way for Cormac, with Father Tormaid bringing up the rear.

On the landing above were two doors. Colin went straight to one, that directly over the hall, pressed the latch and pushed. The stout door shook but did not open. He rattled it, without effect. He spun round. "Locked!" he exclaimed. "What means this?"

Cormac was drawing a key from his sporran. "Sometimes he wanders a little," he said. "He could be doing himself an injury. . . ."

"God in His Heaven—An Colin Mor locked in his own castle!" his brother cried. As the lock clicked back, he thrust the door open, and brushing past Cormac, strode within.

It was a lesser room than that downstairs, but still large and where the hall had been dominated by its table, this apartment was dominated by the great canopied bed in mid-floor. And under the heaped and tossed coverings of that bed a long shape lay, completely hidden. As Colin Og stared, the shape stirred and twitched, and, infinitely slowly, a movement proceeded amongst the plaids and blanketing near the head of that pile. The young man took a couple of paces forward, and immediately there was a convulsion, and the covers were drawn tight as the shape seemed to shrink in on itself. Wide-eyed, Colin stood, rooted, and at his back five men waited, wordless.

The silence in that thick-walled chamber was absolute, though the crying of the gulls came faintly from without. Gradually the stirring began again. A rift, a cavity in the coverings, revealed itself, some way down the bed this time. It grew. A gleam was visible within. Presently the gap was sufficient to reveal most of a long haggard straggle-bearded face from which great eyes peered out of hollow sockets, a very lantern of a face queerly lit.

Colin Og shook his head, and his throat worked as he swallowed. "Father . . . !" he got out. "Mary's Grace . . . !"

"No! No!" Thick, tremulous, the voice came from the bed. "No, I say!" And a long, claw-like hand issued from the covers and gestured urgently away, as though to push the young man back. Thrice that pitiful hand thrust, and then, with a sort of strangled sob, it was withdrawn, and abruptly the bedclothes were pulled over once more and the staring face disappeared.

For a long moment Colin stood dumbly. Then, whirling about, he jabbed a furious finger at the others, standing near the door. "Go—in God's name!" he shouted. "Out! Leave us alone. All of you!"

And all of them went, without a word. Even Cormac, who

wiped a filial eye with a corner of his plaid as he closed the door behind him.

Colin the Great and the Less were left alone.

V

IT was a full half-hour before Cormac MacColl came back, and quietly opened the door of that bedchamber. He found Colin standing at one of the window embrasures, gazing out at the enclosing hills. Their father still lay hidden, motionless save for an occasional shudder.

Colin did not turn his head. "I can make no impression on him," he said, even-voiced. "None. He will not listen."

"No," Cormac agreed. "That is the way of it. I warned you. . . ."

"He seems to think that it is my ghost that is speaking— that I am dead!"

"That is a sad delusion that he has had this long while."

"But why? How should such come to him?"

The other shrugged. "Who can tell? As well ask where the wind comes from. My sorrow—he has many as strange delusions, I assure you."

Colin shook a troubled head. "It is a fearsome thing, this. What sickness is this—what plague of the mind? For how long has he been stricken thus?"

"For more than a twelvemonth. It was on a foray into Mackenzie country. Just a small bit of a tulzie it was, but he was struck on the head from behind. Only a Mackenzie or a Campbell would do the like. He lost his consciousness for six days, and for a month after spoke no word. Since then, this has been the way of it. . . ."

A muffled groan issued from under the piled blankets.

"You mean that he lies like this—bedridden? He is no more than, than . . ."

"Than a living corpse, brother. For a twelvemonth he has not stirred from this room. You will see why it was I must take the lead, in Clan Colin. When the chief cannot rule, lesser men grow bold. I was forced to act."

"Yes. Yes . . . but surely there was no need that Lochgarve should die? And Alastair of Glenoran. And old Martin. These were our friends . . ."

"My good Colin—a dead friend is better than a live enemy!"

Behind them, the bedclothes heaved, and a gabble of words came therefrom, muffled, unintelligible. Colin Og was turning thitherwards when his brother's hand restrained him.

"It is no use," he said. "In all these months he has uttered no word of sense. He has lain there, and that is all that he has done."

Colin stood, eyes downcast, and with the patched toe of his shoe he stirred and tipped the edge of a white sheepskin rug. Staring at it without actually seeing it, something of its quality impressed itself on him nevertheless. His nostrils flared too, and he sniffed, questingly. His glance covered the rest of the floor, reed-matting over stone flags, and numerous other sheepskins, all snowy white. And still testing the air with his nose, he turned to his brother.

"It does not smell like a sick man's room—it smells more like a lady's boudoir," he said. "Bog myrtle, and lavender. And all these white fleeces . . . this bedchamber has changed indeed, Cormac."

It was the other's turn to look out of the window. "We do our best for him," he answered, after a moment. "We can do no less, little as it is. You would not have him stinking?"

"No. No . . ." Colin was looking at his brother's back, curiously. "You have changed in three years, too, Cormac."

"Why not? They have been full years. And it is said that . . ." He stopped, and turned. "But you will hear all, in due course. Come you down and eat, first. You can do nothing more here . . . and I am hungry, if you are not." And jerking his head, he moved towards the door.

Colin glanced from him to that untidy heap on the bed, half shrugged, half shook his head, and followed on.

On the landing, as Cormac closed the door behind them, and turned the key, Colin stepped over to the second door and reached for its latch. It too was locked. His frown was quick.

"What is this?" he demanded. "Have you turned jailer, as well as Captain, in Duncolin?"

His brother's frown was quick, too; they were extraordinarily alike in that moment. "Your room has been kept for you. It was better locked . . . to keep your property safe, see you. You ought to be thanking me! I have not the key, here—it is below. You shall have it. But come you down, man, and eat—there are viands spoiling." He laughed then, if shortly. "You are changed too, it seems. If I mind aright, it was eat first and talk after, Colin of my heart! Come, you."

At the foot of the steps, the fat seneschal was waiting. At Cormac's nod, he drew aside a hide curtain in the walling of the stairway, and with some difficulty insinuated his head between the iron bars of a narrow unglazed window. "Hallooo-o-o!" he bawled. "Hark ye! The Sons of Colin eat! Above there! They eat!"

And from the battlements high above the cry was taken up. "The Sons of Colin eat! Hark ye, all men—the Sons of Colin sit down to eat!"

And with one or two preliminary groans the pipers' strains swelled forth, to drown those of the outraged seabirds, in the bubbling triumph of *An Colin Mor's Banquet*.

If it was not actually a banquet, it certainly was a very adequate meal—quite the best that the returned exiles had tasted for many a month. An Colin Mor's table had never lacked for furnishing. Fish and fowl and beef, oaten cakes and honey and cream, *uisge beatha* and the red Portugal wine, served to indicate that though Duncolin's lord might be temporarily preoccupied, a proper appreciation of what was due and fitting was not lacking in his hall. If the prodigals made no mention of the fatted calf, nor indeed seemed to notice what they ate, the explanation lay not in the quality nor abundance of the victuals. Though, of course, a certain abstraction did not prevent them doing justice to it all, quantitatively at least.

Colin went straight to his old seat at top-right, and after a moment's hesitation Cormac seated himself directly opposite, leaving the great chair of bog-oak empty at the head of the table. The others took their places thereafter, some distance down the great board, only Father Tormaid's position seeming to cause any difficulty. Numerous individuals thronged in and sat down at the lower end, only some of whom Colin recognized, and still fewer of whom offered him any sort of greeting. There was no woman present.

The Sons of Colin ate and drank. There was little conversation. One of the pipers, blowing his way down the turnpike stair from the parapet-walk, to pace round and round their table, saw to that.

It was with Colin finished, and pensively crumbling a bannock between his fingers, that Cormac leaned forward across the table to speak, to shout.

"You will be for sleeping, now? You look weary, brother. When did you last have a night's sleep?"

Colin, who had barely closed his eyes for forty-eight hours, shrugged, then nodded and smothered a yawn. But though those eyes were dark-rimmed and heavy-lidded, they were not dull nor sluggish with sleep.

His brother was looking down the table and signing to the corpulent seneschal, when Colin forestalled him. And his action was not heavy nor sluggish, either. Rising to his feet, he turned, and stepping over the bench on which he had been seated, strode straight across the flagstones to the wall, where a small and ragged tapestry was slung amongst the other hangings. He whipped it aside, to reveal a narrow door set deep in the masonry.

Above the piping, a shout or two penetrated. This door was not locked, but Colin, opening it, found it barred by an outthrust arm, as Iain Cam ran up behind him.

"Out of my way, oaf!" he rapped, and barely giving the man time to withdraw that arm, he drove a furious left elbow backwards into the other's chest, at the same time shooting out his left leg. Iain Cam tripped, staggered, and fell with a crash. Colin, his right hand still on the latch, pushed open the door without so much as a backward glance.

Another brave fellow—never the seneschal—had launched himself forward. Colin sensed his coming, and swung round, bracing both arms against the doorjambs just as the man's hands grasped his shoulders. Bringing up his knee into his assailant's middle, Colin leant back against the support of his outstretched arms, and exploded into a violent kick. The fellow hurtled back, cleaving a way through others who had come up, right to the great table, over which he fell in considerable chaos.

There was the briefest pause. Even the piper was silent.

Cormac MacColl spoke into it, as he came forward unhurriedly around the head of the table. "No need to use that stair, brother," he said, in what passed for a level voice.

"Why not? It leads to my own room." Colin did not sound level, at all. He had been exerting himself, of course, after a heavy meal.

"Your room has not yet been prepared for you. Another would be more convenient, meantime . . ."

"Not to me. Is that all?"

"The door at the top is locked . . ."

"Only with a small bolt. I know—I made it!" Colin's stare at his brother was direct and keen. "What ails you, Cormac *avic*—what affrights you that I should visit my room?"

The other opened his mouth to speak, and shut it again, and the click of his teeth could be heard in that silent room. Then, through those same excellent teeth, his voice grated.

"Nothing ails me. Nothing in heaven or hell affrights Cormac MacColl! Go you up, then, with my blessing!"

His brother lifted one eyebrow. "In Duncolin, I would do that same, with or without any man's blessing," he said, deliberately, and turning, started to climb.

It was a narrow dark stairway, contrived within the thickness of the walling, a private access from the great hall to the master of Duncolin's apartments. Even if any man had tried to restrain him, once within that restricted and unlit stairway he could have defied it. No man did try, now. His hands on the smoothworn stones at either side, automatically following the course his boyhood's fingers had traced, Colin climbed. And behind him, some little way behind, a single pair of feet followed his own.

At the top of the stair, a hand outstretched in front of him felt for and found the timbers of the door. It did not give to his push. He knew where the bolt that held it was placed. Putting his foot directly behind it, he set his hands on either wall of the stairway, tried his stance and flexed his muscles. Then, drawing his foot back a little, with all his might and every thew and sinew brought into play, he thrust outwards and forwards—that same outburst of violence that had flung his attacker below back across the table. There was a splintering of wood, and the door flew open. He had useful feet, that man.

There was a stifled scream from within. A pace inside the room, Colin stopped. At the farther side, her back pressed against the other door, a young woman stood, wide-eyed.

"Marsala!" the man cried. "God's shadow—Marsala!"

The girl's lips formed a name, but no sound issued therefrom.

She was a tall raven-haired young woman, proudly fashioned but not proud-seeming at that moment, still-faced, with a skin of alabaster and eyes dark as peat-pools—but troubled pools. That she was beautiful no man and few women would have denied, but that her beauty was of the sort that might well occasion more pain than joy, more tears than laughter—specially to herself—would be conceded similarly. Clad in a waisted full-skirted gown of fine-spun stuff, flax-blue, with a great square white collar, she made a graceful, grateful, picture against the harsh stone walls of that narrow room—had anyone been in a state of mind to notice it.

Colin Og, who was not normally at a loss for words, was stricken to incoherency. "You . . . ! What . . . what means this? How comes it . . . Marsala . . . ?" Helplessly, his eyes on hers, he shook his head, defeated. Ladies, from Rome right to Dumbarton, could have told a different story.

The young woman did not help him, at all—though that

she was not unmoved seemed likely from the tumult of her bosom and the pressure of her hands against the door behind her. And her eyes were eloquent, at least.

Actually, it was Cormac, framed with the narrow doorway just behind his brother, who came to their aid. "A family occasion," he mentioned, with his own easiness. "Brother . . . and wife!"

"Wife!" Colin whirled round, the word a bark. His eyes stabbed his brother's. "What did you say?" A hand reached out and grasped a fistful of Cormac's doublet.

The other's gaze, after a momentary dart to the farther door, met his. "Wife, I said, yes. Marsala and myself were handfasted last year. . . ."

"Handfasted! Mother of God—you, you Judas! You knavish cockatrice! You snake in the grass! I do not believe it. Lies—all lies." With a furious shake, Colin released his brother's doublet, all but overbalancing him, and swung round. "Marsala—this is not so? It cannot be. . . ."

Great-eyed the young woman stared at him, and though at length she shook her dark head, slowly, the words that her lips reluctantly formed were affirmative. "Yes," she whispered. "Yes, God forgive me—it is true. . . ."

"No! It cannot be. It is a trick—another trick. Always, you were promised to me. Our fathers pledged it, when we were children. . . . Always, I have loved you! You . . . you did not hate me. You said that you liked me better than Cormac—always you said so. Your father, Torquil Macleod—he is my friend. He would never permit this, this treachery . . ."

"Softly, brother. Watch your words, will you," Cormac said, at his back. "Torquil Macleod did permit it. We were wed at Eynart, in his presence. . . ."

"Wed? Handfasted, you said, damn you . . . !" Colin had not turned.

"Handfasted, yes. In the presence of Torquil Macleod and all his people, and my . . . and our Clan Council. It was decided upon by our clans, and done properly, fittingly. It is no trick, believe me. It is . . ."

"Marsala," Colin interrupted, "is this true? For sweet Mary's sake—say that it is not true!"

The girl was biting her lips. "Colin . . ." she began, "I . . . I . . ." Her voice faltered, as she looked from one to the other. Then she seemed to wipe her lovely face of all expression. "You would not have me make my husband a liar?" she asked, tonelessly.

"God—or the Devil—did that same long ago, I think!"

The laugh at his back was not entirely without mirth.

"Much could be said," the young woman went on, with a kind of weariness. "But what is done is done. I am Cormac's wife. . . ."

"By handfast only!"

"Yes. Does the word for it matter?"

"By all the saints, it does!" Quite frankly, Colin Og transferred his gaze from her face down over her shapely but slender figure. And under that barefaced scrutiny Marsala Macleod did not shrink nor flinch. Indeed, almost she seemed to draw herself up, to display her lissome womanly person, not boldly or brazenly but with that proud calm that seemed to be part of her, even in her distress. She did not speak.

Cormac MacColl did. "There is plenty of time yet, brother," he said, cryptically.

"When *was* this?" Colin demanded of the girl. "When were you handfasted to him?"

"After harvest," she replied, low-voiced. "Eight months ago."

"Eight months!" The significance of his exclamation was unmistakable. "A year and a day is all the time you have. Four months to go. If there is no child of a handfast marriage in a year and a day, it is no marriage!"

"Much may happen in four months, Colin *avic*!" his brother suggested. "And cannot a handfast marriage be turned into a permanent one?"

"Not without the consent of all parties. And of the clan!"

"Leave you all parties—and the clan—to me," Cormac advised.

60

" 'Fore God, I will not!" Colin Og exploded. "Over much has been left to you. You have been very busy while I have been gone, brother—your hand has been little idle, I think. Time it is that I took a hand, in Eorsary!" He swung round to the young woman. "Even if the hand that I thought was mine is snatched from me and given to another, Marsala Macleod!" His voice was bitter.

She met his accusatory gaze, hurt-eyed but unflinching. "I am sorry, Colin—I am more than sorry. Believe me, I did not know. . . ."

"You knew that we were promised, trysted. You knew that our father trysted us as children, for the clans' sake. . . ."

"And for the clans' sake, our fathers changed their minds!" That was Cormac.

"Torquil Macleod, then, must be as different a man as An Colin Mor!"

"My father thought that you were dead," Marsala Macleod informed quietly, level-voiced. "And not only my father. All of us thought so. I thought so. . . ."

"That is so," her husband agreed, pleasantly. "How fortunate that rumour so often lies!"

Slowly, this time, Colin turned to his brother. "So! That is it. Clear, it is, at last. You lied, as ever. You lied . . . and she was ready to believe you! You are paired, indeed. Dastards! God have mercy on you—for I will not! I am not dead, as you will discover." His voice rose. "I am back in Duncolin, and Duncolin will know it—Clan Colin will know it! Now—leave me. Get from my sight, both of you, in your sin. Go, before I am sick. Out with you!"

"Colin . . ." the girl began, and a hand came out towards him. "Colin, see you . . ."

But she was interrupted, strongly, if sardonically. "Your pleasure is our command, brother. In your present temper, I swear, you are better alone. You are tired, of course—rest is what you need. Rest and sleep—a deal of sleep. Afterwards, you will look at matters with a clearer eye, I think—more kindly, charitably. If you will come to your room . . ."

61

"This is my room. Take yourself and your woman out of it!"

Cormac frowned, and then shrugged. "Very well," he said. "Come you, Marsala."

The girl seemed slow-footed, and her husband strode over, took her arm, and propelled her to the small door to the private stair. As she passed Colin her eyes searched his face. But he did not look at her. In the doorway she glanced back over her own shoulder and that of her escort. "Mary-Mother, pity us all," she said. "If you cannot think kindly of me, Colin, think of me not at all. I do not . . ."

The ravished door slammed behind her and her husband.

For long Colin Og MacColl stood staring, unseeing, out of the narrow window to the sun-drenched hills. At last, he moved listlessly to the bed, his own bed, and sat down heavily. Apart from the permanent mattress of sheepskins, covered by a single plaid, it was not made up. The man did not consider that— even if the bed and that room were not entirely outwith his reeling thoughts. And still he stared.

Presently his eyelids drooped for very weight, and gradually his weary body sagged over and over till his shoulder rested against the bed-head, where it slipped and slipped. When eventually he slumped inertly in a twisted huddle on to the bedding, he did not stir despite the discomfort of his position. He did not waken.

He did not waken, either, when some time later the door to the main stairway was thrown open, a somewhat dishevelled Tormaid was thrust inside, and the door slammed shut again, the lock clicking.

The representative of Holy Church rubbed a bruised brow and cheekbone tenderly, sighed, shrugged, and yawned cavernously. *He* did not waste any time on staring. Lifting Colin's legs up on to the bed, and straightening his cramped posture, he lay down beside him, starting to mutter a prayer suitable to the occasion, brief necessarily, but powerful, scorching in its aim and intensity. Unfortunately, he was unable to get beyond the phrase "may they shrivel unshriven on the blazing brander of Beelzebub . . ." thrice-repeated, before the snoring of his frail flesh overtook the intensity of his devotions.

VI

IT was dark when Colin Og awoke. With the sigh of the waves outside, and the snoring of Father Tormaid at his side, he thought for a moment that they were back in the black hold of the *Florabel* again, and that all the troubles that came thronging to his fuddled mind were but a nightmare. But the stability of the bed beneath him, and the absence of the creak and groan of timbers, speedily brought him back to reality. He sat up and touched his companion on the shoulder, but Tormaid slept on. Wrinkling his brows into the dark, Colin swung his long legs over on to the stone floor, and stiffly stalked over to the deep window embrasure.

The narrow lattice, filled with a grille of interlocking iron bars, faced almost due east. And above the black mass of the enclosing hillsides faint feelers of light were reaching up. Away beyond that land of soaring mountains, it was dawn. Running a hand through his tousled curling hair, and a distasteful tongue over a dry and unsavoury mouth, the man stepped across to the door, lifted the latch, and pushed. With no result; the door still was locked. Frowning blackly, he strode to the lesser door, that with the broken bolt, and opening it, felt his way down the inky shaft of the little staircase. Before ever he reached the foot, he heard the snores of men from within the great hall. The bottom door, opening outwards but bolted from inside, gave to his pressure—but only an inch or so. No light gleamed through the crack thus opened, but Colin required no light to perceive the situation. The great table had been dragged from its place in the centre of the room and put against the wall to block the door. Knowing that table, of solid bog-oak and as ancient as the room, he knew also that nothing was to be gained by pushing at the door. He was a prisoner in his own home.

Somehow the man managed to check the upsurge of his

fury, and the peremptory shout upon his lips to those sleepers within. This business looked like demanding more than fury and shouting. Clenching a trembling fist and swallowing the bitter gall of his wrath, he stood there for a few moments, motionless. Then, turning on his worn-down heel, he climbed the steps again to his own room.

This time, no protesting groans and turned shoulders sufficed to keep Tormaid happily wrapped in slumber. He was shaken till his teeth rattled, and dragged to the upright.

"We are locked in—prisoners!" Colin Og cried at him. "Captives! The blackguards, the curs—they have the audacity to insult Colin Og in Duncolin itself! They shall rue this day. We are prisoners, do you hear!"

"I know it, yes." Tormaid nodded, and yawned hugely. "I heard them turning the key in the lock when they put me in, Heaven harry them!"

"They have barred the door down below, with the table. They are sleeping in the hall, on guard. What do they—what does my precious brother think to gain by this?"

The priest shook his head. "Loth I am to speak any word against your own flesh and blood, Colin *avic* . . . but it is in my mind that Cormac mhic Colin is an ambitious man!"

"May be. You think that he intends to try and keep the captaincy of the clan, by main force?"

"I think that he intends much more than that. I think that he intends to take more than your wife from you, before he's done!"

Colin's intake of breath was audible. "You know about that, then. You know what Marsala Macleod has done?"

"I know what Marsala Macleod has had done *to* her," Tormaid corrected. "I had just a word or two with her before they parted us . . . that is where I got these lumps on my head! Och, you cannot see them, but they are there, believe me— curses on them for sacrilegious reprobates, for desecrators of Holy Church, for profaners . . ."

"Yes. And Marsala Macleod?"

"She said that she was sorry. . . ."

65

"I heard her at that, myself!"

"She thought that you were dead. Your tryst had been for the sake of the two clans . . . and the welfare of the clans remained. She said . . ."

Colin stopped him, abruptly. "Spare me what she said—spare me her woman's excuses. I have heard enough of such. Cormac, at least, makes few excuses."

"Excuses! What need has the bold Cormac for excuses?" the other demanded. "Cormac holds the whip, here in Eorsary, and the man with the whip needs no excuses, ever. He has An Colin Mor in his hand, and therefore Clan Colin. He has Marsala Macleod in his hand, and therefore her father and the Eynart Macleods. And now, he has you in his hand, likewise . . ."

" 'Fore God, he has not!" That was an explosion. "He cannot twist me in his hands. Short of slitting my tongue—or my throat—he cannot silence me. I am no frail and ageing man, wandering in my mind and shrinking from a shadow. I am no weak and fickle woman to be cossetted and coaxed. I . . ."

"You might be made as frail and shrinking as your father, Colin *avic*—and not by any cossetting and coaxing!" the priest suggested, significantly.

"What? What daftlike folly is this?"

"Folly, yes—and mortal sin. But not daftlike, Colin—never daftlike. I managed a word down there with Alan Glas the Cook, too, and it was an ill word that he told me, a word to wring the bowels of you. He says that An Colin Mor, whom God pity, has been kept down below in the dungeon, like a bear in a pit, since the day that he was struck down . . . and Alan Glas would not like to be swearing that it was a Mackenzie that struck that blow, either! Locked up, he has been, your father, down there in the dark amongst the rats, in the . . ."

"No! Mother of God—no! I will not believe it," Colin burst out. "No man born of woman would do that to . . ."

"Alan Glas swore that it was so. He would not lie to the

Church. He says . . ."

"Alan Glas would lie to St. Peter! This could not be. The clan would never allow it."

"The clan does not know. Only Cormac's own creatures know. All the castle servants are changed, save only Alan Glas—good cooks being scarce, and Cormac fond of his belly— and none may leave the castle. A terrible death is promised to any who will speak a word. . . ."

"But he is in his own room—my father. You saw him. . . ."

"He was moved up there early in the morning—yesterday morning—when Cormac got back in his galley. Cormac and his wife have made that their bedchamber ever since they were wed."

"A-a-ah!" Colin Og saw in his mind's eye a picture of that room through the wall. He saw the soft white sheepskins on the floor, and the silken draperies on the walls. He even smelt the bog myrtle and the lavender. "Sainted Mary . . . !" he muttered.

"Alan Glas says that Cormac mhic Colin is the Devil Incarnate. He has worse than murdered his own father. . . ."

"And she . . . she knows! Knows all this, and yet beds with him. I had rather see her dead."

The priest shrugged. "Women are the strangest of God's creatures . . . as you and I have discovered ere this, Colin *avic*. They think in a different fashion from men—for which perhaps a wise Creator is to be praised! Myself, I would accept them as they are. . . . But perhaps Marsala Macleod does not know it all. Alan Glas says that Cormac told him that his father must be kept in dark and quiet, on the word of this new doctor he has. Old Seumas Macbeth is dead, you see, and there is a new man, MacPhail—him you would see below with the humped back, and a carrion-crow if ever I saw one. She— Marsala Macleod—may have been told the same. Alan Glas says that she is no better than a prisoner here, like his own self. . . ."

"I wonder that Duncolin has not sunk under the very waves for shame, and all in it!"

"Well it might, yes. I will breathe the more freely myself with the smell of it out of my nostrils."

"Ye-e-es." Colin stared towards the grey oblong of the window. "We have come a thousand miles to reach here, to Duncolin. I little thought that we would be seeking to get away from it so soon! But get away we must."

"I am not contradicting you!" his foster-brother agreed grimly. "But how? Myself, I have a modicum of faith—but of the impractical sort. I have not the blessed Paul's proficiency in the matter of locks and bars and earthquakes. *Non omnia possumus omnes*. I can pray passing well, of course . . ."

"Pray you, then—and let me think!" Colin commanded. He strode across to the window, and stood gazing out, his brows knitted. "But do it quietly," he snapped back, over his shoulder, as Tormaid's sonorous voice commenced the assault on his Maker.

All the efficacy of prayer was required, for Duncolin was not built as a place of easy egress or ingress. Its granite walls were massy, its doors stout and studded, and its windows tiny and filled with wrought-iron yetts or grilles. The sea was all about it, except for a narrow isthmus, artificially ditched and spanned by a species of drawbridge. A rat might get in or out, or a bat, but not a man, without its lord's permission.

For long Colin stared out, more or less unseeing, while the young morning grew upon the bald brows of the aloof mountains and its pallid shadowless luminosity spilled over into that great gut of the hills and reflected from the steely mirror of the loch. At his back, on the bed, Tormaid evidently grew so exhausted with the fervour of his praying that presently he was snoring again.

Colin considered the cot-houses and cabins now becoming visible against the loom of the land. Some were not a quarter of a mile away. In them were his own people, the clansmen who knew him, and, he had believed, loved him—at least owed him allegiance as their young chief. Surely amongst them some there must be who would help him, answer his call? But how

68

to make them hear that call? To shout would only inform his jailers, if the noise of the waves did not drown it. A signal? What signal that he could improvise would be understood? And, anyway, his message received, what could these people do? Duncolin had withstood the assaults of whole clans. . . .

With daybreak a breeze had sprung up, and to its sighing about that tall tower was added a creaking sound, a multiple sound, dolorous and discordant. Colin knew that noise of old; he had listened to it many a time on his youthful bed, and shivered. But never had he heard so much of it, such a chorus of creaks and groans. It came from above, and to the left of his window, but he would not be able to see the source of it all therefrom—even by inserting his head, if it would go, through one of the gaps in the iron grille. He knew that by experience. But the association of ideas brought to his mind the memory of another window that did face north, and from which a boy had seen things that afterwards he had sometimes wished that he had not seen. And with the thought of that window another memory long buried jumped to the forefront of his mind. He half turned to the spent supplicant, shrugged, and then made for the private stairway door.

This staircase was within the thickness of the outer north wall, and halfway down between the two floors a small window opened, unglazed, and covered by a draught curtain of heavy hide. Out of that slot of a window, once, fully a dozen years before, a small boy had let himself down by an improvised rope, trying to reach the rocky plinth on which the castle was built, in a forbidden attempt to follow his great father on a disciplinary visit to a neighbouring chieftain. Unfortunately, he had misjudged the length of rope required, and in consequence had hung precariously between window and sea till such time as his anguished cries had attracted attention and he had been hauled back up to safety and well-merited retribution. He could remember Cormac's jeers even yet.

Feeling his way down the steps, Colin found the tiny window opening, little more than an arrow-slit behind its curtain, stuffed with old sheepskins—no doubt to counter draughts.

69

Withdrawing these, the man considered the aperture revealed, sourly. It was very small, smaller than he had recollected; probably the fact that when last he had considered the thing tactically—or considered it at all—he had been a boy of twelve, accounted for that. Though the stonework splayed outwards towards the staircase wall, the actual opening was no more than two feet in height and half that across. And halving that width again, a rusty iron bar ran from lintel to sill.

That bar, of course, was not new. It had been there at the time of his escapade—but loose in its sockets, and he had been able to work it out. Thereafter, it had been mortared in again. Now, the man bent his eye on that mortar. It was old Duncan Gow the Smith's work, and far from up to the standard of the ancient rock-hard oyster-shell pinnings of the original builders. Already it had crumbled a little around the iron, with over-much sand to it. When he shook the bar its lower end moved perceptibly.

Colin reached within his crumpled finery for his dirk—still retained, though unhappily his rapier remained downstairs in the hall where he had doffed it on sitting down to eat. Round the rust-discoloured mortar on the sill, he chipped and prodded—and if his dirk suffered, so did the mortar. Soon it was breaking away in sizable fragments, and eventually he had the root of the bar almost uncovered.

Turning his attention to the upper socket, he found it a different proposition. Here, the corroding properties of rust and rain and salt spray had had less opportunity to penetrate, and the mortar remained largely inviolate. Nor did the back-breaking posture that he was forced to adopt, help. Presently, sighing, he gave it up, and stood and frowned at the thing. Then, abruptly, he returned to the attack on the base with renewed energy.

After a deal of digging and delving he had this end free. Grasping the bar at its foot, he worked it back and forwards. It gave, a little. Taking a deep breath, the man wrenched with all his might. And the bar came away in his hand, as it were by the roots, the new mortar still attached to its upper end.

Laying it down, Colin stooped to peer out.

By twisting his body sideways, he managed to get head and shoulders through, but stuck, wedged, at the barrel of his chest. Wriggling, he got himself back again, and tried once more, turning the other way round. With the same result. He felt as though he could almost make it, but breathe in as he would, twist and edge, the unyielding stone jambs were just too much for his torso. Perhaps, without his clothing. . . .

The man was withdrawing himself again, when he remembered the creaking sound. Turning his head to stare upwards, he caught his breath. Directly above him, two storeys higher, that ominous boom projected at parapet level. And from it depended now, not the three danglers of yesterday, but many, serried ranks of hanging men, bumping and jostling each other in the breeze. Nine, eleven, twelve, thirteen, Colin counted—and then another. Fourteen. An Colin Mor's gallows-tree had fruited indeed. And not one of the new crop wore the tartan.

Colin Og withdrew thoughtfully, and climbed to consult his spiritual adviser.

"Eleven of them," he repeated. "Go and count them yourself. All from the ship, I should say—the *Florabel*. There is the master, the two mates, the boatswain, and most of the crew."

"God rest their miserable souls!" the cleric observed. "And Macdougall, and the Skyemen, and the others?"

"I did not see them . . . though the light is not good."

Tormaid yawned. "It is high-handed, of course, and a slight, an insult to yourself, whose prisoners they were. But so long as Macdougall and the rest have escaped, these are no great loss. You promised that scurvy master a tongueslitting . . ."

"*Dhia*—but do you not see? This is more serious than Cormac's slights. This carrion cannot sail our ship for us. I have told you about the window. I had hoped that if we could get through it, we could drop into the sea, swim round to the *Florabel*, and get away on her. These creatures would have been glad enough to sail her away from here, for us."

"M'mmmm. If Cormac mhic Colin had been letting them!"

"The culverin is still aboard—and the galley in poor order for the sea," Colin reminded.

"Macdougall and the others might serve at a pinch. Sufficient to get us furth of Ardcoll." The priest rubbed his chin. "But I am doubtful of the propriety of this window-louping and sea-jumping, for a clerk in Holy Orders. I . . ."

"You will be a clerk without your Holy Orders, Tormaid *avic*—without anything. Believe you me, if we get ourselves through that window, it will be with no more to us than what we were born in! Your churchman's habit will not embarrass you."

The other swallowed. "D'you say so! Och, but it may be we will not be getting through it, at all." Tormaid had never been so fond of the water as was his foster-brother.

"Come you, then, and we will see," the other declared, and led the way down, stripping off his coat as he went.

While Colin went down to the foot of the stair to listen at the barred door for any hint of stirring amongst the sleepers inside, Tormaid considered the diminutive window, head ashake, before gingerly seeking to insert some part of his person within its jambs. Muttering, he peered down, and then up. He shuddered at the former more noticeably than at the latter.

But it was neither the one nor the other that suddenly brought him backing into the stairway again, as Colin climbed up. "Look!" he pointed. "No swimming round to the ship, I think." And he made way for his companion.

Colin Og stared out, as he was directed. Away over to the left, north-westwards, the Florebel lay in mid-loch, her sails furled, and at anchor. Cormac MacColl, it was apparent, included thoroughness amongst his many qualities.

"Damnation!" Colin observed, with feeling.

"Just that," the cleric agreed loyally—though perhaps with just the merest hint of relief.

The young chief glared from him to the window, and back. Then reaching up behind him, he commenced to draw a some-what torn and far from immaculate shirt over his dark head.

"You are still for the water?" the priest demanded.

"I am for the *shore*," he was told, briefly. "And so are you. Off with those clothes, man."

"Mary-Mother—it is not suitable. A priest must respect his cloth. . . ."

"A priest must respect Holy Writ before his holy cloth! Have you not read that the body is more than raiment? That ye shall take no thought wherewithal ye shall be clad? Consider you the lilies of the field, Tormaid *avic*!" Colin kicked off his buckled shoes. "Sainted Peter—I believe that it is easier for a rich man to enter the Kingdom of Heaven than for a frocked priest to get through the eye of this needle! Haste you—before the sluggards below are stirring." And unbuckling his belt, he let down his breeches.

Tormaid shook a protesting head. "Not breeches . . . ?" he pleaded.

Colin shrugged. "I swim better wanting them." He stripped off his hose. Stooping, he extracted his dirk from the heap of his clothing, and straightened up with it, stark naked. "This will serve me for costume," he said, and put the weapon between his teeth.

Crouching to that window aperture again, sideways on he edged his way through. The stone was harsh and sore on his bare flesh, but he was a much easier fit than heretofore. By deflating his lungs and twisting and depressing one shoulder and then the other, he managed to work his chest through. One hand below him on the outer walling supporting him, he wriggled forward.

"Thank the good Lord that he did not make us women!" he observed, through his clenched teeth. "The chest is the worst of us."

Tormaid, reluctantly disrobing, muttered something unintelligible.

Colin twisted his torso so that he was looking down, with both hands against the wall below him. Directly beneath, perhaps forty feet down, the masonry met living rock. Fortunately the builders had made the most of the space available, erecting their walls almost flush with the edge of the rock. Still, the face of the crag itself sloped slightly outwards, in its ten or so feet descent to the present water's level—and went on sloping beneath. It would be necessary to dive well outwards, to clear it. That was going to be a little difficult.

Tormaid's voice came from behind, in a penetrating whisper, his breath on Colin's bare back. "How much water is in it? Och, we will kill ourselves, man. It will be too shallow, altogether."

"Ten feet and more, there will be. The tide is not far off the full," Colin called back, the dirk permitting. "We will do fine and well—and there is sand at the bottom!"

"Lord have mercy on us—we will be broken in two halves! I am no solan-goose, I tell you. And see you, Colin—they will be hearing us and seeing us from up above, from the parapet. The watch . . ."

"Not them. We have a fine screen hanging between us— fourteen guardians, and all protesting!" Colin spared a hand to remove the knife from his mouth for a moment. "Now quiet, Tormaid, and listen. You are a longer man than myself by an inch, maybe, but no wider in the shoulder. You will get yourself through this. If you mislike the diving, come out feet first, and jump. You will have to push yourself off from the wall. You will clear the rock, and to spare. Swim across to yonder bit where the alders come down near to the shore—where we used to play Catch-a-Campbell. We can get up into the birch wood from there, under cover. I will be waiting for you. You have it?"

"How can I jump, when I have nothing to jump from . . . ?"

"Och, man—make yourself a rope from the plaid on the bed. I did that myself, one time. Tie it to something—anything that is as loth to come out of this window as your own self! By it, once you are out, you can pull yourself up and jump from the sill, here. . . ."

"Merciful and Mighty—what am I! A hairy ape? This is no ploy for a Highland gentleman! Och, Colin . . ."

"Quiet you. I'm off. I will see you in yon alder bushes." And Colin Og restored the dirk to his teeth.

Easing his way forward, his arm holding him out from the walling, the man reached the point of balance, and beyond. Only his bent knees, within the window-frame, prevented him from toppling over. The strain on his stomach muscles was intense, he was beginning to get cramp with the twist on his body, and other unspecified parts of him were crying out against the harsh caress of rough-hewn granite. With a last glance around him he straightened his knees, tensed his arms to lift himself off the dragging stone, and pushed himself forwards. Over he went, his hands going before him down the masonry. As his thigh scraped over the sill, he thrust mightily, with hands and knees, launching himself outwards, and as he felt a toe rasp on stone, he kicked backwards with all his might. One foot beat only the air, but its fellow struck home. In a wide arc the man fell clear.

Down fifty feet he plunged, his arms closing before him like a spearhead. With a strange impression of deliberation the water rose to meet him, and with a convulsive twist he wrenched his body to meet it at a shallower angle. Cleanly he struck the surface, five feet clear of the rock face, and the shock of it was like an explosion within him. For a numb moment he was deprived of all consciousness, and then his eyes opened to perceive the pale bottom coming up at him. He spread his palms as though to ward off that thrusting wrinkled sand. But his hand touched nothing more solid than a waving frond of weed. The upthrust and resistance of the water, his own momentum, and the angle of his body, contributed to force him up. With the pallid gleam of the sand levelling off below him and giving place to the still more wan glimmer of morning light, his progress changed from descent to ascent. He broke surface, gasped, shook the water out of his eyes and his hair from his face, twisted on his back and waved a hand towards the castle window. Then he turned, and commenced to swim strongly for the shore.

He realized, for the first time, how deathly cold was the water.

The point on the shore where the alders came down closest to the water was no more than two or three hundred yards off. Colin, though somewhat out of practice, covered it promptly enough, with an unobtrusive but steady sidestroke. At the weed-covered rocks, he was turning to reassure himself by a quick survey that the coast was clear, when a gleam of white caught the corner of his eye, and there was a sizeable splash below the castle rock. The Church, it appeared, had finally taken the plunge.

Dragging himself out of the water, and creeping over the slippery rocks, Colin ran, bent double, over a narrow stretch of sandy machair, and into the cover of the alders.

Dividing his attention between all the surrounding haunts of men, silent yet, and Tormaid's epic and eye-catching approach, Colin waited and shivered.

With the priest, looking markedly unpriestlike, puffing and snorting like any grampus, spitting salt water, anathemas, and maledictions concurrently and tenderly rubbing a number of angry scrapes and abrasions about his unprotected person, Colin led the way uphill, through scattered bushes where shaggy cattle snorted and stared—as well they might—and into the deeper cover of a large wood of birches and juniper and rustling dead bracken. Barefooted, they trod carefully, heedful of brambles and thorns, heedful of beasts and shadows and their own nakedness. At the top of the ridge, eventually, they looked down into a shallow green valley in which were two houses with the great mist-wreathed heather hillsides rising beyond, and back over the sickle of weed-bordered bay and the croft-dotted braes, to where Duncolin rose proudly from its rock. A single plume of blue smoke was rising from one of its tall chimney-stacks, now. And even as they looked, a sound was borne to them therefrom on the chill south-west breeze. Rising high, the horn sounded to all the wakening world. Then, as its echo died away behind them amongst the hills, faint but clear the words came.

"The day is fine, God is good and An Colin Mor has slept and risen! No man shall keep his bed. Eat, Sons of Colin!"

As the stirring strains of *Duncolin's Breakfast* were blown to them from the skirling pipes on the castle parapet, the fugitives eyed each other, unspeaking, and then turned to hurry down into the farther trees.

VII

AT the edge of the wood, behind the very last juniper bush, the two men stood and eyed the house, doubtfully. Within its small garden ground it was larger than the other cot-houses and cabins of that neighbourhood, of two storeys, stone built and reed thatched, and with something of a farmery at the rear. Its cattle stood about it, still with the bemused stolidity of the night, but smoke was rising from one of its open chimney-stacks.

Father Tormaid scratched an unshaven chin. "It is an ill thing for gentlemen to be chapping at a tackman's door in the morning, and not a stitch of clothing between the two of them," he declared.

"Think you I don't know it!" Colin growled, sourly. "But what choice have we? Hector Ban is a good man, and will know his duty towards his chief's son."

"Yes. Och, yes. But . . . there could be women in it. Hector Ban has a wife and a daughter too, as well as a son."

"What of it?" That was bravely put.

"Och, see you, it is not . . . I tell you, I am not the man to be standing about before the ladies, in a state of . . . in this . . ."

"Mary of Grace—are you ashamed of the way the good God made you! Do you think that any woman worthy of the name will be the worse for the sight of a man that has lost his shirt!"

"Och, the shirt is the least of it, Colin. . . ."

"Damnation, man—if their eyes are offended, they can look elsewhere. We want clothes and food, and Hector Ban can give us them. A plague on his women!"

"Amen—so be it's a plague of blindness! But maybe young Kenneth will come out to the cattle . . . or Hector himself, if we but wait a small piece longer. . . ."

"We have waited over long as it is. I am cold, and hungry—and every minute that we waste we give to Cormac. I . . ."

A black-and-white mongrel dog settled their argument for them. Emerging from the steading behind the house, it slunk round the garden fence, stopped suddenly, sniffing the air, and then threw up its head in their direction and began to bark, loud and long.

Colin swore, and pushed his companion's shoulder. "Come, you!" he commanded, and hastened towards the garden and the door. Unhappily Tormaid scurried behind him.

There were some currant bushes in that garden, and behind one of them the pair sought refuge, the wretched dog barking its head off a yard away.

"Which was Hector Ban's room?" Colin whispered urgently. "If we could attract his attention . . ."

"I do not know, at all. I . . ."

Tormaid stopped. A soft woman's voice was upraised in singsong chiding. "Och, Luath, Luath—wheesht you, now, wheesht you! Och, the noise of you . . ." And then a young woman was round the corner of the house, as the dog had come, and her words died on her.

From this angle the currant bush was no protection for them. Like a pair of scalded cats the two young men scrambled to get to the other side of that shrub—and Colin Og, for all his brave words, was not the hindmost.

And after an initial strangled gasping, the newcomer found her tongue again, if not her words. Lifting up her voice in an ever-mounting eldritch screech, she splintered and shattered the morning. Stooping, she picked up the foot of her apron, threw it completely over her head, and turning about stumbled blindly whence she had come, ululating shrilly.

"Tortured Timotheus!" the priest muttered. "Martyred Mathias . . . !"

He had no time for more. While the distressed lady's screams were still ringing in their ears, above the miserable dog's baying, the front door of the house was thrown wide, and a plump and matronly woman was framed therein. She stared, eyes wide.

"Merciful Creator!" she said.

Once again, the men were in the wrong position. Tormaid leapt backwards to get round his shrub, collided with a gooseberry bush, and yelped his concern. Colin, advisedly, stood his ground, but plunged hasty hands in essential modesty.

"Good morning . . . and your pardon . . ." he began, and got no further.

The woman opened her mouth on a great breath, shut it almost with a snap, backed a couple of paces, pointing with an accusatory finger rather distressingly at Colin's person, and quavered, "Hector! Hector!" before dropping her hand and slamming the door shut. As an indication of her feelings, it was all remarkably effective.

Colin gulped in his righteous wrath. "The ill-natured harridan!" he cried. "The old witch! The . . . the Jezebel! What way is this to treat a son of Colin, to treat any gentleman . . . ?"

"It could be she did not see that we were gentlemen . . ." Tormaid was suggesting, when a movement at an upper window made them both look up. An elderly shock-headed man was peering down at them, open-mouthed, tugging at his beard.

Colin Og gestured urgently, imperiously, with the hand that still clutched his dirk, and the face disappeared.

"Slug-abed!" he accused. "Droil! Sloth! Lying sleeping while we shiver out here. . . ."

The door opened again, and the bearded man, wrapping a plaid around him, looked out. "God save us all!" he said. "What sort of a ploy is this?"

Colin Og drew himself up to his full height, with surprising dignity. "Hector Ban MacColl of Balnafail," he intoned, "I demand shelter, food, and clothing, in the name of An Colin Mor!"

"My goodness, mercy me, indeed whatever!" the other ejaculated.

"Exactly."

"Man, man, Colin mhic Colin—what is the meaning of this, at all? This is not decent, see you . . ."

"Decent be damned! I tell you I need shelter and clothing and food. . . ."

"My, oh my, the sorrow of it! Cormac mhic Colin spoke the truth, then. First it was An Colin Mor, and now Colin Og! The pity, the tragedy of it!"

"Mercy on us—don't stand there mouthing sorrow and woe, man. Do something . . ."

"Crazy mad—like your father. Sorrow on the House of Colin. Cormac was right—Cormac spoke truly."

"Cormac said that, did he? Cormac said that I was mad—like my father? When did he say so?"

"Yesterday, it was—yesterday, Colin mhic Colin. First the word came that you were dead. And then, that you were home, but . . ." The older man looked up and down his naked visitors, and at the knives in their fists, and spread his hands. "Just that," he ended up, helplessly.

Colin glanced at Tormaid, behind his inadequate bush, and as he did so his eye perceived a face peeping from one of the ground-floor windows—the young woman, evidently recovered from her shock. "Let us inside, for the favour of Heaven!" he cried. "Would you make An Colin Og a peepshow for your mannerless women!"

The other looked about him quickly, anxiously, combing fingers through his beard. "Och, mercy me, mercy me—this is bad." He sighed. "Come you in, then—but not for long, see you, not for long, at all."

"No? Your hospitality lacks something, I think, Balnafail."

"Och, it is Cormac—it is your brother, Colin mhic Colin. He will . . . he is a hard man to cross." The older man's hand went up to his throat involuntarily. "Indeed, it is as much as my life is worth. Step in, then, the two of you. . . ."

As they crossed the threshold, nothing loth, Tormaid's voice and hand rose. "God's blessing on this house, and all within it . . . if He can find it worth His while, whatever!"

Colin cut short Hector Ban's agitated catalogue of the dire risks that he was running. "The fact is, Balnafail, that you are so afraid of your own skin that you will not afford your chief's son anything to fill or cover his?"

"Och well . . . it is difficult, difficult. If An Colin Mor's sons would speak with the one voice, see you . . ." He sighed gustily. "But so be it you will leave my house quickly, I will give you a bannock and some meal, and maybe a shirt to cover your nakedness . . . if you will swear to tell no man Balnafail gave it."

"Mother of God—has it come to that in Eorsary!" Colin cried disgustedly. "Give us a stitch of plaid, then, to wrap round our middles, and let us go."

"Yes, then. Wait you here."

Colin and his foster-brother, looking if possible even less appropriately caparisoned in a pair of dirks, indoors, waited— by no means in silent gratitude.

The sound of women's voices upraised from the depths of the house might have been significant. At any rate, Balnafail was back without any undue delay, carrying a coarse linen bag, not noticeably bulging, and two lengths of old and stained tartan plaiding. These his visitors seized and wrapped around their waists as rough-and-ready kilts. Tormaid took the bag.

"The Lord provideth!" he observed, doubtfully.

"The door of Balnafail is wide open, indeed," Colin agreed.

The tacksman ran a hand through his plentiful grey hair. "It is difficult, Colin mhic Colin. I have a wife and a daughter to me. They would fend ill, and me hanging from a rope on Duncolin's walls!"

"There is always the heather, Heaven be praised!"

"My son said that same. One of the family in the heather is enough. . . ."

"Kenneth? Is he in the heather, then?"

"He was, yes. Now he has sold his sword to Mackenzie of Gairloch."

"He fell foul of Cormac, did he?"

"That is so, to our cost. Now he is no more than a hired fighting man in the tail of the bloody Mackenzies. Others there are, too, in like case. At my years, I do not seek to join them.

And there are the women. . . ."

"Yes. There are the women," Colin Og agreed heavily. . . .
"Perhaps you deserve our sympathy. We will relieve you of
our company, then—take ourselves off."

"That would be best," the other concurred promptly. "But
you will be careful? It would be the great pity if any man was
seeing you leaving this house. . . ."

Colin snorted. "That is what it has come to, has it?" he said
bitterly. "I must not be seen leaving the house of a tacksman
of Ardcoll! Changed days, indeed. Come, Tormaid—let us
disembarrass Balnafail. Our thanks, Hector Ban, for a handful
of meal and a stitch of rag. They will not be forgotten!" And
bowing ceremoniously, the heir of Ardcoll, Eorsary, etcetera,
marched for the door.

"Sodom and Gomorrha!" Tormaid mentioned, conversationally. "It shall be more tolerable for Sodom and Gomorrha
in that day . . . !"

The older man, in the doorway, fingered a fleshy lip, pink
above his beard, and pointed a hand. "The wood," he said.
"You will not be seen, in the wood . . ."

"You are right," Colin gave back, over his shoulder. "We
will not be seen in the wood—today, or any day!" and turned
to stalk openly down diagonally across the green pastures and
bog myrtle of the little valley.

Across the chuckling stream and up beyond, towards the
outliers of the heather, Tormaid had to hurry to keep up with
the long striding of his companion. Neither man spoke; they
had sufficient scope for thought.

But however deep their preoccupation, it was not long before
the tender state of their bare feet forced itself upon their consciousness. Even above the level of brambles and thistles, there
are a surprising number of sharp, jagged, and unkindly objects
to harass the unprotected sole of the foot. The conviction grew
upon them that in the circumstances they might have been
well advised to have given footgear priority in their demands
on Hector Ban's reluctant hospitality. Before they were half a

mile above the house of Balnafail, Colin had changed his
direction, was no longer heading straight up for the brown
flanks of the great hills, but slantwise towards an area of
shelving moorland, faded green cut and slashed with the black
of peat workings, and dotted with stacks of drying turf, in the
midst of which, barely distinguishable from the peat-stacks save
by a slender column of smoke lifting into the morning air, a
cot-house of stone and turf crouched.

As they drew nearer, two figures were to be observed
working in the peat bog, a man cutting leisurely, and a woman
suitably doing the carrying and stacking. At sight of them, the
man perforce rested on his spade to watch their approach,
while his companion worked on.

But while they were still something over two hundred yards
off, a change came over the scene. The man with the spade
called a brief word to the woman, pointing. Straightening up,
she stared, and shouted back. Her voice held high-pitched
alarm. Admittedly the two young men approaching must have
seemed rather unnecessarily berserk for the hour and circumstance, but it was hardly likely to be any sort of raid on a peat
bog.

Colin Og raised a hand in reassuring salute.

The effect seemed to be quite other than was intended. The
woman skirled something unintelligible but eloquent, kilted up
her skirts, and turning about, bolted. She ran towards the cabin,
floundering across peat mud, splattering through standing
water, leaping from tussock to tussock, with all the urgency of
a deer in flight but something of the aspect of a milch-cow
desperate for the byre. The man looked from her to the waving
newcomers, suddenly raised his own hand before him, not to
wave back but to make the sign of the Cross between himself
and them, and dropping his spade, swung on his heel, to go
louping after the woman.

"Hounds of God!" Colin protested, wrathfully. "What ails
them, now?"

"Did you see the creature—crossing himself against *me*, a
priest of Holy Church!" Tormaid cried.

Sourly his foster-brother turned on him. "A strange priest you look this day," he declared. "Unfrocked, by any standard! You would do well to forget your priesthood for a space, it seems."

The other frowned. "A priest does not put off his priesthood with his clothes, Colin mhic Colin," he reproved, formally. "God is not mocked in His servants. . . ."

"Tell you that to Murdo the Peat, then!"

"It could have been yourself that upset him—your madness. You may be the crazed one, to all Eorsary!"

Colin stared at him, glared at him. "Damnation!" he said. Tormaid nodded stiffly, and they strode on, some distance apart. Fortunately for their dignity, there were few stones or sharp objects on that peat bog.

At the low-browed cot-house, they found the door shut and barred against them. After fruitless thumping on it, Colin went to the tiny unglazed window, over which a sheepskin hung within. This he pushed aside with a stick from the woodpile.

"Murdo the Peat!" he shouted in. "Open your door."

No sound issued from the black interior.

Colin slapped at the sheepskin, angrily. "Knave! Churl! In the name of An Colin Mor—open!"

A woman's stifled wail was all his answer.

Tormaid took a hand. "Murdo the Peat, and Seana daughter of Callum," he intoned. "In the holy name of Mother Church, I, Tormaid the Priest, command that you admit Colin mhic Colin, son of your chief."

The Church was no more successful than the State.

"Devil roast you!" Colin roared. "Open, or I will pull your miserable hovel stone from stone!" He looked doubtfully at the squat three-foot thickness of the walls as he said it. "I will burn your thatch over your heads." For which lie God forgive him, with the roof solid turf. "I will hamstring your cow. I will tear you apart with my two hands. I will . . . I will . . ." He came to a stop, helplessly.

Once again the loyal Tormaid came to his aid. "You are accursed!" he boomed, deep-voiced. "In the name of Mary

85

and all the saints, I curse you. I curse you under your roof and under the heaven, in your goings out and your comings in, in eating and drinking, in waking and sleeping, in your labour and your pleasure. I curse you in your mind and in your tongue, in your heart and in your belly, in your bowels and your loins and in the unseemly fruit thereof! In all such and more, I curse you . . . if you do not open to An Colin Og."

The answering silence was as profound as the scope of the maledictions.

Colin opened his mouth, shut it again, shook his head, sighed, and in a different tone, spoke: "Look you, Murdo," he complained, "all we want is some old brogans for our feet."

"That is so," Tormaid agreed. "Two pairs."

There was a faint whispering audible from within, and the sound of movement. Then the sheepskin curtain was lifted and a rawhide thonged shoe came flying out, narrowly missing Colin's head. It was followed by two more, and then a fourth, and the curtain fell back.

"The open hand of Clan Colin!" the young chief thereof burst out. "This, and thus." He raised his voice. "See you, a bite of bread and a slice of cheese would go well with the brogans."

There was no further stirring from within the house.

Colin sighed and picked up the shoes. He shook his head over them. One pair was split in sundry places. The other was split, and also had holes worn in the soles. The latter he handed to Tormaid. "Heaven pity you amongst the ant-hills," he mentioned.

They searched in the turf huts at the back of the cabin, and found two or three eggs, screwed the neck of a cockerel, and drew themselves a far from clean wooden cogue-full of milk from a gaunt but acquiescent cow. And discerning no further benefit to be gained from the wretched establishment of Murdo the Peat, their footgear donned resignedly, they turned their faces to the hill once more.

"If we are to win an honest meal, and decent clothes to our backs, we will need to seek them furth of Eorsary, I think—

and at speed," Tormaid said. "For certain, the word is being spread that you are a madman—and our people do not love madmen. Until we get ahead of your brother's messengers, Colin *avic*, I fear me we will obtain the same reception everywhere."

The other nodded. "I believe you. My admirable brother does not give the grass time to grow under his feet—or under his belly, the crawling snake! We will shake the dust of Eorsary from our fine new brogans . . . but we will return, I call Heaven to witness!" Colin looked back, down the hill. "I would have a word, two words, with Torquil Macleod. It is Eynart for us."

"Eynart, for sure. Torquil Macleod may be able to tell us a thing or two. . . ."

"He will do more than that, if I have my way."

"Yes, then—when we get there. Cormac the Twin will try to stop us."

"Let him try."

"Assuredly. But there is no call to help him. It could be wise to hide till night—to travel by dark. Or, at the least, to move with circumspection, to get off this open hillside, go by woods and corries and hidden ways. . . ."

"No, by the celestial host—I will not skulk and creep about Eorsary! I am An Colin Og, and this province is my birthright. I walk in it, upright, by no man's courtesy. Come, you!"

VIII

TO reach Eynart from Ardcoll, it was necessary to sail across the Bay of the same name, or else to travel right up the peninsula of Eorsary to its root amongst the stern mountains of Ross, and then southwards down the mainland coast; the former a voyage of a dozen miles, the latter a journey of over thirty. Since it was probable that in the Ardcoll area all boats would be watched—and even if not, could be overtaken quickly, once observed, by superior rowing power—and the length of the overland journey held no attractions, Colin Og decided to compromise. They would work their way up the long promontory for seven or eight miles, try to obtain a boat, and seek to make the passage across the great bay under cover of darkness.

The Eorsary peninsula consisted, in the main, of two parallel lines of hills, or ranges, divided by a deep valley, Glen Coll, many miles long, near the western and seaward end of which lay Ardcoll with its loch. There were sundry other valleys and ridges and outliers of hill, but these constituted the principal features. The obvious and simplest route up the peninsula to the mainland was by this great valley, Glen Coll—but it was therein, threaded by the ages-old drove road, that the population of Eorsary was congregated. For men not desirous of attracting undue attention, the higher ground was indicated.

They were on the north side of the glen here, of course, and it was on the south coast that they must look for their boat. But they were in no doubts that the wisest course was to work their way along at a high level on this side, and do their crossing later on. Despite Colin Og's objections to skulking and creeping, he was courting no large-scale trouble at this stage, endowed only with his dignity, a rag of kilt, and a damaged dirk.

So, all morning, the two young men pushed eastwards,

through tall heather and blaeberries, tussocky deer-hair grass and the outcropping lichened gravel of the high tops, keeping in the main to the northern faces of the hills, that looked out over the scattered islets of the Sound of Inver, to the companion promontory of Stoer, and the widening Hebridean sea, all sparkling colour in the May sunlight.

They saw many sheep, more cattle, and a herd or two of deer amongst the high corries, but few men, and of these all save two were afar off, down on the lower slopes, working at their beasts or their peats or their patches of tilth, or else out in boats on the glittering waters of the Minch at the fishing. And the two whom they did approach were not really men at all, but youths, herders of the shaggy hill cattle, who lay on their backs beside the embers of a fire of heather-roots and bog-fir after their midday meal, watching the clouds at their sailing across the blue vault of the sky. These, unaware of their approach until they were almost up to them, eyed the newcomers with no alarm and little surprise—for they themselves were not so differently clad, only the one having a shirt to add to his philabeg, or small kilt. They accepted wisely without spoken question, that these were a pair of travelling men heading south for the Macrae country, and while they had no food to spare for their visitors, they blew up the fire again for them so that the eggs could be baked in its ashes and the cockerel roasted after some fashion. The resultant repast, with oatmeal and good burn water, had at least the sauce of hunger to commend it. And the oatmeal would swell satisfactorily in urgent stomachs in due course.

From the young herdsmen, Colin and his companion, by dint of seemingly casual questioning, elicited the information that these were difficult times when it behoved men to watch where they trod—though needless to say, swack and independent young fellows the like of themselves did not let such conditions cramp them unduly. All the same, Eorsary looked to them like a good place to be thinking of getting out of; it might not be long before they were consigning their cattle to the oldsters or the devil, and following their visitors south in

search of the fuller life, and a less chief-ridden existence. Yes—
they were having trouble with their chief. They expected that
most folk had trouble with their chiefs—that was the way of
the world, as all knowledgeable men were aware. But they had
more than usual to put up with. The old man—the famous
Colin Mor of the Battles—was never seen. Some said that he
was dead, some that he was merely sick, some that. . . . The
speaker tapped a freckled forehead significantly. Anyway, his
son ruled in his place. And this son had a very heavy hand. He
liked his own way, did their brave Cormac, and the clan had
to like it, too—or swing for it! This hero, Cormac mhic Colin,
if he was not such a warrior for the battles as the old man,
was an ill man to cross. And cunning, with his tongue behind
his hand. He had got the Macleods of Eynart in his pocket,
and, as likely they had heard, had set the Macraes and the
Macdonalds at each other's throats to the south of him, and
the Macleods of the Lews ravaging the Mackenzies in the north,
while MacColl waited to glean the pickings. He was a crafty
fox was their Cormac—but he had his points, of course, as
chiefs went. At least he did not run away to live amongst the
Sassunachs and worse like his brother had done—and died
there, by all accounts, as was but just and suitable. . . . Still
and all, if this Cormac continued to get much more of his own
way, Eorsary would be no place for free and footloose stalwarts
like themselves. It would be the road and the heather for
them. . . .

Colin, idly, wondered whether many in Eorsary thought as
they did?

The bold herdsmen could not tell, nor greatly cared.
Amongst the younger ones, perhaps; their fathers, the aged
and the dodderers, as ever, would accept anything for peace.
Themselves, they were made of sterner stuff. Stretching
luxuriously on the short scented heather, they nodded weightily
at the voyaging white cloud galleons.

Colin and Tormaid stared into the heaven, too, and for a
while the questing bees, the shouting larks, a tinkling burn
and the soft sigh of air over high places made all the sound

there was—most suitable to profound postprandial contemplation. So much so, indeed, that presently Colin was yawning hugely, and his foster-brother was moved to express the opinion that perhaps David had been played a scurvy trick when he had been made a king instead of a herdsman, and that Solomon might not have been so wise as was made out, or he would have handed back his kingdom to Zadok the Priest and reverted to the paternal hillsides. Which sentiments, however apt and philosophic, were received with sudden doubt and suspicion by the pastoralists, as coming from a supposedly wandering cateran. As a result, one or two searching enquiries followed.

The travellers found it expedient to continue their journey fairly promptly, bees and larks and burns notwithstanding.

By mid-afternoon, a wet grey mist had crept in from the sea, first to blot out the colours from the hills, and then to blot out the hills themselves. The two wayfarers walked lower on the braesides, and made no complaint. Even when the mist graduated to a steady and persistent downpour, they found no fault. Heather-stepping is warm work, they had little to soak, and so long as they kept moving its chill caress was grateful on their bare torsos; also, it disposed of the midges. Moreover, such weather would tend to restrict observation and observers. Indeed, presently visibility was reduced to a murky three hundred or so yards, and Colin decided that a better opportunity for traversing the deep rift of Glen Coll was unlikely to present itself. So, crossing the ridge by a *beallach* between two summits, they slanted down to the bracken braes and scattered birchwoods of the valley floor, forded the peat-brown tumbling waters of the Coll River, slipped unobtrusively across the sheep-dotted haughlands beyond, and were back amongst the wooded hillskirts opposite, without sight of men. They smelt the tang of peat-reek on the damp westerly air just after they had negotiated the river, but glimpsed nothing of the source thereof.

Heartened by their success, and the dour unflagging quality of the rain, it occurred to the travellers that perhaps there was no need to wait for nightfall for their crossing of Eynart Bay. The present obscurity, if it lasted, probably would be sufficient for their purposes—unless their luck was very bad. And Colin Og at least was very much of a believer in the theory that one's luck was largely what one made it. What were they waiting for, then?

They tackled the long southern wall of Glen Coll, at a pace that soon had their chests heaving and the sweat mingling with the rain that streamed down them, plastering the hair to their no longer white bodies. Hillmen as they were, the fact that they had not done much climbing of recent years was forcibly borne in on them. But Colin was not going to admit as much to Tormaid, naturally—and as naturally, Tormaid's less well-disguised distress had no ameliorating effect on his companion. They clambered up some twelve hundred wicked feet in just over twenty-five minutes. And still the rain held.

The descent of the farther side, though easier on the lungs, was harder on the feet. Tormaid's observations on the state of Murdo the Peat's footwear accompanied them like a litany down over the outcrops, screes, and loose rock of that sea-exposed and weather-eroded hillside. It was a surprisingly different terrain from that of the morning. A wild goat or two was all that they aroused thereon—and continual cataracts of tumbling stones. By the time that they reached the foot and the steep rocky shore, Tormaid was limping and leaving behind smudges of what he asserted was his own life's blood, entirely irreplaceable, at every step.

On this harsh and inhospitable coastline, the haunts of men were few and far between. Only the two houses there were in a stretch of ten miles or so, and these were only occupied periodically by fishermen, when the salmon were in season. Fortunately May was within that season, and it was to be expected that the fishers and their boats would be there. One of these bothies, they calculated, would be something over a mile back, westwards, towards Ardcoll, whilst the other, if they were where they thought they were, would be fully three miles further to the east. Tormaid's feet, and the fact that the easternmost house lay only a few miles west of the small township of Aranbeg, indicated that they move west.

Turning right-handed, the two men scrambled over the jumbled rocks, stony strands, and waterlogged hollows of that savage seaboard. The long swell broke on the barren shore with a recurrent sigh, infinitely sad against the constant background of the sibilant hiss of rain on water.

They came on the cottage rather sooner than they had anticipated, the scent of the peat fire coming to them on the westerly wind. It loomed out of the grey curtain of the rain within a little fold of the steep braeside, and below it a jut of rock had been added to with rough masonry to form a little breakwater and jetty. Towards this the men headed.

Unfortunately, there was no fishing-coble moored to the jetty. Presumably the fishers were at sea. But there was a smaller boat, drawn up on the shingle just below the clutter of poles for drying the nets. A shoulder to it seemed to suggest that it would run down to the water without much difficulty. The only drawback was that no oars were visible. The men glanced up at the bothy, speculatively. There was a semi-ruinous stone-and-turf outhouse alongside the cottage—no doubt where the fishing-gear was stored. Nodding to each other they climbed thitherwards.

In the pitch-scented and dripping interior they found, amongst the nets and lobster-pots and creels, two pairs of oars. These seemed to be rather long and heavy for the small boat, but would probably serve. Hoisting a pair of them on to Tormaid's shoulder, Colin led the way back.

They were barely down on to the shingle, when a peremptory voice jerked their heads round. A large and brawny woman was standing within the doorway of the bothy, eyeing them, arms akimbo.

"Good afternoon, mother," Colin greeted her, bowing, hurriedly polite. "Wet, it is."

"Do not be mothering me, ruffian!" the lady cried. "Where are you for, with those oars?"

"We were thinking of borrowing the small bit of boat,

93

there—just to save the walking, see you. My friend here has a sore foot to him."

Thus introduced, Tormaid made as much obeisance as the oars permitted. "God bless your house, and all within, daughter," he said, with authority.

"Hark at him!" the woman gasped. "Blasphemers! Rogues! Thieves! Shameless, godless . . ." She was thrust aside, and a still larger female emerged from the house.

"*Dhiaol!* Robbers, is it! Let me at them!" And she brandished what appeared to be a very substantial poker. At her back, a third face appeared, feminine still but thoroughly formidable.

"Ninian save us!" Colin cried, and turning about ran for the boat. With a sort of hop, skip, and jump, Tormaid followed, the oars bumping wickedly on his bare shoulder.

The three ladies came after them, in full cry, the third helped on by a long-handled birch besom.

Colin reached the boat, and applied an urgent shoulder to its prow. It moved only slowly—and there was a good dozen yards to go. "Hurry, man!" he yelled. "What are you doing?"

Tossing the oars into the boat, Tormaid stooped. "I have a sore foot," he complained. "Mary-Mother, this is a . . ."

"Push—or you will have a broken head, and worse," the other cried. "Much worse. Push, I say—or it will be easier to say what you won't have!"

"Peter and Paul aid us!"

The boat was rumbling forward over the round stones at a fair pace—but nothing to the pace and the clamour with which the salmon-fishers' women bore down on them. The Amazons were charging on a wide front, a notably wide and overwhelming front, and the strand seemed to tremble beneath the very weight of their onset—as well it might. Glancing over his shoulder at the fearsome sight, Colin gulped.

"Keep them off," he panted. "I'll finish this. Fight them off, man. Quick!"

"Fight . . . ? Me? Och, mercy me—not fight! Not with . . ."

"Quickly. Take an oar. Swing it round your head. 'S'death, man—hurry!"

Unhappily Tormaid grasped an oar, and thrust it out towards the oncoming billowing femininity, doubtfully, with considerably less authority than he would have used to exorcise Lucifer himself. "Back!" he croaked. "Wait, you. Back, I say. . . ."

It was neither his oar nor his words that gave the onslaught pause, however. It was solely the broomstick. The matron with the besom, though the shortest of the trio and by no means the most slender, was, surprisingly, the most agile on her feet, and had got slightly in front of her colleagues in the race. Using the handle of her besom to help her along may have contributed. But on round, wet and slippery stones, even broomsticks can have their drawbacks. In mid-career it slithered over one smooth stone, and then another, and ended up between its bearer's bare red legs. The resultant fall was cataclysmic, indescribable, partaking of the nature of an earthquake or other Act of God, as the first of the Furies sprawled apparently in all directions, arms and legs waving like windmills. Into some outflung portion of her person or her besom crashed both her companions, and the disaster was complete. The scene was awe-inspiring in the truest sense. Tormaid's eloquence deserted him, as he gazed dumbfounded, his oar like a magic wand before him.

But Colin Og MacColl was of sterner stuff—also, he was facing in the other direction. Grunting, he kept the boat moving in front of him, till with its stern in the water, he glanced backwards.

"Mother of God!" he breathed. "Aren't you . . . the terrible man . . . with an oar!" Swallowing, he shook his head over the dire prospect. "Och, Tormaid—a little mercy you might have had, and them women!"

"But . . . but . . . Look you . . . I, I . . ." the priest gobbled. "I did nothing, at all! I . . . ."

"Do not stand there shaming yourself further! Help you with this boat. . . ."

Glad enough to look elsewhere, Tormaid tossed the oar back

95

inboard, and gave weight as well as tongue. Up above their knees in the lacework of the combers, they got the craft's prow round, heading for open water, and threw themselves over the gunwales.

"Take you the oars—I will navigate," Colin exclaimed, "Pull, you."

Angry shouts from the shore seemed to indicate that there still was ample fight and breath left in the pursuit. Sorting themselves out of what truly seemed to be unsortable, the ladies barely waited even to adjust their clothing before hurling themselves onwards, down to the water's edge.

Tormaid, the unwieldy oars shifting and slipping about unhandily, scarcely needed Colin's urgent injunctions to row as though the devil's dam was after him.

Kilting their skirts in the shallows, the women's advance came to a halt ten yards or so from the boat—but not their voices. In detail and at length they dealt with the situation and the characters and antecedents of the ravishers. Tormaid's face grew steadily redder—though possibly the vehemence of his pulling accounted for that.

"Shut your ears to it," Colin advised, shocked. "It is not suitable for a priest to hear such things. *Dhia*—you might think that these women were Campbells!"

"You should have told them who you were!" Tormaid gasped. "They . . ."

"What time have I had to tell them anything, at all?" the other demanded. "There is no telling in it."

There was not, save from the landward side. And there, the telling began to tail off—not seemingly from exhaustion of energy or material, but out of an alteration in perspective. One of the women took a moment to address her companions instead of the boaters. Then she pointed to them with her poker, and lifted up her voice again. But this time it was to laugh. The others seemed to consider her point of view, and then began to punctuate their shouting with laughter also. The rain-filled air vibrated to their unseemly mirth.

"What is this?" Tormaid complained. "What is there to be

laughing at? This is . . ."

"Quiet, you," the other directed, "I cannot hear what they say."

Admittedly the derision had more volume and vigour to it than clarity, and the creaking of the oars and the splash of the waves did not help. It was some time before Colin made out sufficient to grasp the sense of it.

"They are saying that we are drowned men. They are saying that the sea will cool our, our—well, will cool us. They are saying that the boat will sink under us."

"More empty curses. Now, if . . ."

"They sound devilish confident."

"Let them. Mother Church is not afraid of the mouthings of such."

"Mother Church looked middling like it a small time ago!"

Tormaid applied himself to his oars, with dignity.

They were a fair distance out, half a mile probably, and the women's voices like their persons long faded and died away behind the rain screen, when Colin Og, staring downwards, spoke.

"There is a deal of water in this boat," he said.

"The rain, it is."

"There is more than there was, I think."

"There is more rain," his companion pointed out.

That was true. The rain had changed its character. It was heavier, with larger drops, and visibility was improving. More wind was becoming evident.

Colin frowned into it. "The weather is going to clear," he declared. "A pest on it."

"Amen," the other concurred. "These oars are plaguey ill to handle."

"Och, you are doing fine and well. But, see you—it is getting lighter all around. . . ."

Undoubtedly the gloom was thinning, and the heavier rain was but the tail-end of the downpour. It was difficult to tell, on featureless water, how greatly their range of vision was increasing, but presently behind them the loom of the land began to show, and it was apparent that soon they would be visible to all who cared to look.

"Pray brother Cormac's eyes are not so sharp as his wits!" Colin observed.

"And salmon-fishers seldom sail far from the land," his companion added, gloomily.

However, though the clouds lifted rapidly so that only the hilltops were hidden, and the rain ceased abruptly and land and sea was as open again to their view, as to others', no boat could they spy on the face of the waters. The Bay was empty, save for its scattered skerries and the one island a couple of miles out from them. The voyagers heaved sighs of relief—till Colin, able to bring his attention nearer home again, found the water in the boat halfway to his knees.

"Merciful Mary—look at that!" he cried. "We are filling. That is no rain. The sea is coming in on us."

"No!" Tormaid denied emphatically, alarmedly. "No. Certainly not. It is the rain. It was heavy, before it stopped. . . ."

The other dipped a finger into the slopping water, and tasted it. "Salt," he declared. "Salt as tears and sweat. We are afloat in a sieve!"

The priest's anguish came forth in Gaelic, Latin, and a little English, graduating from sheer groaning, through disjointed pronouncements to full-blooded denunciations and supplications in approximately equal proportions. All his life he had hated water in any but the smallest quantities—possibly as a result of a diluted milk supply entailed by his mother's fostering activities.

Colin's reaction was more practical if less Heaven-conscious. He was peering at the boat's timbering. "Look," he cried, "she is splitting at every seam. The sea is pouring in on us. Those devil-spawned women laughed to some purpose. This boat is a wreck."

It was true. The craft, long unpainted with pitch, and allowed to lie on the beach exposed to sun and weather, had split along her upper seams. The lower ones, being bedded in the shingle and kept moist by pools of rainwater, had not shrunk so badly. Thus, when launched, the inflow at first had not been very noticeable, but as more water seeped in and the boat sank lower, so the higher seams came under pressure, and the sea was spurting in on every side.

Momentarily, Tormaid's indignation outweighed his alarm. "Hell swallow them!" he exclaimed. "The wicked shame of it, to be keeping a boat in such a condition! Murderers, assassins, they are, just! The sin of it . . ."

"The sin of it is that we have nothing to bail with!" Colin cut in. He whipped off one of his brogans, and attempted to use that, but the limp sodden thing was worse than useless and he desisted, and started to use his cupped hands—with only moderate success. Doing so, he gazed around them urgently.

They were not exactly in mid-bay yet, the shore that they had left being no more than a mile away, whereas the nearest Eynart shore was four times that. But directly in front of them now, considerably less than the two miles off, lay the Bay's only real island, Calinish, a small place but inhabited. Colin pointed it out, amidst his splashings.

"It is farther to go on than to go back," he said. "But there will be no women waiting for us!"

"Och, dear Lord, what a choice—the water or the women!"

"The water we have both ways—the women only one!"

"Yes, yes. Let us on, then, and Saint Peter aid us. We should have his sympathy, and him no Triton!"

"Trust you more in your muscles than in St. Peter," Colin advised. "Row, man, as you never rowed before. I will throw out as much of the sea as two hands will hold."

And so they laboured, mightily pulling and mightily splashing, and the boat forged ahead, though ever lower in the water. Fortunately, the sea was fairly calm, or at least smooth over the long Atlantic swell. Heroes they were, in the stature of their struggle.

But it was a hopeless battle. The lower the boat sank, the heavier she was to pull, and the slower was their progress.

With the island still a good half-mile off, the gunwales were almost awash and the craft foundering. Gasping for breath, Colin shook the closed-eyed, open-mouthed, scarlet-faced Tormaid's knee.

"Over with you!" he cried. "Swim! Hold on to the oars. . . ."

The other, either from exhaustion, mental stress, intensity of devotions, or sheer reluctance to part from even the slender support that the thwart offered him in a dissolving situation, sat still. Indeed, he continued to row, automatically.

Colin stood up, precariously, grabbed a shoulder to shake it, found his stance slipping away from under his feet, and collapsed on top of his friend. And with infinitely less of fuss and splatter than had attended her onward progress, their boat sank quietly beneath them. The waters that had lapped around their middles merely closed over their heads.

The new situation, and the chill of the sea, revived them, and after a little inevitable and unprofitable splashing, Colin got his noisily-blowing colleague inserted between the two oars in front, and himself behind, and thus, swimming with their feet, they struck out for the island shore.

It was a long swim in the cold northern sea, and both men were already tired by their exertions, but the oars, their size now a benefit, would help to support them, and though the reluctant Tormaid was not so strong a swimmer as his companion, his love of life was no less vehement. Also, an incoming tide and the lack of combers tended to assist them.

For all that, after perhaps ten trying minutes of it, Tormaid was unfeignedly grateful when Colin shouted and gestured over towards their right, where, twenty or thirty yards away, the dark line of a skerry showed between the surges of the swell. Towards it they steered their oars.

After barking knees and toes on outlying bastions, and becoming somewhat entangled amongst trailing seaweed, the weary swimmers managed to haul themselves up on to what proved to be a fairly large reef of rock, flattish-topped, alternately swept and exposed by the seas. Dragging their oars after them, the men crouched thankfully on its solid foundation, their heads down between their knees, and gasped and fought for breath, the water swirling about their middles at every wave.

Presently Tormaid was sick, and probably felt the better therefore, though he did not say so. After a space, their breathing quietened towards nearer normal, and though their teeth chattered incessantly and they were racked by convulsive shudders, something of strength flowed back into them.

"The first time that I have praised God for a skerry!" Colin mumbled between blue lips. Heedfully he got to his shaking feet, keeping a firm hold of his oar, and peered around.

Between them and the island, now about five hundred yards distant, the black of weed and the white lace of foam indicated two or three further sets of skerries. In rougher weather these would have been the fangs of the very jaws of death for swimmers, but in this calm sea they might serve instead as stepping-stones for the weary. They still would require careful negotiating, of course.

The MacColls were prepared to give them that—Tormaid emphatically so. In fact, once he was safely on each of even these limited patches of terra firma, he was loth indeed to leave it. But the rising tide added point to Colin's impatience. The first gap was about one hundred and fifty yards, the second only half that, the third as far again. So swimming and climbing out and resting and swimming again, with many a scrape and a bruise from unyielding rock, they progressed. And slowly but surely the island drew near.

So intent were the refugees on their painful and piecemeal approach, that they were entirely startled when presently a hail reached them, and from no great distance. In process of clambering on to a weed-girt skerry, they stopped and stared.

"By Our Lady—more women!" Colin whispered.

Tormaid's groan was more eloquent than any words.

Only a couple of hundred yards from them, on the sandy island beach, two women stood, gesticulating. At first glance it was a distressingly similar sight to that they had fled from on the Eorsary shore. But a second glance revealed that these women were not brandishing weapons nor shaking fists, but waving them towards a line of rocks a little way to the men's right. A brief scrutiny disclosed that this was continuous, a reef running out from the land and only partly submerged in places, that would provide a causeway by which to reach the shore. Accepting this as a well-intentioned gesture, Colin slipped back into the water, to swim heavily the intervening score of yards, his foster-brother following, if with less alacrity.

Tormaid's alacrity diminished still more, abruptly, a minute or two later, when, stumbling and slipping along the weed-grown reef towards the waiting ladies, he became aware that as well as one brogan, he had lost the rag of plaid that had served him as a kilt. Feeling his position keenly, as befitted a man of religion, he completed his passage to the beach on all fours in the interests of safety, and well behind his companion.

The women seemed to be watching their approach with a nice mixture of warm sympathy and frank admiration. The contrast to their earlier reception was striking. Colin felt his elementary faith in womankind returning—especially as, even in his semi-exhausted state, he was not totally unaware that both ladies approximated to what is frequently described as fine pieces of womanhood. Save in age, there was a notable similarity about them, in figure, feature, and fiery red hair, which suggested that they might well be mother and daughter. But neither was so old nor yet so young as to invalidate their essential femininity.

Colin drew himself up, and raised a hand in some sort of salutation. "Heaven smile on you," he observed. "We are two travelling men whose boat had the misfortune to sink on us." He still shivered, and there was a certain rattling of teeth about that.

From the back, Tormaid muttered something indistinguishable.

The younger woman giggled and glanced away, as young women are apt to do—but only momentarily. Her companion nodded. "We were after seeing that, yes," she said. "The great splashing you made." That was pleasantly conversational.

"My friend is no great swimmer," Colin pointed out.

"Och, like porpoises you were—just porpoises," the lady declared, and laughed heartily.

Her more youthful companion peered round at Tormaid, who was now standing very close behind his foster-brother, and trilled with deliciously uninhibited appreciation.

Colin frowned doubtfully, and coughed. "We have lost all— er—especially my friend," he said. "He . . . I . . ." In dignified patience he waited while a further accession of glee subsided. "We cast ourselves upon your shore and your mercy. We crave the hospitality of Calinish." The only flaw to that was an involuntary shiver at the end.

"Och, yes," the more matronly agreed, cheerfully, and nudged the younger with a well-turned elbow. They smiled at each other with entire understanding.

"I will take the fatter one . . ." the girl began, when she was interrupted.

"Not so. *I* will take him," her probable mother asserted. "He is more the size of Seumas Gorm." And her mirth bubbled up once more.

The other accepted that with dutiful promptitude. She stepped forward, and took Colin by the hand. "Come, you," she invited.

"Ummmm . . ." that man said, and glanced quickly behind him.

The older woman made for the shrinking Tormaid purposefully. "Lonely it is, on Calinish, when the men are out at the fishing," she mentioned. "Just the two houses there are, on the island. No more than the two of us. Come you up."

"Er . . . you are very kind," Colin said. "But . . . what we need is a little food, some clothing, and . . ."

"And a boat to take us across to Eynart," Tormaid put in, hurriedly.

"Yes. We are for visiting Macleod of Eynart," Colin Og explained. "And in something of haste." Calinish had always been Macleod property, though Iain Cam had included it in

An Colin Mor's resounding list of titles.

"Och, yes—a meal and maybe a shirt you shall have. But the boat you must wait for," he was assured. "There is no boat on the island till our men return from the fishing, see you."

"And . . . and when is that?" Tormaid gulped.

Both women smiled benignly. "Not until tomorrow's morn."

"That is so," the younger agreed, dimpling. "I am Anna." And she wiped a smear of blood and salt water from Colin's chest with the hem of her skirt.

"And I am Mairi," the older informed. She stripped off a sort of outer bodice that she wore over her ample bust, and proffered it to Tormaid, to that modest man's considerable comfort. Also she took his arm. "That is my house, there, with the white cow in front."

"Indeed. . . ."

"And that is mine," the girl Anna pointed out, indicating a second whitewashed cottage further along the flank of the one hill that made up Calinish. "Welcome, you are," and she patted her captive's shoulder.

Colin Og looked from one woman to the other, and then to his foster-brother, and burst into sudden and wholehearted laughter. "Sustain and preserve us!" he cried. "Here is hospitality indeed! We prayed to the saints—let us be grateful for what they send us! Myself, I am a man of simple tastes."

Tormaid drew a great breath. "But I . . . I am a . . ."

"You are a poor travelling man sorely in need of a little loving kindness!" Colin declared, promptly and strongly. "We are in these good ladies' hands, till a boat comes. Myself, I ask no better—even if I was An Colin Mor himself!" and he glanced sidelong at the older woman as he spoke.

"With whom the Devil fly away!" that matron added, vigorously.

"Exactly as I thought," Colin nodded. "You see, Tormaid, how fortunate we are?"

Tormaid looked speculatively at the large lady who beamed on him, and remained silent.

Intercepting his glance, Mairi smiled and, tugging his arm, jerked an authoritative head upwards, up towards her cabin.

Colin chuckled. "Go, you—your goose is cooked, brother."

Tormaid drew himself up, bodice tied precariously about his middle notwithstanding, and inclined his head. "I go with a quiet mind . . . since I have no choice," he announced. And as an afterthought, when already he was on the move, "But only so far . . ."

"Excellent sentiments!" his foster-brother flung after him. "I will have to be thinking about the same, my own self." *Sotto voce*, he added, "Praise be to all saints that I am no churchman. . . ." before he succumbed to the drag on his own arm.

Early next morning four weary and none too hearty fishermen were prevailed upon—mainly by their wives and sister, undoubtedly—to ferry the two cheerful strangers across the remaining stretch of bay between their island and Eynart proper. The fact that their passengers, as well as being unsuitably bright for the time of day, were clad in some of their own best clothes may have had something to do with the oarsmen's taciturnity.

Be that as it may, they boorishly put their wives' guests ashore on an outlandish bit of the mainland coast, when by only half an hour's more rowing they could have done a gentlemanly job and deposited them below Eynart House itself.

Still, the travellers' spirits were not to be damped by such pinpricks, after all their more dramatic experiences, and swearing by all that they held holy to return their borrowed and far from magnificent plumes before the next Lord's Day, they bade their involuntary benefactors farewell, and turned to serious business.

IX

THE House of Eynart was a very different sort of establishment from the Duncolin of An Colin Mor. A castle there had been here too, at one time, but successive razings of it—largely by MacColls—had so discouraged its owners that one of them had eventually let it lie, built for himself nearby a less pretentious but infinitely more comfortable house of two storeys and a thatched roof, around which farmery, barns, cattle-pens, and his dependants' cottages and cabins had clustered like chickens round a mother hen, in a huddle of domestic felicity.

It was almost noon before the travellers reached this pleasant scene, and threaded their way through the township, no man hindering. At the porch of Eynart House, a certain amount of beating on the door brought a hastening gillie; his master, being only a two-feather man, chieftain of an isolated branch of a larger clan, could hardly rise to a seneschal.

"Torquil Macleod—is he at home?" Colin demanded.

The gillie blinked at the authoritative tone, from one so dressed. "Himself is round at the still-house," he informed. "Busy, he is."

"Go you, then, and announce me."

The man sniffed. "Announce yourself, brolachan. Me, I am busy too."

He was turning away when Tormaid's hand reached out and jerked him round. "Fool!" he cried. "You are speaking to An Colin Og."

The other gaped, blenched, and swallowed twice. "Come, you," he muttered, and led the way.

To reach the still-house it was necessary to cross the garden, a pleasance of bushes and flowers and paths that unsuitably brought a frown to Colin's brow; the place spoke to him too loudly of Marsala Macleod.

106

In the dim recesses of the still-house a group of four men were talking, and before ever their guide opened his mouth Colin swore beneath his breath. Beside the spare figure of Torquil Macleod, stood Iain Cam MacColl of the Cairn.

The gillie lifted up his voice, suitably prompted by Tormaid. "An Colin Og, Heir of Ardcoll, Knight of the Holy Manger, to see Eynart."

That achieved its effect. After a moment's staring all four men came striding towards them. Torquil Macleod was first—but Iain Cam was only half a pace behind, and his hand reached out to the older man's arm. There was a confused jumble of exclamation.

Colin Og's voice prevailed. "Torquil Macleod, old friend, I greet you—despite the bad company you are keeping!"

Macleod shook his grey head. "My boy—is it yourself, in God's name!"

"None other. To the sorrow of some—but not to yours, I hope?"

"To yours also, indeed, Eynart," Iain Cam said, warningly. "This one is sorrow to all men."

"Quiet, ruffian!" Colin cried. "Would you interrupt your betters with your lies!"

"Whatever your trouble, I am glad to see you, Colin," Macleod declared. "For long I have thought you dead."

"You are grown credulous, sir, surely—and my brother clever."

"Do not heed him, Eynart—he is mad, and dangerous," Iain Wryface exclaimed. "Have a care or he will do you an injury. I told you—yesterday he turned his cannon on his own people, for a mere whim. During a meal in Duncolin he assaulted myself and another without cause. He has been frightening the glens-folk by running naked . . ."

"Torquil Macleod—must I listen to the insults of this, this upstart, in your house as well as in my own! Give me a sword, and I will teach him his place. . . ."

"Softly, Colin, softly," the older man said. "My house it is, yes—and MacColl of the Cairn my guest. Like yourself. In my

107

house, let us talk reasonably, as gentlemen. . . ."

"I have nothing to say to this bravo that would not be better said with cold steel," Colin interrupted. "I came to talk to Macleod of Eynart—not to my brother's lackey. Out with you, creature!"

"God's death—I represent the Captain of Clan Colin . . ." the stooping man began, when his host held up a veined hand.

"I think that you should leave us, my friend—it is fitting," he said. "Later we will continue our conversation. An Colin Og and myself would speak privately."

Iain Cam bit his twisted lip, glanced at his two companions—both strangers though dressed in MacColl tartan—and shrugged. "Very well," he said. "I will be outside." He jabbed a finger at the older man. "But I warn you, Macleod—there is danger in this for you. Watch you where you step." And tugging his bonnet over at a more acute angle, he swaggered to the still-house door, his colleagues behind him.

In silence the others watched them go.

Torquil Macleod was a grave fine-featured man in his early sixties, a man who had found less peace in his life than he had sought. To Colin he turned now, and sighed.

"This is not the welcome I would have planned for you, boy," he said. "I am sorry. But you . . . you are well?"

"I am, yes. I am not mad, either, if that is your meaning."

"I did not think it."

"And yet you believed Cormac's other lies—about my death?"

The other spread out his hands. "What reason had I to doubt it?"

There was a moment's silence.

"I have seen Marsala," Colin observed, at length.

"Yes," her father said. "Poor Marsala."

"Poor Marsala!" the other barked. "Poor Colin, is it not? Marsala looks to have settled herself very comfortably."

"You think so? I hope that you are right."

"Other sentiments might do you more credit, Torquil Macleod!"

"You say so, Colin? Is a man's credit more important than his daughter's well-being, I wonder?"

"If the man is a chief, then his credit is his people's," Colin pointed out.

"Ah, yes—his people's." The older man shook his head. "Perhaps I have thought *overmuch* of my people's well-being, and insufficient of my daughter's. It was not by her choice that she was married to Cormac."

"Handfasted, you mean."

"Handfasted, yes. That was the best that I could do for her."

"You mean . . . ?"

"I mean that Cormac was very pressing. For the clans' sake. . . ."

"I see. For the clans' sake, then, she married Cormac and forgot myself!"

"I cannot say what she forgot. But for the clans' sake, yes, and my own, she married Cormac."

"For the clans' sake—and yours, Torquil Macleod! Mine—even my memory—did not enter into the matter?"

Eynart looked at him, directly, sombre-eyed. "You are bitter, Colin. But tell me, are you sure that had it indeed been *you* that she had had to marry, it would not have been for the clans' sake, likewise? Can you swear otherwise?"

The younger man frowned. "I . . . I . . . She was fond of me, I swear . . ."

"Fond, yes. But that is not what I asked you to swear, my son."

"Damnation—how can I swear? How can I tell? How is a man to tell, with a woman . . . ?"

"Exactly. How is one to tell, with a woman! Marsala was only a child when you left, Colin—but she is a woman now. And she is not the sort who opens her heart for all to read."

Torquil Macleod wagged an unhappy head. "I do not know, at all, my own self. I have had no joy, no pride, in this business, God knows. . . . Had her mother been alive, perhaps. . . . But I am only an old done man, and foolish."

109

"You are a . . ." Colin stopped himself, as with an effort, and took a turn away and back on the stone flags of the still-house floor. "See you," he said, tense-voiced, "it was only a handfast marriage that you allowed. You had your reasons for that, surely. And a handfast marriage can be broken."

"If there are no children within the twelvemonth . . . and if the parties desire that it be broken."

Deep-voiced, the younger man spoke. "There is no child yet, I think. And the parties can be constrained."

"I will not constrain Marsala again."

"No? But, by God's shadow, I will constrain Cormac! With your help."

Macleod drew a long breath. "My help, Colin?"

"Yes, then. I need men, to teach Cormac his lesson."

"You do, yes. Many men. But not my men. Not Macleods. . . ."

"Why not? What other men am I to find?"

"That I do not know. But . . . look you, Colin—I cannot have my people suffer in this. And suffer they would. It would mean war, no less. Cormac is not lightly going to be persuaded. We are a small sept—I cannot muster a full hundred fighting-men. Cormac can raise eight hundred—more, at need . . ."

"These are my father's men—not Cormac's. They will not fight against An Colin Mor's heir."

"Are you so sure, boy? You have been long away—and Cormac's grip is tight."

"Give me a few men—give me but fifty—and I will prove just how tight is Cormac's grip!"

Torquil Macleod ran a hand through his grey hair. "I cannot do it, Colin," he said. "The cost to my people is too great. Whoever won of you, they must lose. I will not let them do it. We are a small peaceable folk. . . . Besides, on Marsala's marriage, I signed a bond with him . . ."

"Not with Cormac! With my father, surely?"

"With the Captain of Clan Colin, duly appointed, and acting for An Colin Mor. What is more, my chief did likewise—Raasay did. I cannot break my own bond, nor his."

Colin Og ran a hand over mouth and jaw. He looked at Tormaid, who throughout had stood back modestly in the rear. He shook his head. "You are a great disappointment to me, Torquil Macleod," he declared, warmly.

"I know it, boy—and I am sorry. But I can do no other."

"And that is your last word, then?"

"It is, yes. For your immediate personal wants, of course, I will do all that can be done."

"For my personal wants, I can look after myself . . ." Colin was asserting, when Tormaid intervened, practically.

"Clothing, we could be doing with, and arms . . . and footgear," he suggested.

"There speaks the wiser man," Eynart approved. "Rome has not stolen all your native wit, then, Tormaid? Faithful yet, I see. Colin—you are more fortunate in the quality of your foster than in your true brother, I think. . . ."

"I am, yes. Than in the quality of my true friends likewise, perhaps!"

"It may be so," the older man acceded gravely. "At least, my table is yours. You will not refuse my poor hospitality?"

Colin bowed with stiff formality. "That would be altogether lacking in respect to my father's friend," he announced. "So long as I do not have to eat in the company of Iain Wryface."

"That can be arranged, I think. Come you both to the house."

Torquil Macleod did arrange it, though not without a certain amount of unpleasantness. Iain Cam and his henchmen departed on horseback for Eorsary, breathing threatenings and slaughters. Colin and Tormaid did justice to a satisfying meal in the kindly house of Eynart, and learned in the process much that it was expedient for them to know about the methods and activities of Cormac MacColl. They left the table to go upstairs, for the ravishing of their host's wardrobe, in a thoughtful frame of mind.

Later, left alone to select and try on the most suitable of Macleod's offerings, their thoughtfulness developed into

111

something of a council of war. Their problems were not far to seek, and the remedies less than self-evident. That prompt and drastic action was called for was not in doubt, but what action possible for them to take could be effective?

Colin eventually summed up the situation thus. They had two immediate tasks. One, to raise a force of men able to act at least as a nucleus around which a revolt against Cormac's power could be organized. Two, to ensure that Marsala Macleod's marriage was broken. And since, he argued, the effect of the latter might bear strongly on the former, it seemed wise to attempt it first.

Tormaid wondered whether that was Colin the tactician speaking, or Colin the jealous?

Authoritatively put in his place, he was given to see how much depended on this marriage. Break it speedily, effectively—above all, before Cormac achieved an heir—and the effect on both clans would be enormous.

But how was this breaking to be done, speedily or otherwise, Tormaid wanted to know? What chance had they to break anything—except their own necks? For that matter, what chance had they to do *anything* effective—even to gather a few men together? They might get a cateran or two out of the heather—broken men with their hands against everyone. But what use were such, against the might of Clan Colin?

There were other clans besides Clan Colin, the other pointed out. Had not old Hector Ban of Balnafail told them that his son Kenneth had gone to sell his sword to Mackenzie of Gairloch, and others before him? They might pay a visit to Gairloch, themselves . . . but not until they had tried to loosen that handfast marriage of Cormac's a little. . . .

In that spirit, then, they took their leave of Torquil Macleod, dressed now as Highland gentlemen should be dressed, in philamore—Macleod, necessarily—doublet, bonnet, thonged hose, brogans, broadsword, and dirk. Mounted on a pair of sturdy shaggy long-tailed ponies, they rode away northwards once more, on the long road to Ardcoll.

X

SOME twelve miles north of Eynart, not far from the root of the Eorsary peninsula, the tail end of a mountain range came down to the sea, finishing in great black cliffs which soared hundreds of feet above the restless waters. To circumnavigate this obstruction the drove road had to turn away inland, to climb through long folds of rolling heather moorland, over a bare shoulder of hill, and down steeply into the gut of a rocky ravine wherein a white river boiled and plunged. The road necessarily was narrow here, a mere track over which the horses picked their way in single file.

The travellers were perhaps halfway down this chasm, glad enough of its shade and the cool sound of cascading water, in the heavy heat of late afternoon, when the noise startled them. Ominous, like distant thunder, there was a rumble overhead. Glancing up, directly above them they saw the entire rocky hillside on the move. Great boulders were hurtling down from a high overhanging cornice, and their weight was bringing down all the precipitous slope of scree and loose stone below. Even as they stared, they sensed the tremor of the ground beneath their ponies' feet.

Colin's shout and action were simultaneous. "The river!" he bawled, and threw himself off his garron, to race headlong down through the rubble and ferns towards the stream, Tormaid only a couple of bounds behind.

The river, in the process of the ages, had cut a deep channel for itself in the solid basalt floor of the ravine. Colin, in the desperate moment of realization, had remembered this. Under the jut of that wall of basalt they might just conceivably find shelter. They would find no other in that bare and barren trough.

They had no more than sixty yards to go, but it seemed to take them an eternity. Not so much running as falling and rolling, they flung themselves down that steep uneven place.

Time is not to be reckoned in seconds and minutes in such circumstances, but by the fleeting span of opportunity. And by every standard their opportunity was fleeting. Without wasting a fraction of a second to turn and look behind them, they could hear and feel how ill went the race against them.

At the brink Colin, still leading, did not so much as pause—he could not have done so had he wished it. A dozen feet below him, the peat-stained water rushed, not in a deep pool as some corner of his mind had hoped, but in shallows over grey basaltic shelves, foaming round great jagged rocks, eloquent testimony to other stone-falls. Launched into space as he was, kilt, plaid, and sword flying about his ears, he twisted violently to prevent himself from being hurled on to one of these rocks, and at the same time to fall as flatly as might be. Into two feet of water he dropped, practically on all fours. Vaguely he knew that wrists and knees had jarred, and then he was throwing himself backwards towards the bank that he had just left.

Tormaid, though a yard or two behind, was also a yard or two to the right, and struck a rather more favourable spot to jump, with the beginnings of a pool below him. But he had a narrower escape, for all that. Almost exactly as he struck the water, a huge boulder, forerunner of many, bounded in his wake and crashed into the river only a foot from him. Actually, the wave that it threw up cast him back a little in the way that he wanted to go. Dazedly he floundered amidst a welter of spray.

The noise was now stunning. Colin, grasping at a projection of the rocky wall, yelled to his wallowing companion. His voice was drowned in the roar. Frantically, he threw himself forward through the water, to grab at his friend's thrashing arm, his shoulder. Stumbling, he dragged Tormaid back. Subconsciously, he crouched, head down, adding to his physical stress. Almost, he held his breath.

And then, with one of his hands reaching for the bank, the avalanche reached them, overwhelmed them. In indescribable fury the cataract of rock and rubble and soil thundered over them, and the boiling river seemed to rise up in steam. Like a waterfall the torrent of stone shot over the lip of the little cliff above them, in its impetus plunging clear of the huddled men beneath. In a daze they pressed back against the rock wall, and the surge of the displaced water rose in a wave and covered them.

Battling to keep their feet, to draw breath, to avoid being swept down in the stress of waters, they were only dimly aware of the earthshaking concussion of rocks great and small, of the deafening noise, of what was happening to the river. To stay alive was their one preoccupation, demanding their every faculty.

Somehow, Colin's questing feet found a basalt ledge behind them, and another, following the striated formation of the rock. Backing against that wall he climbed up, dragging at Tormaid to do likewise. Knocking his head on the overhang above stopped him. But still the water was swirling about their faces. And it was dark. . . .

Eventually what was happening became apparent to them. The mass of material that had descended upon them was filling up the trough of the river, leaving only this cavity beneath the overhang as a sort of tunnel through which the water was being forced.

The knowledge had an immediate and shocking effect on both of them, the fear of being buried, trapped, overwhelming them. For a moment Colin at least knew panic. Almost, he gave way to it—and then quelled the urge fiercely, and forced himself to consider.

Their only hope lay in the steep fall of the river's bed. This was bound, surely, to have a loosening effect on the packing of the debris at its lower end. There would be a pull downstream. . . . But how far did this landslide extend on either hand . . . ?

Gesturing and pushing at Tormaid, Colin plunged right-handed with the current.

Short as it was, that was a nightmarish progress. Tripping,

115

pitching, buffeted against their wall, knocked down by pendants and projections, under water much of the time and in complete darkness, they floundered on desperately—for approximately how long neither could ever say. Their advance partly involuntary, swept on by the current, thrust hither and thither, choking, barely sensible, they fought their crazy incoherent battle for space and air and light.

They achieved the last first. A faint greenish glimmer ahead, wavering and uncertain but unmistakable, caught their despairing attention, and drew them on. Frantically they struggled towards it. It grew in area and intensity—but it became little clearer. In a cavity of the bank, where, standing on a small ledge, they could keep their chins well above water, the men stared, panting.

Obviously it was reflected daylight, shining through water. Somewhere not far in front was a gap—but presumably there was either a buttress or a heavy overhang of their wall between.

Colin shook his companion's shoulder, and gasped in his ear. "Dive . . . ! Under . . . and out."

The other's answer was not intelligible, but Colin did not wait for comment. Drawing as deep a breath as his heaving lungs would hold, he ducked beneath the water and forced himself, part-walking, part-swimming, towards that shimmering light.

It was not so desperate a venture as he had feared. A large boulder had wedged itself against the bank at an angle that left a narrow and tapering gap between, and the rubble had packed itself up beyond. Through this aperture the light percolated in one direction and the water flooded in the other. Indeed, so strongly did the current stream through this bottleneck that Colin was carried thither willy-nilly. Forcing himself downwards—for the gap was widest at its base—he used his hands to fend himself off from the harsh rock rather than to propel himself forward. In the very jaws of it his sword, trailing from the belt slung across chest and shoulder, caught and held him, and for an instant panic came close again. But a furious tugging released the weapon, and the surging tortured water carried him through. Up into blessed light and air he struggled, to lie gasping, half in the water and half out.

The man found himself in something like a crater, a hollow of soil and gravel and stones that seemed to have caved in from the general level of the avalanche's deposit, revealing this small glimpse of the river at the foot.

The landslide itself seemed to be over, though tricklings of small stones continued down that scarred and dust-reeking braeside, sounding thinly. A smaller sound still, and close at hand, drew the man's eye. Projecting nearby a little way out from the piled debris was the faintly-twitching single hoof of a brown pony.

A puffing and gasping behind him heralded Tormaid's emergence. But Colin had no eyes for him. A movement from the hillside above caught and held his glance.

"Mother of God!" he swore.

Up there, near the brink of the ravine, a man on horseback shouted, waved, and pointed. Beside him two riderless garrons stood. Even at that range—over quarter of a mile—the man's peculiar carriage identified him as Iain Cam of the Cairn. An answering hail from much closer at hand sent Colin crawling to the lip of their hollow. Upstream, perhaps two hundred and fifty yards off, and not much above their own level, four men were picking their way cautiously towards them over the rubble and loose soil—the two MacColl-tartaned strangers from Eynart, and a pair of wild-looking gillies.

Colin slid down again to his friend. "They are almost on us," he whispered. "Four of them." He jerked his head upwards. "Wryface keeps well out of trouble's road. Is the Church too weary for a fight?"

Tormaid groaned, but his hand went to his sword-hilt. "The Church is never too weary to fight," he asserted, sighing. "Four, just, you say?"

"Four, yes. The two bullyrooks and a pair of caterans out of the heather. Child's play! Searching, they are, for our corpses." And he laughed softly, and drew Torquil Macleod's broadsword. He also unbelted and laid aside the heavy kilt and plaiding of the sodden philamore, for ease of action, his foster-brother following suit.

Panting still, they crept up to the very rim of their crater, to peer over. Undoubtedly Iain Cam from his lofty viewpoint could see them, but equally evidently the four men in the gut of the ravine did not realize the significance of his hailings and waving. They were pressing on, but warily, for the terrain made bad going, and they were scattered over a sizeable area, scanning and searching the debris. The nearest, one of the gillies, was no more than fifty yards off.

"The saints willing, and that man is yours," Colin whispered. "I will throw him down to you. Dirk work. Down you, and look dead."

So while Tormaid lay sprawled on his back lower in the hollow, his companion lay on his face at the top—and kept one eye, under his arm, trained on the advancing cateran.

The fellow saw him, aided perhaps by Iain Cam's distant warnings, when a score of yards away. Shouting in his turn to his colleagues, he came running, a *sgian dubh* gleaming evilly in his hand.

Striving desperately to prevent his chest from heaving, Colin lay inert, waiting. Had he not been An Colin Og, Heir of Ardcoll, the Hundred Glens, and all the Islands of the Sea, etcetera, he might just conceivably have felt an uncomfortable anticipatory sensation of cold steel between his ribs.

Ten yards, five, three—the man stood over him, stooping. And even as the creature stooped, dirk raised high, Colin exploded into life like a coiled spring released. His arms wrapped round the gillie's knees, and as the fellow toppled forward, Colin's head drove up into his middle, folding him exactly in two. A single convulsive heave, and the unfortunate went head over heels down the slope, to Tormaid's waiting arms. One of those arms rose and fell, twice, and the incident closed abruptly.

This extremely brief episode had taken place just within the lip of the hollow, and so probably had not been fully visible to the other searchers. But certainly Iain Cam had seen it all, and the alarmed urgency of his hailing could not be lost on his henchmen below; also, the casualty's own shouting had ended in a sudden strangled yelp which ought to have told them something. Wriggling back to his former position, Colin once again investigated.

The situation had developed, as was to be expected. The gentry in the MacColl tartan were now making hotfoot for the hollow, swords drawn, while farther back, the remaining gillie was coming on strongly.

Colin calculated swiftly, and nodded to himself. The pair of sworders would reach them first, and from their appearance would be handy men at cut and thrust. They bore the stamp of the professional. But then, so did An Colin Og. Tormaid could deal with the gillie. He whistled a few staves beneath his breath as he waited.

Their panting breath heralded the bravos' heavy approach over the loose rubble. Their quarry drew himself up tensely, his broadsword hilt gripped in his right hand, the folds of his soaking philamore in his left.

The foremost man saw him when a dozen yards off, and cried out his news. Colin did not move a muscle. He could not use the same tactics as with the first gillie; while he wrestled with the one, the other would run him through. Whatever he did would require to be timed to a second. Less. A man can move yards in a second, and a sword can bite. . . .

When the fellow's foot was on the very rim of their crater, Colin sprang into violent action. Leaping to his feet, in the same movement his left arm was flung over, and the wet plaiding hurled directly in the face of the oncoming assailant. There is a lot of cloth in a philamore, and weighted with water it can have a considerable effect. Momentarily enveloping the man's head, shoulders, arms, and even his sword point, it brought him up short, with a muffled oath. Colin's right hand was only a little behind his left, and the oath changed abruptly to a horrible scream as the broadsword drove home into the midst of the heaving folds of Macleod tartan.

The second bravo was only a few yards behind his friend. He came on, sword high. Colin wrenched at his own weapon, to free it, but his victim had doubled up over it, and whether he was clutching it with his hand or merely with his ribs, it resisted its owner's tugging. With only instants at his disposal, Colin reversed his tactics, launched himself forward against the wounded man, and hurled him back, plaid, sword, and all, into the arms of his oncoming colleague.

It was not entirely a successful manoeuvre, but it gave Colin a vital second or two. The casualty collided with his companion but collapsed as he did so, causing the other only to stagger and sidestep. But the impending down-drive of the sword was deflected and nullified.

Colin wasted no moment in throwing himself after his victim. Leaping over the fallen man, he grasped the other round the middle, pinioning his left arm, his dirk arm. Reaching up, he gripped the sword arm just below the elbow, before his opponent could shorten his weapon for an inward or jabbing thrust. Calling on every last ounce of his strength, he held him thus.

So they strained, chest to chest, eye to eye, panting in each other's faces, while at their feet the third man squirmed and twitched. Almost motionless they stood, though with every muscle in play, nearly in a state of mutual checkmate. Nearly but not quite. The fingers of Colin's left hand were moving, groping, seeking. They sought a nerve, under the elbow, where it crossed hard bone, a nerve that a drunken surgeon of the Papal Guard had shown to him in a den in Rome.

Grunting in the extremity of their effort, they swayed. The bravo was slightly the bigger man, certainly the heavier and more stockily built. But probably Colin was the fresher, for all his recent exertions; he had not come running over the debris of a landslide, nor indeed laboured mightily to create that landslide. Also, he was less hampered by his clothing, in shirt and doublet only.

His groping fingers suddenly sank home, and he felt the other wince and shrink. The grimace on the face so near to his own was eloquent. Through clenched teeth, he spoke.

"So you thought . . . to kill . . . An Colin Og with . . . his own rocks!" he said. "More than rocks . . . more than hired swords . . . you will need!" Relentlessly he kept up the pressure on that nerve. He could feel the arm sagging. "Say your prayers, hireling . . . or you die unshriven!"

A different expression had come into the fellow's eyes. Colin recognized it, and grinned. "Fool to . . . challenge Colin Og," he jerked. "Wryface . . . up there . . . knows better. Die, fool!"

The man's mouth gaping to the numbing pain, the sword dropped from his nerveless fingers with a clatter.

Instantly Colin acted. Thrusting with all his might, he flung the other from him, and as they disengaged he brought up his bare knee to the man's groin. As the bravo bent, yelping, Colin bent also—for the fallen sword. He grasped it, not by the hilt, but halfway down the blade, and straightening up, hurled it, in the same javelin-like throw that he had used in the *Florabel's* lazaretto. It took the other full in the throat, as he sought to struggle upright.

"So perish all traitors!" the younger man panted.

"Prettily done!" Tormaid mentioned, at his back. "But could you not have left one of them for myself?"

Slowly turning, Colin found his foster-brother wiping a dirk on his first victim's bonnet. "You had the gillie," he asserted, and swallowed his unruly breath. "What . . . have you done with him?"

Tormaid pointed down into the hollow, where by the welling water the second cateran lay, arms outstretched.

"Good," Colin nodded. "Four scoundrels suitably dead."

"Not so," the priest corrected. "Three, only. This poor creature of mine was so much concerned with what you were after doing to these sword-wavers, that he had no eyes for such as myself. I had no heart to dirk him unawares, so I let him have a dunt on the back of his thick head with the hilt— and there he is! *Ille crucem sceleris pretium tulit, hic diadema!*"

"Man, Tormaid—you are weak, weak! That is the worst of religion . . ."

"Worst, nothing. Are we not seeking a tail for ourselves out of the heather? Well, then—there is the first of it!"

"M'mmm. Well . . ."

"Very well, indeed. My man he is, for hereafter . . . and more use to us than your three corpses, there!"

"I do not know. . . ." Colin was stooping, and fingering the clothing of the man at his feet. "It will be good to wear the MacColl colours again . . . after so long," he observed. "I think I have made no holes in it, with my swording!"

Tormaid looked at the other bravo, and scratched his head. "I am not so sure about this fellow," he objected. "A bloody mess you have made . . ."

"Och, man—with a drop of water, a needle and a yard of thread, you will be fine, just fine. It is . . ." He stopped, as his eyes lifted to the ravine top, and he pointed, unspeaking.

Iain Cam was riding away along the ridge at a full canter, the two riderless ponies behind him, northwards.

"Well may he," Colin Og nodded. "I will speak with that one, again."

XI

COLIN OG had to wait some time for that promised conversation with Iain Cam of the Cairn, whatever his eagerness. Likewise his wider purpose, urgent though it was, since it could only be achieved by guile and the adroit handling of circumstance, demanded patience. And Colin Og MacColl was not, in essence, a patient man. The days that followed the affair in the ravine, then, though they had their small activities, were trying ones for the dispossessed Heir of Ardcoll. And therefore, in the very nature of things, they were still more trying for his companion Tormaid.

In the hinterland of Eorsary, amongst the great mountains that reached from the peninsula's root into the wild fastnesses of north-west Ross, they lingered and made such preparations as they could. So near and yet so far. But Duncolin was no fragile nut to crack, as none knew better than they. And since whatever they were to achieve entailed the circumvention of Cormac MacColl's far from sluggish wits, it behoved them to go more warily than was his brother's norm or pleasure.

The plan of sorts that they did work out was arrived at more by a process of elimination than by constructive design. What they could by no means do so infinitely overwhelmed what was even remotely possible, that they had little choice. Only circumstance, in the shape of Tormaid's Divine intervention, or Colin's less ambitious luck, resolutely and promptly grasped, could sway the issue. And circumstance can be deplorably fickle even when fortune is said to favour the bold. In the case of the brothers MacColl, the question as to which was the bolder was a matter for debate.

To winkle Marsala Macleod out of Duncolin was the immediate and formidable task. Hours of wit-cudgelling and debate only underlined two prerequisites for any sort of success. One was that Cormac must be decoyed away, with much of his strength. The other, that Marsala must issue from the castle, if not by her own will, at least by permission of her immediate gaoler—since she would issue under no other conditions. To make reasonably possible, much less to ensure, both of these conditions was the size of their problem.

Cormac being Cormac, and with a name for cunning that obviously had not been lightly won, had to be outsmarted. Colin, who knew his brother fairly well, decided that to counter his cunning only the invoking of his cupidity could succeed— together with his pride, perhaps. And to such an end the only means that he could think of laying hands on was the *Florabel*. And to lay hands on the *Florabel* demanded manpower. Hence the delay.

Tormaid's action in sparing his gillie now turned to their advantage—a fact which Colin was by no means allowed to forget. The man, a hairy and uncomplicated individual calling himself Rob Molach, and some sort of Mackenzie out of Kintail, had been considerably surprised and gratified to find himself alive after the landslide incident, and more surprised still to be presented with his late intended quarry's suit of clothes—such clothes, of a gentleman of the Macleods, as he had never dreamed of being privileged to wear. He swore that he had had no knowledge of the gentlemen's identity—which was probably true—and that Iain Cam had made himself and his late colleague and cousin a considerable offer for their services in helping him to dispose of a couple of Campbell spies—an offer which was still to be redeemed. He also swore, with touching conviction, that his life was now entirely the property of the excellent Tormaid the Priest—though a proclaimed Protestant, he had eventually to be restrained from crossing himself each time Tormaid addressed him—and the high and noble Colin mhic Colin. But, more important, he offered to conduct them to the retreat of a party of his friends, broken men living a lawless life in the no-man's-land between the clan territories.

Thus it was that the travellers came to a disused summer shieling, nestling beside a dark lochan high amongst the peat

mosses and frowning corries at the far head of Glen Druim—
one of An Colin Mor's hundred glens, no doubt, but sufficiently
remote and worthless to be almost unknown terrain. Here they
found half a dozen nefarious-looking ruffians, very evidently
under the command of an enormous bull-like man whom their
Rob introduced with some trepidation as Sorley Dam, leaving
his clan discreetly nameless. This impressive personage, who
suffered variously from a cast in one eye, a lack of ears, and
a broken nose, after a lengthy and unnerving stare with one of
his eyes while the other roamed at large, decided to greet Colin
as one Highland gentleman should greet another, with heavy
formality. He seemed to know all about Colin Og's situation—
in fact, he appeared to be remarkably well informed on affairs
altogether. Though it transpired that he had lost his ears at the
hands of An Colin Mor over some small misunderstanding as
to the ownership of certain cattle, he asserted that he bore the
chief of the MacColls no grudge. He was prepared to co-operate
with the said potent chief's son and heir in the legitimate pursuit
of his inheritance—provided, of course, that arrangements
suitable to his dignity as a Highland gentleman were arrived
at. Colin, without trusting him a couple of yards, agreed to his
terms in the handsomest fashion, and shook hands on it.

They now had a tail of seven, and Sorley Dam declared that
if they gave him two or three days he could double it. Days
were all that they had to give him, there and then, and the
offer was accepted.

While they waited, Colin, with the second stage of his plan
in view, made a small expedition of his own, back into Macleod
country, to Eynart itself—though it was an anonymous and
unheralded call that he paid under cover of darkness to that
too peace-loving place. He returned to the lonely shieling in
Glen Druim, on a borrowed pony, two days later, with a
somewhat doubtful but thoroughly cowed companion, one
Farquhar Macleod, a stiff elderly man and steward to Torquil
himself. Bewildered and unhappy, but willing to do anything—
so long as it demanded no heroics—to be allowed to return
safely to the home from which he had been ravished, he was

put under the care of Rob Molach—now, because of his proudly-worn tartan, a kind of co-opted Macleod.

The stage was almost set.

The day following, when Sorley Dam arrived back at his headquarters, he brought with him more than just the four scoundrelly characters that he had collected from Heaven knew where, but an item of news. It was that there were three men, professed friends of Colin mhic Colin, that had belonged to the Dumbarton ship that was lying in Loch Coll, who now were in hiding with some herdsmen six or seven miles to the north. Sorley had sent some of his men to fetch them in.

At nightfall, they arrived at the little encampment by the darkling lochan—Angus Macdougall, the bold Graham, and the Skyeman cook. Their accession was received with much satisfaction, Tormaid pointing out the efficacy of true faith.

Their story, briefly, went thus. When, that first afternoon at Ardcoll, Iain Cam and a large company of armed men had come aboard the anchored *Florabel*, all her people had been driven off and locked up ashore, the officers and Lowland members of the crew to be summarily hanged at sundown, the seven Highlandmen to be consigned to the *Iolair* as galley slaves. The next day, in retribution, these seven were set to labour, with the MacColl shipwrights, at repairing the damage done to the *Iolair's* bows by the *Florabel's* cannon. Their manacles being removed for the purpose, they made their bid to escape, by jumping overboard. Four failed, and their fate was unknown. This trio that had got away had succeeded by swimming back to the galley itself, hiding under her counter, and, when the search was at its height, climbing back aboard and lying low in her belly till nightfall, when they had crept ashore and headed for the north. Eventually they had found refuge with some Mackenzie herdsmen on the borders of Assynt. And here they were.

Colin Og assured them that they had come to the right place, and at the right time. Tomorrow, God willing, he would start paying his own and their accounts for them.

So, twenty hours or so later, on a grey evening of lowering cloud and threatening rain, eighteen men stared down from an outcrop-strewn shoulder of Beinn Buie, over the scattered township of Ardcoll and the stern castle that dominated it, to the steely mirror of Loch Coll and the further isle-dotted sea. The *Iolair* lay close under Duncolin's walls, guarding a huddle of smaller craft, but the *Florabel* still rode at anchor out near mid-loch. It was the *Florabel* that the men considered most consistently, though sundry points on the loch-shore took their attention too. Colin Og's plans, such as they were, were laid, and his dispositions made. They awaited only the kindly dark.

Fortunately, they had less waiting than would have plagued them had the night been fine. The rain, no unusual concomitant of a West Highland evening, presently enshrouded land and sea, and night strode apace. Under its cover, all but three of the party set off downhill; Rob Molach and another of Sorley's men were left behind with the steward Farquhar Macleod in that high eyrie. Their time was not yet.

Colin led the silent company down, skirting well to the north of the township, and avoiding as far as possible any near approach to farmstead or cabin. By the time that the soft sigh of the wavelets reached them, they were at least two miles round the loch-shore from Duncolin. Following the beach a little farther, they came to the spot they sought—the estuary of a fair-sized stream, with four or five cottages clustered around it, and a couple of black fishing-cobles tied up at a small wooden jetty. This clachan had been chosen advisedly, for though practically every crofter around that seaboard was also a fisherman and had a boat, or a share in one, here was one of the few places where the boats were kept normally in the water moored to the jetty, and not drawn up on the shingle above the tide's edge. With a silent embarkation imperative, this condition was important.

The cottages were in darkness, with only a faint drift of smoke rising from the smoored peat-fires that were never permitted to die out. A scout was sent ahead to spy out the situation, and came back presently with the good news that one of the boats contained its complement of three pairs of oars, and that no sounds issued from the houses. Silently, then, the fifteen men filed down to the jetty.

The boarding was accomplished without noise or interruption, other than that occasioned when from somewhere near at hand a dog barked twice, and froze them all to abrupt immobility. But there was no repetition and no apparent reaction, and the intruders continued with their task. The one high-prowed flat-sterned coble was large enough to carry them all, at a pinch. Four oarsmen seated themselves on the two forward thwarts, while a couple more stood with the remaining oars in the stern, to push her off. Colin himself unhitched the painter from the jetty, and climbed down last into the overladen boat.

Using their oars as poles, the two men in the stern worked the craft out, quietly, till the current of the river running through the little estuary caught her and bore her onwards, the gurgle of water and the hiss of the rain alone breaking the hush. It was not until they were out on to the open waters of the loch itself that Colin gave the order for the oars to be run out. To the creak and groan and splash of them, the coble headed back south by east.

They had no more than a mile and a half to row before the dark outline of the *Florabel* loomed out of the mirk ahead of them. The coble circled the ship cautiously, but there was no sign of life about her; it was after midnight, of course, and no time for life to be demonstrative. Colin instructed the rowers to pull alongside.

They found no rope-ladder over the side, which seemed to indicate that it had been drawn up, and that therefore there were men aboard, indeed. Angus Macdougall, undeterred by such considerations, clambered aboard hand over hand up the anchor cable, and disappeared. Soon he was back, leaning over the side, to whisper that there were snorers in the master's cabin, but apparently none forward. He would let down the rope-ladder.

The whole party aboard, Colin led the way aft. Compared

with his previous performances on these lines, the subsequent developments were entirely tame, flat, and insipid. Only four men were on board, and they were so sound asleep that actually they had to be shaken by their attackers before they awoke to the fact that they had been relieved of their caretaking duties. Philosophically, they uttered no protest amongst their yawns, and gave no indication of being unprepared to do what they were told. A number of *sgian dubhs*, dirks, and broadswords were sheathed regretfully by the boarding-party.

Angus Macdougall, aided by his two seafaring colleagues, now came into his own. He supervised the shipping of the anchor, and the clumsy unfurling of sufficient sail to give them steerage-way, and then repaired to the poop and took the helm. Tacking sluggishly against the light south-westerly breeze, the *Florabel* moved down-loch, towing the coble with her.

So far so good. Macdougall seemed to have everything well in hand, the wind did not look like freshening, and they appeared to have the night and the loch to themselves. But, Colin realized, the testing-time would come when they had to turn due south along the narrow leg of the loch that led to the open sea. Piloting the *Florabel* through that twisting alley between the hills, in darkness and with a crew of landsmen, was going to try Macdougall fairly high. Himself, he wanted to get his brogans back on the shore again, just as soon as was possible. But he would have to see Macdougall through these narrows. . . .

It was Tormaid's suggestion, as they headed into that gut of the mountains, that the coble should be manned and sent ahead to tow them. Colin was doubtful as to the effect of a mere six oars on a vessel so large as the *Florabel*, but Sorley Dam thought that it was worth trying, and Angus Macdougall said that it could do no harm, at least—so long as the wind did not rise.

So the boat, with six stalwart oarsmen, was sent out in front with a cable, and Macdougall shortened even the meagre sail that the *Florabel* was carrying. Without ever letting the ship lose way, the rowers pulled, and slowly small vessel and large headed into the dark trough of the narrows.

Colin was surprised at their progress, that so small a towboat should have any real effect. The ebbing tide aided them also, no doubt. Their passage was slow, inevitably, painfully slow for impatient men, but it was steady, and though twice at bends in that restricted channel the *Florabel* was nearly into difficulties, she never became unmanageable, serious mishap was averted, and way was maintained. The narrow mile was covered, and the increasing swell heralded the open sea.

With the constriction of the dark hills falling away behind them, and the more lively motion of the ship quickly invalidating the oarsmen's efforts, the coble was recalled to her leeward side. But the rowers were not finished yet. Colin Og, repeating his final instructions, and leaving Tormaid and Macdougall in charge of the vessel, with eight men as a minimum crew—but advisedly taking Sorley Dam with him— transferred himself to the smaller boat, and had her prow turned back whence they had come.

As, a little wearily, the rowers pulled northwards again, for the loom of the land, the *Florabel* put on sail and stood out to sea. Speedily the two craft were lost to each other's sight in the rain-filled night.

The coble did not head back into the gaping jaws of the loch, nor yet did it draw in over-close to the savage shore, spectrally white-rimmed in the dark even with such a tranquil sea. Instead it pulled away in an increasingly easterly direction, to follow the southern coastline of Eorsary, keeping a prudent half-mile's sea-room.

Though the oarsmen were tired, there could be no slackening of effort. Colin Og saw to that. It was essential that they reached as far along the promontory coast as possible before daybreak—and already Colin imagined that he could discern just the faintest lightening in the eastern sky. The shortness of these early summer nights was a distinct handicap in activities such as theirs.

Fortunately, the wind was now almost astern, and they made

good progress. An hour of it, and Colin reckoned that they were at least level with Duncolin, beyond its protecting shoulder of hill. But the lessening of the darkness was now unmistakable; moreover, the rain had stopped, and visibility was going to improve rapidly. Half an hour more was as much as they dared permit themselves; observation of this boatload, and any landing that they made, could be fatal for their plans.

When Colin dared not leave the landing a minute later, with all the farther mist-cowled hills beginning to stand out starkly from the shadowy background, the coble was steered landwards.

All these hillsides pastured a thousand head of cattle and sheep, and herdsmen tended to be a sharp-eyed folk. Pulling along the shore, Colin selected a patch of pebbly strand backed by heaped rocks, amongst which bushes of alder and scrub-birch grew. Here they beached their boat, and with some labour drew it up sufficiently far amongst the cover to hide it from any but a searching scrutiny. And wasting no further time, all nine men started to climb directly uphill.

Their position now was about three miles east by south of Ardcoll, but with a great hog's back of hill between. From the summit of that ridge they ought to be able to obtain the vista that they required.

Looking back, now, they could see the *Florabel*, no great distance out on the plain of the sea. She seemed hardly to be moving, with barely any sail on her. She gave the impression of being in difficulties. But none of the men who watched were in any way perturbed; the lame-duck tactics were not for *their* benefit.

The sun was rising, rose-tinting the mist-wreathed brows of the high tops, before the climbers reached the crest of their ridge. Before them, the yawning shadow-filled trough of Glen Coll fell away, with its river and its drove road, losing itself, on the right, in the welter of the mountains. To the left lay Ardcoll, unseen, but with a corner of its loch visible, and behind it the guardian peak of Beinn Buie, on a shoulder of which they had left Rob Molach and Farquhar Macleod some seven hours before.

Thitherwards Colin pointed. "The next move lies with a simpleton and a craven," he declared. "We can do no more than lie here and wait. Pray you that we are not leaning on broken reeds!"

Sorley Dam's pronouncement as to what he would do to any reed that broke under *him* was sufficiently intense to be felt on the said shoulder of Beinn Buie, three miles away or none.

Undoubtedly they did Rob Molach Mackenzie less than justice—whatever might be the position with Farquhar Macleod.

Rob knew what he had to do, and would do it—Tormaid had his word. He had to wait until the departure of the *Florabel* was discovered and the hoped-for subsequent sailing of Cormac MacColl's galley in pursuit, whereupon he was to light a single small heather fire as signal. Then, with the *Iolair* well out of the way—and, it was trusted, Cormac with her—he was to hurry Farquhar Macleod downhill to Duncolin's gates on the borrowed ponies, leaving the third member of the party up on the hillside for further signalling, and there to represent themselves as urgent messengers from Eynart, bearing the word that Torquil Macleod was a sick man and desirous immediately of seeing his daughter, the Lady Marsala—which, after a fashion, was little more than the truth. Marsala would not doubt Farquhar Macleod, her father's steward, whom she had known all her life . . . and was not Rob himself now most respectably dressed as a gentleman of the Macleods? The lady, it was prayed, would not ask too many questions at this juncture, but would prevail upon whoever was left in charge of Duncolin and herself to let her hasten to her father's side—and Farquhar Macleod's anxiety and agitation should be convincing enough, at any rate. How she—or her gaoler—elected to travel there, would have to be the subject of more signalling. It was hoped that she would prefer to go on horseback, for she had the name of being no sailor—but that would be for the remaining lonely watcher up on Beinn Buie to communicate to the waiting main body, when he saw what decision was taken: another single fire should the party set off by road, and two separate fires, some distance apart, should it be by boat. If nobody emerged from Duncolin at all, of course, meaning that their ruse had failed, no fires of any sort would be lit. Except, perhaps, a funeral pyre for Rob Molach and Farquhar Macleod.

Such were the dimensions of Rob's responsibilities.

In the event, the first part of his task was rendered unnecessary—though he carried it out as instructed, nevertheless. Colin's party on the ridge, dozing in the main after its night's labours, was aroused presently by the boom of a cannon echoing from a hundred hillsides. As a sign and proclamation, that required little interpretation. The *Iolair's* armament was summoning Cormac's fighting-men to their duty. The glove had been picked up.

It was almost an hour later before a slender column of brown smoke rising on the morning air from high on the flank of Beinn Buie informed them that Rob was taking his responsibilities seriously, and that the *Iolair* had actually sailed. Looking back towards the *Florabel*, Colin hoped that Tormaid had duly observed the signal likewise. The vessel seemed to have put on a little more canvas, and to be standing farther out to sea, north by west.

The further waiting was a trying business—at least, for Colin Og; his present companions seemed to be well content enough, not unnaturally perhaps. No further signals from Beinn Buie could be expected for a considerable time—two hours, it might be. And until then there was nothing to be done.

They slept. All but Colin MacColl; he did not trust any other to keep awake.

The *Iolair* took just over half an hour after the smoke-signal to emerge from the narrow mouth of Loch Coll into sight and the open sea, her low evil-looking hull thrusting out from the rock barrier just as the first slanting rays of the early sun surmounted the massed ramparts to the east and spilled down on to the furrowed floor of the sea. The *Florabel* was now at least five miles out into the Minch, and turning ever more into

133

the north. Even as Colin looked from one ship to the other, he saw the level sun catch the white of extra canvas as the *Florabel* made sail. Running almost directly before the breeze as she was now seeking to do, she ought to be able to keep the galley well to heel. The lame-duck act would be progressively dispensed with.

For long the one wakeful man on the ridge watched that stern-chase, at first with some little anxiety, and then with increasing composure, as he perceived little lessening of the distance separating the two ships. Cormac's galley slaves were in for a tiring day. Until both vessels were lost to view amongst the islands of that northern sea, Colin stared. It looked as though it was going to be a day or two before he saw his foster-brother again.

Heavy-eyed, but only from want of sleep, the watcher was reduced to fixing his drowsy gaze now on a herd of cattle that grazed slowly uphill towards them—and required to be watched, for possible herdsmen—and now on a pair of eagles that circled endlessly high above in the pale vault of heaven, as the only moving objects in all that far-flung vista. The movement of neither, however, was exactly of a stirring or an exciting nature. Sorley Dam, it was then, shaking Colin's arm and pointing, that ultimately drew attention to the smoke rising once more on the jutting shoulder of Beinn Buie.

"One fire, no more, praise be to God," the large man said, thankfully. "Rowing about in cobles is no diversion for gentlemen, at all. Downhill it will be, now, Colin mhic Colin?"

"Downhill it is, yes—with the hounds of hell at the heels of us!"

Indeed, they wasted no time on the descent of the northern slope of that hillside—they had none to spare. Ponies, even without being hard driven, would cover the three or four miles of track from Ardcoll in twenty minutes—and allowance had to be made for the watcher on Beinn Buie to get his fire burning. Colin's party had little more than ten minutes in which to transfer themselves from the top of the hill to the drove road at its foot—and they must do so inconspicuously. For their descent to be observed would ruin all. Fortunately, that northern and inland slope was fairly well wooded with scrub, and scored with many burn-channels.

So, headlong, the nine men hurled themselves downhill, working slightly over to their right hand to gain fuller advantage of a bend in the glen, stumbling amongst the outcrops, leaping the watercourses, slithering on the treacherous green aprons of wet ground, tripping amidst the clutching bracken, in a jolting, jarring, spine-shaking career. Down amongst the hummocks near the foot of the brae, they had to moderate their pace, but here the cover was closer. Surprisingly, with not a broken bone nor an ankle turned amongst them, they reached the rocky gorge of the peat-brown river. The drove road hugged the river closely here. There was no time to pick and choose their stance. Hurrying, panting, to a nearby bluff that to some extent overhung the track, Colin disposed his little force—four men under Sorley Dam at the Ardcoll end of the bluff, the remaining four with himself at the farther end, some fifty yards on. Promptly and thankfully both groups sank down amongst the bracken and birches.

They had a little longer to wait than Colin at least had anticipated. Presumably they had descended their hill in better time than had seemed to be the case. The bend in the glen hid the road until a mere two or three hundred yards ahead. The rushing waters of the Coll River permitted no other sound within that narrow place.

And then Rob Molach and Farquhar Macleod rounded the track into view on trotting garrons, both with somewhat anxious expressions on their otherwise dissimilar faces. Something between a curse and a groan escaped from Colin Og's lips. Why, in the name of Mercy, had he left it to such . . . !

His lament died on him. Other horsemen were appearing round the bend—gillies on short-legged shaggy ponies, four, five, six of them, no less. Then Colin caught his breath. Two horses followed, side by side, a little way behind, mounting Marsala Macleod and the fat seneschal. Farther back still, at

135

a respectful distance, rode a further four gillies. The whole cavalcade advanced at a slow and dignified trot—no doubt a pace dictated by the portly master of Cormac's household. Cormac mhic Colin's wife had to travel in style. Or, more likely, the seneschal it was who was thus careful for his own dignity and his extensive skin. He it was they had to thank, no doubt, for the breathing-space; the young woman gave the impression of impatience to be on, with her beast half a length in front of that of her companion.

Colin, eyes busy, let them pass Sorley Dam's party, let the six gillies pass himself. Then, with a full-throated shout—for the benefit of his scattered company—he leapt up from his cover and strode out into the middle of the track in front of the man and woman.

"Well met, Marsala, *a ghraidh*!" he cried, doffing his bonnet with a sweep. "You are a pleasing sight—even if in bad company!" And that was all the attention that he paid to the stout man.

There was plenty of attention paid to himself on that piece of road, with a rearing of horses, a scrabbling of hooves, and a confused shouting. Hands flew to swords and dirks—but not Colin Og's hand. Between the seneschal and girl and the four following gillies, Sorley Dam and his men had thrust themselves, facing the rearguard. Colin's own four stalwarts faced the six gentry in front.

For a few moments there was a curious lull, a pause in positive action if not in noise. Startled, awaiting leadership, perhaps a little awed by Colin Og's authoritative and confident air—and not unimpressed no doubt by the warlike appearance of Sorley Dam's caterans—the escort hesitated. Well might it.

It was the fat man who broke the spell—as was only suitable. "Ruffians! Scoundrels! Rogues!" he yelped, in the high-pitched voice of alarmed obesity. It was not very clear whether he addressed the newcomers or his own men. "Devil destroy you— you shall suffer for this . . ."

"Quiet, windbag—lest I puncture you!" Colin barked. "Marsala—I would . . ."

He was interrupted. A shouting at the back, in tones of excited command, ended suddenly in a choking scream. There was a dragging sound, a scraping of hooves, and the crash of a falling body. Then Sorley Dam guffawed loudly. If he had an ungentlemanly trait, it was a tendency to boast of his prowess as a thrower of the *sgian dubh*.

Colin Og did not so much as turn his head. "Marsala," he resumed, "I would talk with you, privately."

That still-faced young woman was biting her lip, her glance veiled. Almost, she seemed to be forcing herself to speak.

But she also was interrupted. Abruptly, a mêlée started amongst the people in front—no sort of concerted onslaught or attack, but merely a spontaneous scrimmage amongst individuals. There was some grunting, a curse or two, and then some mild groaning. Colin waved an impatient hand. But the seneschal, impatient too in his presumption, apparently took the other view. He, evidently, thought such rowdiness was to be encouraged. Emitting an enraged squealing, undoubtedly of an inflammatory character, he urged his minions on, and at the same time, probably involuntarily, urged his garron forward too.

Colin, with the best will in the world to keep this encounter on a suitable plane, with a lady present, was forced to take a hand. He took it, an empty hand, with commendable brevity and absence of display. Not, of course, that he would have soiled his clean steel on such as this pork-bladder, anyway. He took a couple of swift paces forward, hit the advancing garron hard on its snout with his left fist, and grabbed the seneschal's trailing plaid with the other. As the beast reared violently to the blow, and its rider swayed perilously, Colin jerked at that plaid with single-minded vigour. The fat man screeched, toppled, and fell backwards, crashing to the track on the back of his thick neck, and loud was the crack of it. Apart from a species of jellylike trembling, he lay satisfactorily still.

"I beg your pardon, Marsala," the young man said, courteously. "You were going to say . . . ?"

The girl gulped, put thumb and forefinger on either side of

her wide brow, as though to discipline and compress her thoughts, and spoke, levelly, quietly. "I cannot talk now, Colin. Another time. Just now I must go on. I must go to my father. He is sick, and is calling for me . . ."

"He is sick, yes, is Torquil Macleod—but not of his body," Colin declared, deep-voiced. "And, to his shame, he is not calling for you, Marsala *mo chreach*—myself it is that is doing that!"

Under those smooth brows she looked at him. "What do you mean? A messenger came from him . . . Farquhar the Steward . . ."

"The messenger was mine . . . and Farquhar the Steward said what I told him to say. Look, you . . . !" And he gestured towards the front, where, beside the other four of his men who surrounded five apprehensive mounted gillies, a shame-faced Farquhar Macleod sat his pony alongside a beaming Rob Molach.

"Oh!" the young woman said. And again, "Oh."

Colin frowned, and then quickly raised his brows instead. A trifle fleeringly, he spoke. "At least, you could be looking pleased that your father has made such speedy recovery . . . even if you cannot be looking pleased to see myself!"

The other seemed to consider that, but did not speak. She had a gift for silence, that young woman.

Her silence suddenly produced in Colin an awareness of the silence that was all about them, and of the interested regard of all but the injured and the dead. "Cover the Devil's Dam!" he cried, rather rudely. "What are we waiting here for?" The unprejudiced might possibly admit that his exasperation was pardonable, in the circumstances, for, for Colin Og MacColl, he had been very patient: "On with us—Glen Druim it is." Mounting the late seneschal's trembling horse, he grasped Marsala Macleod's reins as well as his own.

"Come, you," he said. "We can talk as well riding as standing. *I* can, at least—and I have a deal to be saying, by Glory!"

And kicking his beast into a quick trot, he led the way

onward along the glen, and down into a haugh where the river shallowed, and they could splash across. He did not once look behind him, to where, on the track, there ensued a swift unhorsing of leaderless and bewildered gillies, a quick but thorough rifling of the sporran and person of the stout casualty, and a cheerful galloping after their patron, by Sorley Dam's satisfactorily mounted adherents. Eight men were left standing—and three lying. Also Farquhar Macleod, if he could be called a man, whom nobody had troubled to instruct as to what to do now, his usefulness being over. Miserable and undecided he waited, a free man—and what is more, alive.

XII

CURIOUSLY enough, despite his previous assertions as to
the great talking that he had to do, Colin found extremely
little to say on that long cross-country ride to remote Glen
Druim. The climb up out of Glen Coll, of course, was steep,
even when achieved at a slant, and though the ponies were
sure-footed and might almost be left to pick their own way,
the narrow cattle and deer paths which were the obvious routes
up through the bracken and heather constrained them to go in
single file. Talking, therefore, was difficult, at least until they
had reached the summit of the ridge. Thereafter, turning and
riding eastwards along the heights, it was easier; though even
so, the peat-hags and the hummocky grass and the burn-
channels demanded no small share of the riders' attention.

But by that time the fiery eloquence had in some measure
died on Colin Og, with his righteous wrath. It was difficult to
maintain the pitch of it, without incidental reinforcement—
especially with youth and beauty, however still-faced and silent.

Indeed, apart from sundry false starts and abortive deliver-
ances, the girl it was who eventually gave him his opening. As
they reached a comparatively level stretch of rust-tipped deer-
hair grass, she asked, "Where are you taking me, Colin?"
Quietly she said it.

"Out of the clutches of my brother," the man told her, over
his shoulder.

"And *my* husband," she gave back.

Colin frowned. "In name, only."

"In more than name, I am afraid." Her voice was level as
the level plain of the sea away below them.

Her companion reined up. "*You* say that!" That was almost
an accusation.

"Who should know better?" she asked, simply.

"*Yourself* should know better!" he cried. "A handfast

marriage is no marriage, till . . . till the good God makes it so!"

"The man has some small hand in the matter, likewise," Marsala mentioned.

"And the woman . . . ?" he threw at her.

Directly she looked at him, steady-eyed, but said no word.

Turning, to his mouth's tripping, Colin cursed beneath his breath—perhaps at the brute's stumble.

They were amongst black peat-hags once more, picking their way. But there was nothing to prevent them from thinking.

When Colin spoke again some while later, on a long brae of short heather, his thinking bore its fruit. "It would not be that your state has become tolerable, Marsala?" he suggested, slowly. "It would not be that you even have come to like being the wife of Cormac?"

He heard her draw a long breath, but she made no other answer.

The man's brows down-drawn swiftly, he made another suggestion. "Or is it being the wife of the master of Clan Colin that takes your fancy?"

"And that is a state to win me the envy of women?" the girl asked.

Surprised, it was Colin's turn to pause. "It could be, perhaps," he asserted, after a moment, ". . . and the right man master of Clan Colin." His voice lifted to that last. He could say no less, surely.

Yet the young woman barely seemed to have heard him. "Rather would I be just plain Marsala Macleod, in Eynart House!" she declared, and there was the hint of a quiver in her voice as she said it.

Her companion found nothing to say to that, at all.

Their route lay parallel to the drove road up Glen Coll, but on the high ground over the ridge to the north, a progress dictated by the need to ensure the secrecy of their sanctuary. After some miles, as the peninsula began to broaden towards its root, they were able to discontinue the bog-hopping and drop down into one of a number of narrow twisting side-glens, all radiating northwards and eastwards. Here the going was much better and frequently it was possible for two to ride abreast.

Here it was that Marsala repeated her question. "You have not told me where you are taking me? Not to my father's house, it would seem?"

"Your father's house would not hold you long, with Cormac returned! I am taking you to where you will be safe."

"Safe?" she wondered. "Safe from whom?" There was weariness there.

"Safe from Cormac. Safe from any man that would hurt you."

"Any man . . . ?"

He jerked his head backwards. "*These* will not hurt you, *a ghraidh*," he assured, easily.

"It is not of these that I am afraid," the young woman said, simply.

He could not mistake the significance of that. "Myself," he said, deep-voiced, "I would not hurt a hair of your head, Marsala Macleod!"

She sighed, though with just the trace of a smile to her lips. "The hairs of my head are not the chiefest of my worries!" she observed. "But my thanks for that, at least!"

The man glanced at her out of the corner of his eye, rubbed an unshaven chin, and rode on a little ahead, in silence.

It was a long way to the shieling at the far head of lonely Glen Druim, and the violet shadows of night were welling out of every hollow and fold and corrie of the high places before the cavalcade reached it. On a small eminence the girl drew rein, and stared down into the dark trough of that hidden valley, and at the black waters of its brooding lochan.

"You will be comfortable there," Colin asserted. "Comfortable—and secure."

Her gaze turned to the man, to consider him, her face devoid of expression, before, touching her mount, she followed on down into the shadows.

There were two bothies or huts of turf and stone and heather, amongst the rock-falls and peat-hags of that desolate place, that blended so completely with the surroundings as to be all but invisible save to the informed. The larger of these, naturally, had been appropriated by Colin and Tormaid MacColl. Now, it was assigned to the young woman. A fresh couch of heather-tops was constructed therein; an odd plaid, some deer-skins, and one or two of the sheep's fleeces that had served the gillies for saddles completed the furnishings. She was allotted a small inlet of the lochan, to some extent screened by stunted alders, for her toilet. By the time that a meal of porridge and cold venison was laid before them, the arrangements for the accommodation of a lady were perfected. With some little pride, Colin displayed them to their visitor.

Marsala saw and studied, and spoke. "I sleep . . . here?" she said. "And . . . and the others?"

The man waved an easy hand. "Sorley Dam and his caterans? They will bed in the other cabin and in the heather. You need not consider them. . . ."

"And yourself?"

"Have no worry, *a graidh*—myself, I shall lie within your doorway, here."

"Indeed! That . . . that is what I feared. I . . . I . . ." She paused, and shook her head a little, helplessly. And then, surprisingly, she smiled. Wanly, and not very mirthfully, it is true. "You have not changed greatly, Colin—for all the grown man you have become."

Doubtfully he looked at her. "Would you wish me to have changed, then?"

"No. No, I do not say . . ." She bit her lip. "Or, perhaps . . . in the circumstances, it would have been better if you *had* changed, Colin. . . ."

"In the circumstances? Circumstances do not change An Colin Og!" the man said, with appropriate dignity.

She might not have heard that last. "Since Cormac has changed so greatly, it might have been better had you changed, likewise. . . ."

143

"And you. Since you too have changed. This is scarce the Marsala Macleod that I left . . ."

She interrupted him, with the first trace of spirit that she had permitted herself. "And how could it have been?" she demanded, reaching out a hand to crumble the peat-soil from the turf walls of the bothy. "How could I have remained unchanged? If I have changed, is it any great wonder? What say has a woman, as to whether she shall change or no?"

Colin eyed her warily. "I cannot say, at all," he told her, but gently. "But, now, you need not fret yourself, *a graidh*. You are safe, and free—and I will sleep across your doorway."

"Free . . . ?" the other repeated, those wide brows raised.

"Free, yes. So long as you do not seek to leave this place, so long as you do not do anything foolish, at all—you are free as the wind itself."

"Oh. My thanks for this freedom, at all events, Colin!" the girl said, gravely.

"It is no more than your due," her companion assured, handsomely. "Come you, now, and eat. Eat, and sleep—and tomorrow you will be another woman."

"I would that I could," said Marsala Macleod.

XIII

WHETHER or not Marsala found herself another woman, in the morning that followed a somewhat restless night, it was deemed that she did—which perhaps came to the same thing. Colin's assumption that she was the released prisoner rejoicing in her new-found freedom was not to be gainsaid.

And if such was accepted as her role, she had little to complain about. She was treated with respect by all, elaborate by Sorley Dam and his minions, protective but of course authoritative by Colin Og. She fed on the choicest titbits, of venison and roe-liver and mountain hare and the speckled brown trout with which their lochan abounded. Offerings of skins, deerhorn implements, even flowers—yellow flags, water-lilies, and the white-tufted bog-cotton—were brought to her. And she had such privacy as the situation, and Colin's assiduous guardianship, afforded.

Nor was the young woman entirely unresponsive to this simple care of men. Since obviously she must, she acquiesced in her position—and without fuss or more than an initial token protest, since she was that sort of woman. With the calm acceptance that she wore like a garment, she adjusted herself to the conditions in which she found herself, conforming to the life that the terrain and the company imposed, and taking her quiet part therein. Other than emotionally, of course, it was no great trial for her. Since childhood, she had been in the habit of taking part in the life of the shielings, that pleasant but essential feature of the Highland economy when almost the entire able-bodied community moved itself with its flocks and herds, up to the high places to take advantage of the rich but short-lived upland summer pasture, to pass the long days and short nights in a carefree existence of lightest labour, extensive lazing, and strenuous recreation. Such life had been her joy—and this, superficially, was little different. If Marsala in any way failed in appreciation of the fact, she had it frequently pointed out to her by her chief protector. Like old times, it was, he averred.

Save for hunting and fishing for their daily sustenance, and keeping a watch against surprise—for all of which there was ample manpower—there was little for them to do but to await Tormaid's return. Colin, alone frequently with the girl for hours on end, in sheerest idleness, lacked nothing of opportunity, for great talking and great deeds. For this, indeed, had he planned. But as so often happens, actuality was but the palest shadow of anticipation. The man's tongue did not fail him, nor yet did the young woman fail to heed and listen. She listened and listened. Indeed, her patient unflagging listening became no small part of Colin's trouble. She was polite, attentive, interested even, especially in his accounts of his foreign wanderings. Yet somehow, the man felt that he was never piercing the armour of her reserve. It was as though there was a wall between them. Colin's efforts to climb that wall met with little success—however high his eloquence took him. It was not the habit of Colin Og mhic Colin of Ardcoll to work round walls, nor yet to burrow under them.

So two sun-filled days passed, and a third, and two grey shadowy nights, and the man and woman were seldom far apart. And if the man discovered therein certain things that he had not known about women, it was as nothing to what the woman discovered about this man—such being the way of women, especially quiet ones.

And on the third afternoon Tormaid arrived back at Glen Druim, and, almost, Colin Og welcomed his company.

Tormaid brought back with him all but one of his crew, including three of the *Florabel's* slumbrous caretakers, who had elected apparently to transfer their allegiance to Colin Og rather than face the wrath of Cormac; about the fate of the fourth of them, there seemed to be a certain vagueness.

The mariners' adventures, as detailed by Tormaid, made epic telling at least. They had observed the smoke-signal from the hill, and so had been ready for the *Iolair's* emergence from the jaws of the loch, sailing away northwards before the wind, and trailing their coat only sufficiently to keep the chase in good heart. With the superior sail that the *Florabel* could make, she was able to outstrip the galley on a following wind—even with an unhandy crew and less than expert navigation. All day, then, the two vessels had sailed north, with no more than two miles or so between them. But towards nightfall the wind had dropped, and immediately the pursuit had begun to gain on them. This was doubly unfortunate, in that it had been Tormaid's intention to draw still farther ahead in the night, enough to be out of sight, and then to turn sharply to starboard into one of the narrow sea-lochs of the Sutherland coast. They had sought to pile on every stitch of canvas available, but still failed to maintain their lead; indeed, in the increasingly still night air, they began even to hear snatches of the cries of Cormac's slave-drivers and the crack of their whips as they urged on the wretched rowers to fiercer efforts. Tormaid, turning ever farther into the east, closer to the coast, had had decision thrust upon him. The island of Handa looming out from the black mass of the land, he had run in beyond it, and whenever its unimpressive bulk gave them fleeting cover from the galley, had driven the *Florabel* straight for the shelving mainland strand. There, in a tiny bay, they attempted to beach their vessel, but reckoning without a hidden sandbank, they had run aground nearly quarter of a mile offshore. With no time to lose, the ship's company had flung themselves over-board, to swim, splash and flounder ashore—but not before Tormaid, with Angus Macdougall and the Graham, had hastily contrived and lit what they hoped were a couple of slow fuses; some proportion of the ship's cargo of gunpowder had still remained in her hold. They had barely reached dry land, however, when the *Florabel*, not waiting for the hoped-for boarding-party from the galley, had blown up with a noise that should have been heard back here in Eorsary. The refugees had made straight into the welter of peat-bogs and lochans that made up that Godforsaken and Mackay-ridden country, and whether Cormac's people imagined them to have perished with the ship, or were merely disinclined for a chase on foot in the dark through such a wilderness, they had been aware of no further pursuit.

Apart from a slight scuffle with some ill-disposed Mackays when they were in process of borrowing one or two miserable ponies to bring them decently on their way, their journey back had lacked incident to the point of dullness. But it had been a long, long road. . . .

Marsala Macleod, surprisingly, proved to be by far the most interested audience for Tormaid's story. In fact, she opened out to Tormaid, seeming to approve of him, and shedding something of her protective shell, in a fashion that was extremely galling to Colin. It may have been the comforting influence of Mother Church, of course, discernible to the eye of faith behind the now distinctly cateranish exterior, but for all that Colin did not like it. Women, he decided, except in their prescribed place, were considerably more trouble than they were worth.

However, fortunately or otherwise, that sorely-tried young man's days of idleness, profitless talk, and unaccustomed intro-spection were over. Tormaid, whilst giving Ardcoll a wide berth, had observed considerable numbers of men, individually and in groups, heading thereto. And Sorley Dam's scouts reported armed parties combing the country and working up the glens towards them. Cormac MacColl, scouring Eorsary for his wife, was bound to find them sooner or later. And no matter what havoc his augmented company could wreak amongst scouting parties, they could nowise hope to resist the concerted might of Clan Colin that would be thrown against them once they were traced. For that, not so much more men, as an army, was required.

The first essential was that Cormac should not get his hands on Marsala again, not for three and a half months—not ever again, indeed. But let her have those months. . . . She was Colin's only trump card in this game that he was playing. Lose her now, and he lost all. They must leave Eorsary, meantime—leave Eynart and Coigach and all that country where An Colin

Mor's writ ran.

Where to go, then? Where, but where they might go with profit, to try to get those men without which the trump card could never be played? Where, but to Larravaig in far Badenoch—that only MacColls might be brought in to do battle with MacColls.

To Larravaig at the head of Spey, then, tomorrow they would go. But, they would come back. . . .

This was not the first occasion on which there had been dynastic troubles within the Clan Colin. Just about a century and a half before, there had been a somewhat similar upheaval, this time between uncle and nephew. The Colin Mor of the day had unhappily died early in life—unsuitably, from over-doses of *aqua vitae*—leaving as heir a son still in his childhood. The chief's brother, one Duncan Dubh, had been appointed regent, as Tutor of Ardcoll, until the youngster entered into man's estate—quite a normal procedure. Unfortunately, Duncan Dubh, after ten years of ruling Clan Colin in the name of his nephew, acquired a taste for power, which took but ill the young man's increasing independence. Bitterness had arisen, factions had developed, and at length the business came to open warfare. Youth and right and legality had triumphed in the end, but not before the clan had been split asunder. Duncan, whose wife was a Mackintosh from Badenoch, had retired defeated, with a large body of his followers, to his father-in-law's country, where they were welcomed with open arms as Heaven-sent reinforcements in Mackintosh's chronic disagreement with sundry Grants and suchlike. So well did the MacColls acquit themselves, and so guileless was the ageing father-in-law, that presently Duncan Dubh was firmly established in possession of lands as much Mackintosh as Grant, his fellow-clansmen around him, and on the old man's death, to all intents Duncan ruled in his stead. Clan Chattan had had something to say about that, of course, but Duncan had married his daughter to a Cameron chieftain, and in alliance with that traditional menace to the Mackintosh chief, he had been able to drive a good bargain. Thus was established the sept of MacColl of Larravaig, a hundred miles and more from its home country.

A sept of MacColl of course, An Colin Mor came to call it, as time went on, though Duncan Dubh and his successors claimed entire autonomy, and indeed seemed to look on themselves as an independent clan. Their chieftains even gave themselves the title of *Mhic Brathair-athar*, Son of the Uncle; but since that might be said to indicate some measure of junior status, in that it was not Son of the Son of, and since they did not change the surname of MacColl, with An Colin Mor recognized everywhere as chief of all the MacColls, the situation remained less than clearly defined. An Colin Mor claimed overlordship, of course, but at that range had never been able to enforce it whilst Larravaig asserted its independence—but not loudly enough to provoke trouble.

But of late the situation had altered a little—or at least, conditions might be manipulated to alter it. Larravaig had quarrelled with the Camerons, the sheet-anchor of their balanced position, and though Lachlan, the present and nineteenth chief of Mackintosh and Clan Chattan, was old, ailing, and unlikely to seek adventures, his son was ambitious and headstrong and known to have his eye on certain lost properties of his house. Mhic Brathair-athar, a bumbling body, by all accounts, was bound to feel somewhat apprehensive, and perhaps was looking round for some alternative support.

Larravaig seemed to Colin Og to be an excellent place to visit at this juncture.

With the white mist-wreaths only beginning to lift out of all the folds and valleys of the hills, then, they hid the traces as far as possible of their sojourn in the shieling, and climbed up out of the head of Glen Druim, eastwards. Colin Og prevailed on Sorley Dam and his men to accompany him, for a Highland gentleman travelling abroad must have his tail, and the bigger the tail the better he was likely to fare; and Sorley, needless to say, was not for staying on in Eorsary meantime, anyway.

Not that they could travel across the breadth of Scotland

just as they were, of course. They must be equipped in suitable fashion, a detail that must be attended to at the first opportunity, *en route*. All told, they made twenty-one souls, with exactly two dozen garrons to mount them.

They avoided the Eynart area and Macleod country, since it was certain to be infested with Cormac's creatures, or at the least, spy-ridden. East by south they went, by narrow secret valleys and great rolling heather moors, by stern mountain passes and still lost waters, with the towering sugar-loaf of Suilven on their left, brooding over a stony wilderness, and all the blue mountains of Coigach on their right, towards the sea. It was barren rock-ribbed country, empty under the sun, and all but uninhabited. Colin chose this difficult route so that they might win out of his father's province unobserved and unpursued. For the same reason, even that night and forty long miles from Glen Druim, they avoided the clachan of Kinlochgorm and camped in a bare and inhospitable corrie where a chill mist-laden wind moaned about them cheerlessly. Marsala Macleod did not complain; perhaps she was too weary for that. Wrapped in plaids she lay amongst great boulders, and slept to Tormaid's great and sonorous singing.

But by noon the next day, things were different. They were now converging on the head of long Loch Broom, and well into the Gairloch Mackenzie country. Cormac would not penetrate here, being no friend of Gairloch nor any Mackenzies. By the same token, of course, Colin was no friend of the Mackenzies either—but that did not mean that they might not have their uses. Such broad-minded attitude was amply demonstrated that second afternoon, when Colin, leaving Marsala in Tormaid's care, paid a brief courtesy call, with the rest of his tail, on the house of Mackenzie of Cuileag, putting to that man, as one gentleman to another, his duties of Highland hospitality to wayfarers in need. The Mackenzie responded only churlishly at first, but a little prompting, and the fact that almost all his menfolk were away at the shielings, eventually persuaded him. The visitors left Cuileag, then, considerably better endowed in clothing, accoutrements—including two sets of bagpipes—food, and general satisfaction. Mackenzie fortunately was of very similar build to Colin—though older, of course—but Tormaid did not do so well. However, Tormaid's needs were distinct, obviously. One or two items of lady's attire Marsala accepted, without much in the way of thanks nor yet of question. Sorley Dam, who might as easily have been a Mackenzie as anything else, blossomed out in some magnificence.

That night, well to the south, they put up at the house of another gentleman of the same too numerous clan—Bruaich, under the shadow of the mighty Slioch. The laird thereof did not happen to be at home, unfortunately—shieling again, no doubt—but his absence did not in any way invalidate his hospitality. One or two of his people, elderly timorous folk, were less accommodating, keeping well out of the way, but perhaps they misconstrued the essentially peaceable nature of the travellers, mistaking them for a raiding party of Macdonalds or the like.

They moved on, after a restful night, up Glen Docherty, around Loch a Chroisg, and into the high hills beyond, shunning the head of Strathcarron, which would be too full of Mackenzies altogether. Above Achnashellach they found a little church, where they sought spiritual and material replenishment. But only the latter they achieved, for the incumbent thereof turned out to be a black Protestant. Colin was disappointed, for he had intended to acquire some suitable priestly habiliments for Tormaid, who would assuredly make a much more profitable and impressive travelling-companion in the character of a churchman than as merely a species of gentleman—especially with a lady to the party. But another opportunity would no doubt present itself. Tormaid, however, indubitably made a notable impression on the unfortunate representative of the Kirk.

Colin was trending, now, ever west by south. This, with Badenoch as their destination, was yet not so foolish as it might seem. To have gone more or less straight thitherwards would have taken them across the main and terrible watershed of broad Scotland; moreover, too long a sojourn through Mackenzie country would be to ensure trouble, with the district rising behind them, and following in pursuit. Also, east of the Mackenzies were the Frasers and the Grants, large, aggressive and ill-disposed clans, that a score of men, even MacColl-led, would be unwise to provoke. The shortest way through and out of the vast and sprawling territories of Mackenzie was undoubtedly to work south-west into that long finger of Matheson country running north-east from Lochalsh. Matheson of Lochalsh was, of course, for reasons of policy, always a friend of MacColl. From Lochalsh, avoiding Kintail and more Mackenzies, they could go by boat to Macdonnell of Glengarry's domains, where, if they used a little discretion, they might not be unwelcome, and so they could cross the country to the Great Glen, and Badenoch lie before them.

By evening they had reached the head of Loch Carron, and were safely into the land of the Mathesons. Since it was important, for their further journeying, that the chief of Lochalsh should be favourably impressed, a herdsman was sought out and enquired of as to where was to be found the nearest *Mackenzie* priest. Informed that there was a certain Father Mungo living between two townships back some nine miles up Strathcarron, Tormaid and Sorley Dam were dispatched thence forthwith, tired as they might be, whilst the remainder of the company sought, politely, and found hospitality at the house of Attadale, a foremost cadet of Matheson. Colin even offered to pay for the provisioning of his men—never for himself, of course—an offer which, fortunately, was emphatically declined. Marsala shared a bed with Attadale's daughter— and slept less soundly than during the nights previous. Tormaid arrived back in the early hours of the morning, with a priestly robe, somewhat on the small side and giving the impression of having been recently torn, and loud in his complaint of the meanness and wretchedness of Mackenzies in general and their clergy in particular, who provided themselves with only one robe and then had no Christian charity towards the naked, the needy, and the stranger within their gates.

So it was that by midday following, Colin's party was able to present itself outside the gates of Balmacara, chiefest seat of the Mathesons, pipes skirling, and with Sorley Dam, dressed in Tormaid's discarded MacColl tartan, sent ahead to announce the arrival of the high and mighty Colin Og mhic Colin mhic Cormac, Younger of Ardcoll, Ardtarff, Eorsary, the Hundred Glens, all the Islands of the Sea, etcetera, etcetera, to pay his respects to the noble MacMathan, Chamberlain of Lochalsh and Representer of Matheson, on passing through his land.

They made a rousing picture as they advanced, with musical honours, to receive Matheson's welcome, well mounted, Colin with a fine new—to him—blue bonnet clasping the two eagle's feathers of his rank and a sprig of yellow broom, his MacColl doublet above a pair of Cuileag's tightfitting Mackenzie trews, and the lot set off and enhanced by a brilliant plaid of yellow-and-black Macleod, with badger-skin sporran, buckled brogues, and, of course, broadsword, pistols, and dirk completing his costume. Close at his back rode Marsala, with a plaid of her own sett about her arisaid of crotal brown, and a fillet of scarlet silk binding her raven hair, whilst Tormaid, in sober black, rode at her side, his feet almost touching the ground on either side of his short-legged pony. A little way behind, the rest of the cavalcade rode, in loose order, motley as to garb but uniform in the bristling array of its armoury.

MacMathan received them well, and though he asked a number of questions, indicated no dissatisfaction with the answers. A small cheerful man, with a pot-belly and a bald head, he enjoyed good company and fine talking and was evidently prepared to pay for it. He had heard of the illness of An Colin Mor, but not of the return of Colin Og, nor therefore of the troubles that had followed. His guests did not vex him with details. He had heard of Torquil Macleod, too, though not of his daughter, and professed no surprise that the young woman should be travelling in the company of the Church and of the heir of Clan Colin—to whom, he rather gathered, she was affianced—on a visit to the eastern branch of the clan. Matheson was something of a Protestant—a state of affairs

154

which would grow, it was to be feared, as they moved south and east—but he was not bigoted enough to consider other people's morals to be any concern of his. The visitors enjoyed two days of his liberality, and on the third were embarked on one of his old-fashioned birlinns, and sailed off across rain-curtained Loch Alsh and into the dark narrows of the upper Sound of Sleat.

Leaving, on their left, and thankfully, the scowling ramparts of Kintail, very hotbed of the virus Mackenzie, and green Glenelg of the trees, and the cabin-strewn braes of Sandaig, they pulled in at the terrible mouth of Loch Hourn. This was the most north-westerly point of the far-flung domains of Macdonell of Glengarry. The Mathesons would row their visitors no farther, not even to Barrisdale, halfway up the loch; Lochalsh and Glengarry by no means always saw eye to eye, and Barrisdale was a prominent man of his clan. So, landed on the barren rocky southern shore of Hourn, under the frowning precipices of Beinn Sgriol, Colin and his party waved a slightly derisive farewell to the somewhat chicken-hearted Mathesons, and turned their faces to the daunting slopes of Knoydart and the second stage of their pilgrimage.

It would be tedious indeed to detail the events and adventures of that long journey across the back of Highland Scotland. Even as the eagle flies, their route extended to almost one hundred miles, and, despite the emblem of the MacColls, there were no eagles in that company. Probably, they doubled those difficult and upheaved miles before they reached the endless rolling ridges of the Monadh Liaths, the Grey Mountains of Badenoch. Let it suffice to recount that they followed the same procedure as on the first stage of their travels, in friendly or neutral country claiming the traditional hospitality of Highland gentlemen towards their own kind, simply but with suitable authority, and in hostile country taking it, still more simply, and with the equally potent authority of nineteen armed men and the anathemas of Holy Church. They used discretion, of course, in not demanding grudging sociability in too frequent succession, and in avoiding the proximity of powerful chiefs and organized communities. They did not go near Glengarry's castle of Invergarry, on Loch Oich, for instance, nor yet Locheil's house of Achnacarry on Loch Arkaig side; though with neither of these chiefs was An Colin Mor presently quarrelling, one never could tell how long memories such people might have. Lesser men might have memories, too, but they usually knew how to keep them disciplined.

Thus, eight days and nights after leaving Balmacara of Lochalsh, they came, strung out, over a long brown heather hill to a wide and open green valley, wooded with scattered pine and birch, and dotted with grey stone houses each with its emerald patch of oats and its black stack of peats. A little church on a knoll beside a blue lochan, and a long low whitewashed house nearby, drew and held Colin Og's eye.

"Larravaig is a richer place than I had thought," he observed, thoughtfully. "Too rich a place to be good for men to live in for long. Let us down, then, and do them the good that they need, in cousinly fashion! Sorley Dam—the pipes!"

They had four sets of bagpipes now, happily, and while Marsala rode a milk-white garron, gaily caparisoned, Colin bestrode a jet-black high-stepping stallion, almost certainly of Arab extraction, with moreover two long-legged deer-hounds to lope at his heels. Such was the gauge of Highland neighbourliness.

Thus arrayed, they descended on Larravaig.

In some measure, Colin's forecast, anent the effects of rich living, was promptly justified. Coming piping down to the meadows near the church, and passing men and women tossing and piling hay therein, Colin had just sent off Sorley and two of the pipers towards the whitewashed house to announce his arrival, when a pink-faced, plump and breathless youngish man came running after them from the field. He was dressed only in a sweat-stained shirt, with sleeves up-rolled, and coarse homespun breeches, and hair and face and arms were coated with the dust and seeds of the hayfield.

"Sirs, sirs," he panted. "This is a pleasure, gentleman . . . and my lady. An honour, it is, I am sure . . . visitors are the rare ones. . . ." He wiped face and close-cropped head with his hand, thereby smearing the dust into streaks. "Is it the house you are for . . . ?"

"Larravaig House, yes—the house of Nicol MacColl, that styles himself Mhic Brathair-athar."

"Myself, that is, sir, yes. I am Nicol MacColl . . . at your service. The hay, I have been at. . . ."

"So I see, sir," Colin said, with upraised brows. "You will have your reasons, I have no doubt. Myself, I am here on a cousinly visit, from the house of my chief, and yours. . . ."

Tormaid stepped into the breach. "You speak with Colin Og mhic Colin mhic Cormac, Younger of Ardcoll, Eorsary, the Glens and the Islands, Heir of An Colin Mor," he intoned, resonantly.

The pink man's jaw—what there was of it—fell ludicrously, and his slightly protruberant eyes by no means receded. "Oh," he said. "Ah," he said, and swallowed. "An Colin . . . Mor!"

"Himself." Colin inclined his head, his eagle's feathers nodding.

"I . . . I did not . . . I had not heard . . ." Nicol MacColl faltered. "I am much honoured—er—much." His very mobile glance swivelled round over the entire company as he said that last, perhaps with just a hint of doubt.

"You are, yes," Tormaid confirmed, heavily.

Colin Og, who had been eyeing the newcomer keenly, calculatingly, decided that a suitable foundation had been laid, and that he might now with profit unbend—after all, he was going to require a great deal from this pop-eyed haymaker. Behind those cod-like features, he thought that he could just discern the possibility of a doltish obstinacy; he might well have to be handled with finesse—and who, at need, could finesse more finely than Colin Og MacColl?

He dismounted from his tall steed, and held out his hand. "This is a great pleasure, cousin," he said, civilly. "We have travelled far to gain it, too."

The other moistened pink lips with the tip of a pinker tongue. "You have?"

"Yes. It is a far cry from Ardcoll to Larravaig. Time it is that they were closer."

"Ah," said Nicol MacColl.

"That is so. But, the saints be praised, our long journey is now ended, and our pleasure commences."

Larravaig blinked quickly. "You . . . you mean, that you go no further? That you travelled all the way from Ardcoll to see *me*!"

"Who else?" Colin returned, simply. "After all, we are cousins, are we not . . . and MacColls!"

"M'mmmm. Yes. Yes. Undoubtedly. . . ."

"This is the Lady Marsala Macleod of Eynart," Colin introduced, "with whom our clan is like to be united."

"Ma'am—your servant. Forgive me . . . my costume . . . my appearance. . . ."

"And this is Father Tormaid Urramach, foster-brother to myself."

"God preserve, advise, and guide your steps, my son!" that man declared, officially, fingers raised.

Mhic Brathair-athar gulped, ducked his head, and goggled, in one.

"My seneschal, Somerled, has gone ahead to acquaint your household of my arrival," Colin added. "Not being aware that you should be sought for amongst the hay!"

"My sorrow that it should have been so," the other assured, with unmistakable sincerity. "If I had but known . . . But, come you to the house. You will be weary, hungry."

"We will not deny it—but do not let us interrupt your—er—labours. . . ."

"No, no. I regret, as I say, that you should have found me thus. But the hay is ready, and the weather is good. . . ."

"You are not short of men, here at Larravaig, I hope?" That was rather sharply put.

"No. There is no lack of men. But there is a deal of hay . . . and a deal of beasts to eat it." The husbandman's voice swelled a little with its own pride. "It is a busy time, at Larravaig."

"It must be, if Larravaig himself must toil and labour like any gillie," Colin Og observed stiffly. "But tomorrow, it may be, some of my men here will spare you that, by lending a hand." He coughed. "It behoves cousins to assist one another, does it not?"

"Eh . . . ah . . . oh," said Nicol MacColl. "H'r'mmm. You want *my* assistance?"

"We want your provender, my friend, here and now," his guest announced, with sudden heartiness. "Listen you to our Tormaid's belly rumbling. We have not tasted food since morning."

"My faith, is that the way of it!" Relieved, obviously, to come down to such essentials, the other gestured onwards, if clumsily. "Follow me then, gentlemen."

"Lead on, Mhic Brathair-athar."

XIV

NICOL MacColl took quite a lot of handling. Colin Og had been right about the possible obstinacy. Deep beneath the vacillating doubtful exterior there was a buried stubbornness, stupid and illogical but undeniable. However far he was to be swayed, threatened, cajoled, even apparently convinced, he was distressingly apt to come back eventually to his original viewpoint. Only with the utmost patience, and out of careful study of the man's hopes, fears, and mental processes, could he be permanently affected. Colin, needless to say, found him most trying.

The Larravaig household was a dull one. He had a plain and simpering wife, with whom he appeared to be astonishingly satisfied, and a sickly and obnoxious infant son of whom he was inordinately proud. Also a soured and long-toothed sister, who seemed to serve in a semi-menial capacity. They lived in uncouth not to say squalid fashion, without graces or any sort of chiefly style, amidst overflowing plenty. Nicol Spliugach, or the Starer, as he was called, actually boasted of the possession of money, gold and silver tokens, and in quantity, a state of affairs practically unknown and certainly unsuitable amongst Highland gentlemen. His talk, when talk he did, was almost wholly concerned with the weather, his crops, his cattle and sheep, and the prices ruling at Crieff and Falkirk Trysts. To imbue such a man with the urge for dynastic adventures was the size of Colin Og's problem.

Early on, Colin convinced himself of the futility of the direct approach. His man just would not respond. Vague threats by the leader of twenty men tend to lose point and pith when the motive is to conjure forth an enthusiastic army of two hundred. Nicol Spliugach was concerned about his position in relation to Clan Chattan and the chief of Mackintosh, but not with sufficient immediacy to force him into any sort of positive action; the old man of Moy was by no means dead, and aggressive action by his son and successor far from a certainty. The present Mhic Brathair-athar was not the sort that met trouble halfway.

By guile only might the thing be achieved. Nicol Spliugach's weaknesses might be exploited, until he was in a position in which he might actually desire to undertake such an adventure. That was going to demand a deal of guile—and of time. Time, however, Colin had in plenty—with Marsala's three months to while away. He and his companions settled themselves in for a prolonged stay at Larravaig, not without distaste—and somewhat to the alarm of its laird.

Nicol MacColl, of course, had many weaknesses, but pride was not one of them, a deplorable and unique position for a Highland chieftain. And pride it was that was the most likely to produce some hundreds of armed men. So far as Colin was able to judge, the fellow had pride in three directions only— in his flocks and herds, his son, and, to a lesser extent, his wife. If anything was to be done with him—as it must—it would have to be through these. Unlikely material, at first sight.

But Colin Og MacColl was a man of initiative, purpose, and ideals. Obstacles, undoubtedly, were made for getting over. And he needed those two hundred men.

After four wearisome and degrading days in the hayfields then, approximately half of Colin's tail, under Sorley Dam, went off happily enough southwards, ostensibly on a mission bearing greetings from An Colin Mor to Cluny Macpherson at Laggan, but naturally with sundry other and more worthwhile instructions. The same afternoon, late, one of the party came riding back to Larravaig hotfoot, to announce that a number of suspicious-looking characters had been observed hanging about the southern fringes of the MacColl land, and Sorley Dam had thought that Mhic Brathair-athar ought to be warned. Needless to say, Mhic Brathair-athar refused to act on any such pointless scaremongering, in which attitude he tended to be supported by Colin Og. But two days later, no more, three Larravaig herdsmen arrived from the high Monadh Liath pastures with the distressing news that the previous night a large herd of MacColl cattle had been stolen and driven off. There had been something of a struggle in the dark with the herders, a few heads had been cracked, and in the morning a dead cateran had been discovered lying on the field of battle, dressed in Mackintosh tartan. Also, in the fight, the Mackintosh slogan of "Loch Moy!" had resounded prominently.

The news set Nicol Spliugach in a fever, but apart from beating his breast and protesting to highest Heaven, he did nothing about it. Colin Og's gallant offer to sally forth and administer a suitable lesson to any Mackintoshes that he could find was alarmedly declined.

However, when next day runners from the north brought tidings of a similar raid, apparently by a mixed band of scoundrelly Mackintoshes and Camerons, there was no holding Colin back. He could not sit still under this insult to the name of MacColl. It was a pity that Sorley Dam was away with half his strength, but he had enough left to supply a stinging rebuke and assert the honour of the clan. It was just a mercy, he pointed out, that all this trouble had boiled up while he was in the vicinity. At the same time, since this seemed most evidently to be a case of Mackintosh and Cameron acting in concert for once, it looked as though it might well be going to develop into a campaign against Larravaig, and he advised Cousin Nicol, while he was away, to summon together all his able-bodied Larravaig MacColls, in a legitimate display of strength and firmness. That was the only sort of talk these gentry were going to listen to. Nicol Spliugach demurred, but Colin insisted, ably backed by Tormaid. Also, his wife, to whom Colin had been showing marked and courtly attention, supported them. Reluctantly, Mhic Brathair-athar gave way. Without committing himself to any promises, he would see what could be done.

Leaving Tormaid and Marsala to the delights of Larravaig House, Colin and nine men moved away north-eastwards towards the head of Findhorn and the scene of the last raid.

Their Larravaig guide, however, proving to be something of a redundancy, the unfortunate fellow clumsily fell into the water while they were fording a rushing river, was fished out amidst considerable excitement, and in the process managed to acquire a broken collarbone amongst other damages, forcing Colin to send him home forthwith.

They managed very well without him, however, even if they never actually reached the scene of the cattle raid. Instead, in due course, they arrived at the house of one Ewan Mackintosh of Dalcroe, whom strangely enough Nicol had mentioned as one of the most shiftless, worthless, and dissipated of his neighbours, though indeed a distant relative. For all that, Dalcroe welcomed his unexpected visitors most warmly, pressing on them much hospitality, liquid in especial, and listening with something like glee to the account of Larravaig's misfortunes, seeming to think the dull fellow well served. When Colin suggested to him, humorously, that he might be doing the handless and ineffective Nicol Spliugach a favour by taking some of his overmany cattle into his own safekeeping for a bit, the Mackintosh positively hooted with mirth. He would do so with the greatest of pleasure, he announced—he owed more than that to the creature. He even knew one or two others who would be happy to do likewise.

Well satisfied, Colin proceeded on his way.

They had to travel more than a day's journey south-west to reach the nearest Cameron country. There they chased a few unarmed Cameron herdsmen, with loud shoutings of MacColl slogans and war-cries, burned a couple of shielings and entertained some of the local ladies, before retiring to MacColl land again with about one hundred head of shaggy cattle. These they drove half-roads home, and then returned to Larravaig and well-earned refreshment. Nicol Spliugach, even if he did not thank them now, might well thank them one day.

That irresolute but obstinate man had done little more than think about collecting together his clansmen. Information that the punitive party had indeed chased a company of the enemy deep into Cameron country, and restored a number of their cattle to Larravaig, seemed to produce but little of enthusiasm or yet of decision. But when, during the next day or two, reports came flooding in of trouble on every side, of a positive plague of cattle-stealing, and even the wanton burning of a MacColl township by a large force of Camerons, Nicol MacColl, with his own clansmen up in arms and demanding action, could delay no longer. The MacColls were to gather, gather.

If this stage had taken an unsuitably long time to reach, and the gathering itself took time likewise, Colin Og at least did not appear to be impatient. Indeed, his attention appeared to be very considerably occupied elsewhere. He was, in fact, paying continual and elaborate attention to his hostess—and she was lapping it up, and purring, as a cat sups cream. Probably it was her first experience of such attentions—for, however much her husband might admire her, he was no Romeo, with manners suggestive of the byre and the stable rather than of the boudoir—not that the Larravaig establishment ran to boudoirs. She displayed neither subtlety, reserve, nor any dissembling in her artless reaction to her guest's advances—but then, of course, Colin himself was entirely frank, open, even blatant in his whirlwind campaign; at all times and in all places, might have been his motto—especially in company, apparently.

His preoccupation was not without its effects on more than his hostess. Nicol Spliugach became increasingly concerned, fidgety and bewildered. Obviously, he had not the faintest notion as to how to deal with such a situation. His sister took to dogging, indeed to positively haunting, Colin and the lady, sniffing almost continuously. Even Tormaid found it fitting, as spiritual adviser, to counsel that his foster-brother be a little more discreet in his amusements, at the same time as expressing some astonishment at his apparent lapse of taste. It was left, however, curiously enough, to Marsala Macleod of all people, to make any really potent protest, with threatened sanctions to underline it.

She came to Colin, the third evening after his return from

his punitive expedition, whilst the lady of the house was putting her objectionable infant to bed. "I would crave a word with you, alone, Colin," she said, addressing him directly and spontaneously for once. "No easy matter, nowadays, it seems."

"With all my heart, *a graidh*," the man responded gallantly.

"Your heart?" the girl wondered. "Have you a heart, then?"

Somewhat taken aback, Colin blinked. "I . . . *you* should not have to ask that," he declared reproachfully.

"I do, nevertheless. If you have any heart, any mercy in you, how can you do what you are doing here? How can you so cruelly destroy the happiness of these people on whom we are living?"

"Happiness? Do you name the dull and brute-like squalor in which this household lives, happiness? I warrant you the lady has known more of happiness this past week than ever she has known!"

"It may be that you interpret the word otherwise than do I." That was coldly said. "At least, you will not deny that you seem to be deliberately seeking to break up their marriage? But of course, you may consider the breaking up of marriages to be your privilege, now!"

"You are unkind, unjust, Marsala . . ." he was protesting, but she went on.

"I only speak of what I see, and have experienced. I urge you, I plead with you, Colin, to cease trifling with this poor woman."

"Poor woman, you say! You are vastly sympathetic towards the lady. Perhaps she may have less reason for your pity than you suggest. . . ."

"You cannot be . . . I will not believe that you can be serious in your . . . assault upon this woman?"

"Serious? Serious enough, *a graidh*." The man smiled sardonically. "Serious enough, I hope, to make her cod-like husband wish to see the last of me!"

"You . . . you devil!" the young woman cried, her usual level serenity strangely shaken. "It is as I said—you *have* no heart!"

"I have a heart, yes—and a head," the man declared, soberly. "But little else, here and now. If I must give play to the one rather than the other, it is because I have the scant choice."

"No honourable man has any choice as to whether or no he will wantonly break up a marriage."

"On my soul, Marsala—I am breaking no marriage. I do not . . ."

"You are trifling with this woman . . . or coveting her. You must stop it, Colin."

"I will, yes—in due course. I tell you, I . . ."

"No—now. You must stop now, at once . . . or I will not stay silent."

"And you would say?"

"I would tell these people the truth—that I am nothing more than a prisoner, taken from my husband's side, and carried hither for your own purposes."

"And what profit would that work you, Marsala? Do you imagine that this bullock of a man would hasten to your rescue—to deliver you back to Cormac? Do you fancy that he would care for your concerns—or for anything other than his cattle and his gold? These, and his wife, perhaps . . . ! That is my difficulty—the man is not to be touched, save through such. And I must have his two hundred MacColls."

"You must have them, yes—and for the same reason that you must have me. So that you may rule Ardcoll. For that, all things are to be sacrificed—men's lives, your own honour, this foolish man and woman, their home and happiness. You will drag them down. . . ."

"Down! They little know how great is their opportunity— how greatly I can lift them up, if . . ."

"If they will but bow down and worship! I said that you were a devil, Colin! I will not let you do this. I warn you—you will go no further with this woman. . . ."

"You are powerfully concerned for the creature, I swear!" Colin declared indignantly.

"I am concerned for more than that one," the girl answered, sombrely. "I have been patient—perhaps too patient. I have caused you little trouble . . ." She stopped, as the door opened, and their pop-eyed host peered within suspiciously, drew back, and then came inside, muttering foolishly. "Remember," Marsala concluded, "I will hold to my word!"

Colin Og looked from the girl to Nicol Spliugach, opened his mouth and shut it again, and rubbed at his chin. It was seldom indeed that that man was at a loss for words.

But it was one thing to raise the devil, and altogether another to lay him—or her—whatever the urge or the pressure, Colin was not slow to discover. However closely he was prepared to carry out Marsala's injunctions, he was not allowed to reckon without Kirsten MacColl. The lady was apparently under no obligation to change her tune, and if Colin faltered in his playing, she would pipe herself. The hunter became the hunted, and the pace became only the faster.

The man, naturally, was at some pains to point this out to Marsala Macleod, but found scant opportunity, with the wife, husband, and the sister constantly on his heels. It was a trying situation.

Happily, Colin contrived that his unseemly ordeal was short-lived. All the following day men were streaming in to the place of Larravaig, in pairs and little groups, in answer to Mhic Brathair-athar's reluctant summons—and apparently to the same man's growing despondency. By evening, practically all the men of the sept were assembled—for the Larravaig lands, though rich and populous, were not widespread as such territories went. Nicol Spliugach, at a loss to know what to do with the throng of them, allowed himself to be led, or pushed, by Colin Og—albeit with undisguised mistrust. Fortunately, amongst the two or three *duin'-uasal*, or small gentlemen, that attached to the House of Larravaig, was one youth known as Alan Liogach, Alan the Stutterer, who, apart from his unfortunate impediment, was much more representative of the ancient honourable stock of the MacColls, being headstrong, quarrelsome, and proud enough for anyone. On Alan Liogach, Colin was forced to put much reliance. Sorley Dam and his party—unfortunately two men short, from undetailed causes—made a timely reappearance, not having been able to trace the apparently elusive Cluny Macpherson, and therefore with their master's greetings intact.

The clansmen were assembled, not entirely appropriately, in the hayfield between the little church and the lochan. Early in the evening, Colin's four pipers were sent down to play suitable martial music to them—Nicol Spliugach, of course, by no means rising to pipers. It was also arranged that ample supplies of whisky should be available, for the due stimulation of the corporate spirit.

These two excellent agencies were allowed perhaps an hour to have their effect, and then two pipers were recalled to lead the chiefly procession down from the House. Sorley Dam, as Seneschal, came first—needless to say Larravaig was un-provided with such a functionary—followed by Alan the Stutterer and Father Tormaid, making way for a resplendent Colin Og and his host, the former with his arm companionably and encouragingly through that of the latter. Behind came Kirsten MacColl, surprisingly with her young son in her arms, and the solid phalanx of Colin's tail brought up the rear. They made an impressive display, much enhanced by the appearance of Nicol himself, dressed up reluctantly by Colin, especially for the occasion.

The dancing of a strathspey was in progress when they arrived at the field, but Sorley put a stop to that with a stentorian bellow, and into the eventual silence, he proclaimed:

"Sons of the Uncle of Colin, Grandchildren of the Eagle, men of the strong arm and the sharp sword—behold the great and noble Colin Og mhic Colin mhic Cormac, Younger of Ardcoll, and so on, son and lawful heir of that mighty prince An Colin Mor, Chief of MacColl and of all of the name and race of Colin, Lord of the Hundred Glens and so on, Keeper of the Keys of the West and so on!" He stopped for breath, and then recollected. "Also, Mhic Brathair-athar, his lady, and his heir." Which was an excellent introduction for anybody, however Nicol Spliugach might seem to frown.

Nicol nevertheless spoke first, briefly, if less than clearly. He said that they were here, unfortunately, and what were they going to do next?

Colin jumped into the rather obvious breach. "Men of the MacColls," he cried, throwing up his hand, "you are here because insolent and wicked men threaten your property, your peace, even your persons. I am here with Mhic Brathair-athar because at such a time all MacColls should cleave together. Who so affronts one MacColl, affronts all!"

Lusty cheering arose from that green haugh to the brown round shoulders of the surrounding hills.

"A time there was when our cousinly houses were divided by faction and strife," he went on. "The time for that is long past. Today we can show Scotland that it is dangerous to insult MacColl. Yet you *are* being insulted, here at Larravaig, day after day. And why? Because your rascally neighbours think that you are friendless. They know that you have quarrelled with the unspeakable Camerons, and that Mackintosh covets your land. What they do not know is that all the power of An Colin Mor is yours, if you will reach out your hand to take it."

Into his dramatic pause, Tormaid the Priest raised his mighty voice. "Terrible is the power of An Colin Mor!" he declaimed.

There was an answering rumble from the crowd, and a cough from Nicol Spliugach.

"Mhic Brathair-athar is a man of peace," Colin resumed. "But he can be pushed too far. Even his gentle lady demands that a halt be called!"

He glanced behind him, and the lady in question nodded and smiled vehemently.

"W-w-w-we all do," Alan the Stutterer announced loudly. "L-l-l-larravaig demands action!"

A second cheer arose.

"Very right. Very proper," Colin commended. "But I have to warn you against too precipitate action, too. You cannot challenge all the might of Clan Chattan and the Camerons by yourselves. That is just what they are after wanting. They would

169

fall on you, and cut you to pieces. Mhic Brathair-athar I am sure will be the first to agree with me, there."

The laird of Larravaig looked perturbed enough, at any rate.

"You must have allies, powerful friends, chiefly confederates. I can provide that, if you will help me. What you must do is this. You must make a demonstration of strength. You must parade in force around this country, but peaceably, avoiding bloodshed unless it is forced upon you. Thus you will show that you are not to be provoked without a fight, and force your covetous neighbours to think again, and to have to assemble large forces if they are to proceed with their villainous campaign. And while they are so thinking and considering, a sizeable party of you should return with me to Ardcoll, where I am at present having a little trouble with a usurping brother, and after settling that small business, we will return here with a thousand broadswords and all the might of An Colin Mor. And no man will trouble you, after that!"

There was a great shout of approval, swelling and swelling again, and it took a considerable time for anyone to notice that Nicol MacColl was speaking—not that he was addressing his clansmen anyway, but only himself, his wife, and obliquely Colin Og.

"That is all very well," he was muttering, "but what is going to happen to Larravaig while all its men are away stravaiging in the West? We shall be defenceless . . . a prey to all . . ."

Colin got at least the gist of this. "Not so," he asserted. "I shall announce beforehand that you are under the protection of An Colin Mor. No man will be rash enough to attack you under the wing of the Eagle of Colin!"

"In that case, why take my men away from Ardcoll?" the other complained. "Make you your announcement, and let us have peace to get on with the sheepshearing. Why should Larravaig folk go traipsing through the land . . . ?"

"Man, man," Colin said, with exemplary patience, "can you see no farther than your nose? The word of my father's protection will only be accepted, for any time, if it is proved and backed by action. Broadswords speak louder than words.

And the only way that I can win you those broadswords is by unseating my brother in Duncolin—and for that I need the help of your men."

"My ten score . . . to defeat your brother's thousand?" Those rolling eyes rolled alarmingly.

"Mary of Mercy—no! Cormac is well hated. The men of MacColl will not fight against me, their natural leader, nor against their brother MacColls from Larravaig—not for Cormac's sake."

"If they hate him, why do they countenance him . . . ?"

"Because they have no choice, no leader, no guidance. Cormac holds them down with a small group of evil and desperate men. But let me appear, with two hundred armed men, and they will rise up and sweep him away."

Nicol Spliugach grunted, apparently less than wholly convinced, a man of a deplorably suspicious nature. This exchange had outlasted the uproar of acclaim, and Colin advisedly turned his attention to the larger gathering again.

"Mhic Brathair-athar doubts you would wish to leave your flocks and your herds, your shielings and your shearing," he cried, "to come with me to Ardcoll, and to come back with those thousand broadswords. It may be that he is right—that you have changed, here in Badenoch, from Sons of the Eagle to sons of the plough and the . . ."

"N-n-n-no! I will go with you," Alan Liogach shouted. "*I* am no c-c-c-cattle-dealer!" and drawing with a little difficulty his somewhat rusty sword, he thrust it above his head.

The screech of drawn steel shivered across that haugh, above the roar of approval—admittedly, it was led by Sorley Dam's practised sworders, the Larravaig men being definitely out of training for this sort of thing. Nevertheless, in a few moments, a positive forest of sword-blades had blossomed out of that hayfield—and if quite a large proportion of them failed to gleam and scintillate in the last rays of the westering sun, that was a minor matter that could be rectified. Nicol Spliugach rather blenched at the sight and sound, and kept his hands tight clasped in front of him.

"I see that Mhic Brathair-athar need have no fears," Colin observed, when he could make himself heard. "Together we will show Badenoch that MacColl is not to be slighted, we will deal with my foolish brother, and we will make the name of Mhic Brathair-athar famous for more than cattle and crops. . . ."

"I want no such fame," that man declared, almost with spirit. "I want only to be left to live in my own fashion . . ."

"There speaks your true man of peace!" Colin interrupted. "And all honour to him. For himself, your chieftain would be content to swallow insults and injury, for the sake of peace. But not in the name of his people, not in the name of MacColl. And not, I swear, in *his* name . . ." And swinging round, he caught the infant from his mother's arms, and held him aloft. ". . . not in the name of the next Mhic Brathair-athar, and all of his name and line, past and to come! This child can be, one day, a great and powerful chieftain, second only to An Colin Mor himself . . . or a landless wanderer, despised and rejected. The choice is yours, not his—and now!"

That did it, of course. The company rose to it like a trout to a mayfly. Deafening cheers lifted and echoed from every hillside. Bonnets, targes, swords, were hurled into the air. One of the pipers grabbed his instrument, and poured heart and lungs into it, his colleagues following suit if not melody. Kirsten MacColl clasped her firstborn in her arms—and some small portion of Colin Og at the same time—and skirled shrilly. And the Ardcoll contingent, of course, did its duty manfully. Even Nicol Spliugach blinked owlishly at his small, sickly, but so important son, as though with enhanced respect.

Colin, who, as has been indicated, had a lively sense of timing, decided that high-tide mark had been reached, and an anticlimax was undesirable. He nodded and jerked his head to Sorley and the pipers, spoke a few words in the ear of Alan the Stutterer, and taking Nicol's arm again, turned him towards the House. Undoubtedly that man was thankful enough to go.

As they moved off, over his shoulder Colin called back.

"Two days hence, then, we start our rounds. Alan Liogach will . . ."

The rest was lost in *An Colin Mor's Wedding March*, as Sorley Dam led the procession back whence it had come.

Two days later, then, a highly impressive body of men, two hundred and thirty strong, set out from Larravaig's green and pleasant strath, quite the most impressive that that place had produced in a century at least, and headed south by east towards the stripling Spey. Ostensibly led by Alan Liogach, but with Colin and his colleagues going along in an advisory, not to say avuncular, capacity, the company was well mounted on sturdy garrons, and equipped with a truly terrifying assortment of weapons of all ages and conditions. Unfortunately its four pipers still had to suffice, but if the music department was weak the commissariat made up for it, being of an amplitude quite unprecedented in the experience of the west-coast campaigners. Mhic Brathair-athar stayed at home without any urging, though his wife was rather less easily dissuaded from accompanying the tourists. Marsala Macleod naturally enough elected to remain behind, and it transpired that it was Tormaid the Priest's duty to stay with her. That peculiar young woman still retained her secret, apparently.

The demonstration of strength and firmness was an enormous success, and an excellent time was had by everyone concerned. Despite their warlike aspect, they were received with the greatest friendliness wherever they went, and they visited almost every establishment of any size in a wide area—of course, two hundred-odd armed men in sparsely populated country tend to be fairly well received. Nowhere did they discover any inclination to disparage the name of MacColl, and though there were a few jokes at the expense of Mhic Brathair-athar, no one could have called them malicious or threatening, and the Larravaig contingent was not so churlish and thin-skinned as not to be able to join in the laughter. Undoubtedly, Nicol Spliugach's credit did not suffer by the expedition, even if Colin Og's suffered still less. If it came to making himself popular, Colin was no more of a laggard than he was with sword or stratagem. It would be a nice point to decide with whom he succeeded in making himself most popular—with his successive hosts or with his borrowed retinue.

Almost three weeks of sheer holiday-making they put in, then, amongst the wide straths and great forests and spreading moors of Badenoch, reaching as far as the borders of Atholl in the south, as Glen Feshie under the snow-streaked Monadh Ruadh in the east, as Tomatin of Moy in the north, and as the distant fringes of the Great Glen itself in the west—and they went there last, in order that the Camerons might have no doubts as to their potency, their popularity, and their peaceable intentions. Thereafter, Colin, considering that a sufficient demonstration had been made, and recognizing that shepherds are more contented when their sheep are sheared, and that harvest would soon be upon them, suggested to Alan Liogach that it was time to redirect their steps to Larravaig. In cheerful, not to say boisterous style, his advice was followed, and their return home savoured of a triumphal procession—even if their ultimate reception was mixed.

Before they dispersed to their houses, Colin had a last word with his exuberant holidaymakers. They had completed the first part of their task satisfyingly, he told them. The second part would take longer, but would be no less pleasant. If he gave them a month to shear their sheep and to cut their oats—the in-gathering could be left to the women and old men—how many would come with him to the West . . . on Mhic Brathair-athar's authority, of course?

There was not one refusal; not a man was going to miss a further instalment, whatever Mhic Brathair-athar had to say.

If that was a long month for Colin Og, it was undoubtedly as long a one for Nicol Spliugach. Long before it was over, he was wishing his visitors away, at any price. That his lady did not agree with him was a large part of the trouble—the trouble for both of the men, indeed: Colin, with a lynx-eyed Marsala to contend with, found Kirsten MacColl very trying. It was a difficult situation, in which perhaps only Father Tormaid found no complaint. He was getting fat, and enjoying the process.

The sheep were sheared, the oats cut, the rain scarcely fell, and not so much as a calf was stolen that month on all Larravaig.

XV

COLIN was able to follow a much more direct route back to Eorsary, at the end of August, than that taken on the outward journey—two hundred and ten Larravaig MacColls, in addition to his own eighteen veterans, ensured that. Few chiefs, however powerful, kept so large a body of fighting-men as that around their doors, especially at this season of the year, whatever the size of following they could raise given sufficient notice. The MacColls were tolerably certain of consistent Highland hospitality all the way, even from such as Glengarry and Macdonald of Sleat. They were not disappointed, and the pitch of their morale was suitably intensified accordingly.

With considerable junketing and high spirits, but entire absence of opposition and other than mildly amorous adventure, they crossed the country in easy stages, by the Corryarrick Pass, Invergarry, Glen Cluanie, and Glen Shiel, to salt water at the head of Loch Duich. Avoiding, a shade reluctantly, entanglement with the Mackenzies of Kintail, they trended a little southwards, up over the high pass of Mam Rattagan, and down to Glenelg, where Macleod thereof had them ferried across the Sound to Sleat in Skye, swimming their garrons alongside the boats. A short day brought them to Kyleakin, where they crossed Loch Alsh back to the mainland, and Balmacara once more. Their swollen numbers strained poor Matheson's liberality to the utmost, but he responded manfully. Thence they proceeded as directly into the north as that country would let them, giving the Gairloch area a fairly wide berth, and on the second day of September they sighted the soaring mountains of Coigach and the blue waters of Eynart Bay beyond. Colin had timed his return, as he did most other things, with some precision, for the very next morning, in the house of some unfortunate Mackenzie mediocrity, he was able to greet Marsala Macleod at breakfast with his sincere congratulations. It was twelve months and one day since her lamentable handfast marriage with Cormac MacColl, and she had borne no child, and therefore she was a free woman once more!

The girl accepted that, as she had accepted the rest of Colin's statements, attentions, and commands, indeed as she accepted the entire journey—save only his conduct towards the lady of Larravaig—with a calm acquiescence, that gave the impression of impassivity, almost of indifference. Colin had come to expect no other, and their relationship had become increasingly formal, not to say distant. That the widening gap tended to be pleasantly filled by Tormaid may have been a sort of compensation, but if so Colin showed little appreciation of it. In fact, his distance-keeping had been inclined to include his foster-brother also, for some time now. That was the worst of women; their influence, however ostensibly pacific, was ever disruptive.

By the same night they were out of Mackenzie country, and into the no-man's-land that backed Eorsary. Far and wide the mountains and the glens marched down to the isle-strewn sea. To Alan the Stutterer, Larravaig's lieutenant in this expedition, Colin threw out an all-embracing arm.

"MacColl's country," he declared, deep-voiced. "Mine . . . and yours! Will you fight for it?"

His wide-eyed companion's reply, though more than usually incoherent, was in the affirmative, indubitably.

It requires at least two parties to make a fight. Rob Molach and another of Sorley's experts were sent forward as scouts to spy out the land, whilst the main body rested amongst the high mosses of the watershed. They were back within twenty-four hours with the information that Cormac MacColl did not seem to be looking for a fight at the moment, that most of the men and young people of Ardcoll were away harvesting or at the shielings, and that the galley *Iolair* was beached under the walls of Duncolin and seemed to be undergoing repair. Cormac was not the man to leave himself totally defenceless, of course, and there were fighting-men around Ardcoll still, but his main strength was dispersed without a doubt. Apparently he had had no word of Colin's approach.

That was all that the same Colin required. Half a dozen of Sorley's men, who knew the district, were dispatched with messages for all the sizeable lairds and *duin'-uasal* of Clan Colin. The remainder of the great company moved forward forthwith, north by west, into the gathering dusk.

All through the night the long cavalcade wound like a snake down through the glens, splashing through a hundred streams, encircling black lochans, following deer, cattle and sheep tracks and no tracks at all, Colin himself acting as guide. As far as possible they avoided townships, houses, shielings, and the haunts of men, and injunctions to silence were rigorously enforced. But when the mists of morning had cleared, and the early sun topping the eastern mountains found them no more than three miles from Ardcoll—in fact, almost at the exact spot in Glen Coll where Marsala and the fat seneschal had been ambushed—Colin reversed his tactics entirely. With the glen widening towards the sea-loch, he marshalled his strung-out following into a much more compact formation, had them draw their broadswords and lay them across their shoulders, dismounted his four pipers and marched them in the van, playing at their most vigorous, whilst Alan Liogach, the four or five other young Larravaig lairds, Sorley Dam, Tormaid, and of course Marsala Macleod, were brought forward to ride directly at their leader's heels. Thus, bravely, flauntingly, now that it was too late for Cormac to do anything about it, to the strains of *Colin Comes!* they followed the river and the road to Ardcoll.

The country became increasingly populous now, and their progress by no means went unnoticed. From every house and cabin sleepy-eyed and mainly elderly folk came flocking, to stare and gape open-mouthed. To many Colin nodded and smiled graciously, and sometimes got a vague wave in response. Small boys, three parts naked, fell in behind them, more forthcoming in their approval, such cattle as were not up on the high pastures fled, tails erect, and dogs too old for the work of the shielings barked dutifully. If the Larravaig people had been more musical, they could have sung the stirring words that went with the pibroch, to the benefit of all.

The sight of Duncolin, grim on its sea-girt rock, drew a gasp from the men of Badenoch, audible even through the piping. Its sheer walls frowned arrogantly at land, sea, and sky, and the eagle banner of An Colin Mor flew proudly above, in the morning breeze.

Straight towards it, nevertheless, the column proceeded, without deviation, falter, or at any rate visible hesitation. Between the houses and buildings of Ardcoll they rode, with every doorway framing its quota of part-clad and concerned watchers, and the parapet of the castle black with figures. Colin's eyes were busy too, but he did not fail to smile right and left as he rode.

To the group of large bothies, directly in front of the approach to the castle, where Cormac barracked his unattached fighting-men and some of his galley slaves, Colin led them. There was a certain amount of shouting and scurrying here, but a very apparent bewilderment as to what was afoot and what was to be done about it. When the numbers of these unseemly early-morning arrivals were ascertained, of course, the second part of the problem at least solved itself: nothing could possibly be done, by two or three score half-awake men, against obviously ten times their number. The two or three score therefore wisely made themselves as inconspicuous as possible, and from a variety of refuges awaited developments.

They had not long to wait. Giving orders for a party to go and free the galley slaves—but to keep an eye on them thereafter—Colin had the bothy area surrounded, and then rode down to within hailing distance of the castle. He did not venture too close to the upslung drawbridge over the channel that separated its rock from the mainland, however, and kept his studded targe well in front of his body. Tormaid and Sorley Dam flanked him; the remainder of the company waited farther back. Musket-balls were chancy things to best in any argument.

As he waited for the pipers to finish, Colin considered. It had all been simple, so far, inevitable almost—no more than the result of numbers, competent planning, and a little luck. Now he was faced with the real challenge, the hard core of the problem. Duncolin was as good as impregnable. Cormac, if he felt himself to be insufficiently strong to do battle or to risk conclusions one way or another, had only to shut himself up in his castle and await a more favourable occasion. That he could probably do something to hasten that favourable occasion, even from within Duncolin's walls, that time was not necessarily on the side of the newcomers, was not to be doubted. His brother was not the man to have overlooked such a contingency. How great might be the support that Cormac could summon to his aid in the circumstances was uncertain, admittedly—but then, so was the fighting ability of Colin's own untried following. So much depended on the clan's reaction. That, inevitably, must be at the back of both brothers' minds, affecting now their every move.

As the bagpipes sobbed into silence, Colin spoke to Sorley, who cupped his hands and raised his brassy voice.

"Cormac mhic Colin, within Duncolin!" he cried. "An Colin Og, Heir of mighty An Colin Mor, rightful ruler of Clan Colin, desires you to speak with him."

Clearly the words came back from the high parapet-walk of the castle. "I am here, and listening," they said. "I bid my brother a very good morning."

Colin took him up, quickly. "A good morning for Clan Colin, yes. I have come to take over my birthright!"

"You are a mite early for that, brother, and our father no corpse!" Cormac's voice was high and distinct, intended for all to hear.

"Our father has died a thousand deaths since you ruled in his stead!" Colin asserted, with equal clarity. "I have come to see to it that his grey hairs go down to the grave in peace." And as an afterthought. "That An Colin Mor deserves, I say." Out of the corner of his mouth, he whispered to Tormaid. "An Colin Mor . . . !"

The priest lifted his sonorous voice obediently, like the pipes of an organ. "Great and noble is mighty An Colin Mor!"

And from all around, from the walls of Duncolin, from the doorways of Ardcoll, from the massed ranks behind Colin Og, hands, swords, and voices were raised in unison. "An Colin Mor!" rang out the tremendous shout, and all the hills took up the cry with their echoes. Unanimity was complete, it appeared.

At this happy juncture, Cormac signed to the piper on duty on the parapet-walk, who promptly burst forth into a spirited rendering of the *Wedding March*. Even as toes began to tap to the lively rhythm of it, Colin Og, frowning, turned round and jerked his head at his own pipers. The first of them to effect any really recognizable results produced a variation on *Colin Comes!*—which, after all, they had been playing all morning—and presently his three companions almost caught up with him. Cormac, from the castle, hastily gesticulated to his immediate supporters, but it was a few precious moments before a second musician managed to unearth his pipes and come blowing to the rescue. Two or three others hurriedly disappeared from the throng at the wall-head, no doubt plunging downstairs in search of further instruments.

The noise was stupendous, awe-inspiring, but undoubtedly four pipers tend to have the advantage over two, even when the latter are professionals—and of course, Colin's men were considerably closer to the main audience. The unbiased observer would have to admit that they won. But it was a vigorous and rousing onset. No question but the two principals took the excellent opportunity to do some equally vigorous thinking.

When there could be no doubt about the issue, Colin Og silenced his champions with a magnificent gesture of the hand, and, taken by surprise by the comparative hush, the Duncolin pair allowed their effort to droop and die, mournfully.

Cormac made a quick recovery. "You said something of bringing peace to our father's grey hairs, brother," he called into the sudden lull. "Is this how you bring it—with a thousand alien swords?"

Colin, whilst denying the alien, saw no reason to waste breath denying the thousand. "Not so," he cried, "Sons of Colin they are, to a man. Our cousins from Badenoch. MacColls of Larravaig, men of Mhic Brathair-athar!"

He nudged Tormaid with his elbow, who, with only a moment's hesitation, shouted, "Mhic Brathair-athar!" at his loudest, turning his head. Behind him the serried ranks of Larravaig perceived their cue, and raised a thunderous cry, "Mhic Brathair-ath-a-a-a-ar!" Sorley's foremost instrumentalist caught Colin's eye enquiringly, and raised his mouthpiece to the ready. But Colin, for the life of him being unable to think of any stirring music appropriate to either Nicol Spliugach or to Larravaig, shook his head regretfully.

Cormac had no answer ready on this occasion, so his brother went on.

"I come in peace—but prepared for war, you see. And I ask, as our father's elder son, that you bring me out here the keys of Duncolin!"

"*Bring* you . . . ?"

"Just that. Bring them to myself, here, Cormac—personally."

"Would you not prefer to come into Duncolin for them—equally personally, brother?"

"With a hundred men at my back, only!"

Cormac laughed pleasantly. "You flatter me, Colin. I think that so many might be an embarrassment. Myself, I find crowds distasteful."

"You will come out here, then?"

"I think not, no. I am very comfortable where I am. Moreover, I cannot yield up the keys of Duncolin, even to you, brother, without the authority of the clan council which appointed me to rule Clan Colin in our father's sickness."

"And in my absence!"

"That you will have to ask of the clan council," Cormac declared smugly.

Colin snorted. This could go on indefinitely. And he found all this shouting trying. Sustained argument could not advance his cause. He spoke with deepened voice. "A truce to this windy chatter, man!" Stern, he was. "You have usurped my place in Clan Colin, and tyrannized our people. I have come to take that place again. Do you yield it peaceably—or is it to be war?"

"Take what you can, brother—but I yield nothing. Not even my wife, whom I think I observe hiding amongst your bravos from Badenoch!"

"That is no wife of yours, nor of any man's—yet. That is Marsala Macleod, a free woman these three days. Your hand-fast is loose, see you. Twelve months and no child. Do not tell me that you had forgotten, Cormac!"

"I tell you only that she has been, is, and will be my wife!"

It was Colin's turn. "Come you and take her, then!" he invited.

At his back the girl caught her breath in a sob—though of course neither of the brothers could be expected to hear it.

"I will, then—in due course," Cormac assured, with a curious evenness for a man who had to shout. "Meanwhile, I hold you to account for her, brother. And I do not price her lightly!"

"You are in no position to demand any price—for Marsala Macleod or for anything else, Cormac. Your day is done. You would be wise to accept the fact."

"I accept only the expressed will of Clan Colin, through its clan council . . ."

"Which council you hold in the palm of your hand! More than that you will require."

"What more I require, I will take, I assure you."

"And that is your last word?"

"My last word . . . ? No, perhaps not." Cormac turned, and pointed to one of his companions. "Here, see you," he called, "is my last word!"

There was a moment's pause, and then a flash, a puff of smoke, and a shattering roar, as a cannon was discharged from the parapet. Like a thunderbolt, with its sphere of smoke rolling after it, the ball crashed home, amidst a great shouting, rearing of garrons, and general uproar. But, fortunately, apart from mangling a couple of galley slaves and demolishing a corner of their bothy, it did no material damage.

When the pandemonium had died away a little, Cormac's voice came again from the castle, mockingly. "There are many more answers where that came from, Colin—you were good enough to provide me with ample supplies of powder and shot from your ship, you remember! Now—take yourself off, before I blow both you and your rabble back to Badenoch!"

Colin began to answer, but at the noise from behind him, turned his head. His company was tending to take Cormac's advice forthwith, evidently impressed considerably by its first experience of artillery. He frowned blackly, bit his lip, and then shrugged.

"Get back amongst the houses, then," he ordered angrily. "He will not fire into the houses. Scatter yourselves—but be ready to come to my call, and quickly."

Before he had finished speaking, the host had begun to disperse, in highly mobile fashion. In a remarkably short space of time, only a comparative handful of people remained with Colin Og about that open space before Duncolin—Sorley and his veterans, the survivors of the *Florabel*, Tormaid, and strangely enough, Marsala Macleod.

It looked as though Cormac MacColl had won the first round.

But Colin was not prepared to accept any such interpretation of the situation. He spoke a few words to Tormaid and Sorley Dam, dismounted from his restive horse, and then strolled forward, nearer to the drawbridge and the castle, alone. He did not hurry, but his glance was keen.

"Your noisy display settles nothing and proves nothing," he declared, to the frowning walls of Duncolin. "Save only that you are irresponsible, and quite unsuited to hold any sway over our people. You would kill blindly even your own kin. That will not be forgiven. Let there be no more bloodshed amongst Clan Colin. This dispute concerns myself and you, brother. I make you an offer. Let us fight this thing out here, before our people, and let the winner rule the clan, in the name of An Colin Mor!"

There was a slight pause, before Cormac's voice replied. "You are becoming vastly concerned at a little blood-letting, to be sure. For why, I wonder? You have been less tender in the past. And was it to fight a duel with me that you fetched all your hundreds from Badenoch?"

"They were brought that I might speak with you on at least equal terms. Else, as well you know, there would have been no speaking, at all! But now, I speak. I offer you the decision of fair fight, with pistol, broadsword, dirk, or naked hands. I offer you what I need not offer—what is my birthright, and what I have the power to take."

"There you lie, brother. You have no power to take Duncolin!"

"I have power to starve you out of Duncolin."

"Again you lie. So long as a boat can sail this western sea, we will not starve!" There was truth in that. A besieger could not prevent boats, launched from anywhere on the lochshore or beyond, reaching the castle rock under cover of darkness, short of maintaining a permanent and unbroken cordon of boats of his own, well beyond cannon-shot—which would be well-nigh impossible. "And would you starve your own father?"

"I shall starve no one," Colin proclaimed, a trifle hurriedly, "if you will come out and settle the issue with me, here. I *challenge* you to do so!"

"And if I refuse . . . ?"

"Then I brand you now, before all Clan Colin, before all Scotland, as a coward and a craven . . ."

"No! I say that you shall not!" Surprised, Colin turned to find Marsala Macleod at his side. Her voice was tremulous, but strong enough and crystal clear. "There must be no duelling. You must not do it, either of you!"

"But, Marsala—surely you would not have . . . ?" Colin had begun, when Cormac's shout overbore him.

"There speaks my loving wife!" he called. "Heed you her, Colin."

"Cormac! You must not fight," the girl cried. "I beseech

185

you—not this crowning folly!"

"Thank you, my dear, for your kind concern. It warms my heart. And I think that you may well be right about the folly. Your advice is probably sound. A duel might be unwise. It would be a tragedy if we killed each other, and left Clan Colin without a leader at all!"

Colin was frowning. "Marsala—I would ask that you do not interfere in what is no concern of yours."

"No concern of mine! Is it no concern of mine that, that . . ." She hesitated, biting her lip. "Oh, why must violence be the only . . ."

Harshly the man interrupted her. "A decision there must be," he said. "Is it not better that two men should reach that decision, alone, rather than that many should fight and die?"

"Why should *any* fight?" she demanded. "Why should your decision not be reached by discussion, by arrangement? Why must . . . ?"

"Would you discuss with a viper whether or no it shall sting you!" Colin gave back. He jabbed a forefinger towards the castle. "*You* must have tried discussion with that man ere this! What has it ever availed you? I would as soon trust the word of Lucifer himself!"

"And are you so much better, then? Has Nicol MacColl of Larravaig any reason to trust *your* good faith? Or have I?"

Shocked, Colin stared. "My word is my bond!" he cried. "No man will question the word of An Colin Og . . . !"

"Not to his face, perhaps," Marsala said, wearily. "But what he may think . . ."

From Duncolin, Cormac's voice sounded. "Pray speak up," it came jeeringly. "I cannot hear how my wife and my brother may be deciding my fate! That is unmannerly, surely!"

He was ignored. Marsala turned to the priest. "Tormaid—you at least profess to be a man of God. That is, surely, a man of peace. Will you not speak for Holy Church? Will you not tell him. . . ."

"The Church can speak with other voice than peace," the cleric declared, heavily. "She can wield the sword of justice as

186

well as the Cross of Mercy. The bruising of the serpent's head is . . ."

"Oh, you are wrong, wrong! That is hypocrisy. . . ."

"Tormaid," Colin cut in, cold-voiced, "take Marsala back, out of danger's way. Bestow her comfortably, where she shall come to no hurt."

At the note of finality in his tones, the young woman bowed her head, sighing, and turned away, her cloak of acceptance resumed, before Tormaid's hand was on her arm. Colin watched them go, sombre-eyed.

He turned back to Duncolin. "Have you made your choice, then, Cormac?" he demanded.

"Assuredly," the other answered. "Our Marsala is right. The Sons of Colin are too precious to risk in a duel. One, we might spare—but not two. Never two. No, brother—you must think again."

Beneath his breath Colin cursed. "You brand yourself coward, then?" he called back, aloud.

"No man has yet called me that name—nor will, I think." That was easily, almost casually, said.

The other drummed fingers on his targe. Somehow or other, this brother of his must be enticed out. "Then, if you are so careful for your own skin, will you choose a champion to fight me?" he called. "And abide by the results. Can I offer you better than that?"

"You are very anxious to display your prowess, Colin," he was answered. "But it seems to me that the matter at issue between us deserves more settlement than the mere hazard of single combat."

"Pick ten champions, then, to meet ten of mine. Or fifty! Let us match our men . . ."

"And how could I trust you not to throw in your horde from Badenoch, if the tide should turn against you? How can I trust you not to do that same, in any event?"

"You have my word . . ."

A hoot of laughter came from the castle, to be taken up and echoed by others lining that parapet. Colin flushed, and swore.

"Since I should require rather more surety than that, brother mine, I think that I will remain comfortably here in Duncolin. Now, my throat is sore with much shouting. I intend to slake my thirst forthwith, and commend my example to you. Go away, now, Colin—enough is as good as any feast!"

And waving to his pipers, Cormac MacColl retired along the parapet-walk, and passed within the gabled cap-house that covered the stairhead, to musical accompaniment.

More or less automatically, Colin's stalwart quartet struck up the inevitable *Colin Comes!* But despite their loyal and resounding efforts, their hero followed them back to the scattered buildings of Ardcoll in a preoccupied and less than appropriate fashion.

Thus was initiated the siege of Duncolin, certainly not the first though it was likely to be the last.

XVI

COLIN'S army quickly settled itself in at Ardcoll, satisfied its various appetites, and very largely went to sleep; after all, it had been travelling all night. Colin himself held a council-of-war, with Tormaid and Sorley Dam; the Larravaig lairdlings he left to snore.

Certain dispositions, of course, were accepted without discussion. The rounding up and rendering harmless of the landward detachment of Cormac's leaderless fighting-men. The provision of guards and sentries. The institution of a permanent patrol of three boats, to enforce as far as possible the seaward blockade of Duncolin. The organization of scouting and foraging parties. Leadership in all such devolved inevitably on Sorley's hardened ruffians.

These were straightforward matters, but there were others demanding much discussion and decision. Principally, they concerned the reaction of Clan Colin as a whole, and its various chieftains and lairds in particular. How quickly could Cormac get out his orders to them from his beleaguered fortress, and what would be their response? What, conversely, would be their response to the messengers Colin himself had sent them? Were they going to look on his arrival as a threat or a deliverance? In the former event, they would have to be dealt with piecemeal, and any signs of leadership amongst them would have to be promptly quenched. In the latter, they must be encouraged to show their support actively. And soon. Time was the prime consideration. In time, Cormac could draw aid to himself, could organize a counterblow. In time his own raw levies from Badenoch would wilt in their enthusiasm, and turn their eyes back towards Larravaig. In time, and no extended time at that, his cause could be lost irrevocably.

Colin would have liked to have made, personally, a hurried tour of the clan notables, leaving them in no doubt as to their duty and their profit. But he dare not leave the vicinity of Duncolin. He could summon the chieftains to meet him here— but it might be unfortunate if they came in the wrong spirit and with large numbers of fighting-men at their backs.

One or two he did summon, that lived close at hand, dispatching envoys to escort them in unattended. Three of these, Colin interviewed, after a brief sleep, in the priest's house beside the church—its incumbent, a backslider and timeserver indeed, was safely walled up in Duncolin, so Tormaid naturally took possession in the name of Mother Church, it being quite the best house in the immediate neighbourhood. The three tacksmen, or landholders under the chief, Glengarve, Innisbeg, and Balnafail—that Hector Ban whom the naked refugees from the castle window had so alarmed and offended one early morning some months before—greeted Colin with wary affability, considerable general concern for his welfare, and a noteworthy desire not to discuss either Cormac, armed strength, or dynastic matters whatsoever. The harvest, the weather, and intermittently Colin's health were their evident and determined preoccupations. Their men, it seemed, were all confirmed shieling addicts, and so neither suited nor available for armed adventures.

Though Colin found difficulty in keeping his temper with them, at least they were apparently not anxious to rush to Cormac's aid. If they were typical of the rest, the situation might be less serious. Clan Colin, it almost seemed, was less warlike than its leaders.

That night again, there was no great deal of sleeping permitted to the liberators—though some may well have been snatched without permission. Colin Og spent most of the hours of darkness, lengthening now with autumn, in a boat seaward of Duncolin's rock. As it was a wet night, with a chill and gusty wind, he found as little comfort as profit in the exercise. But apart from two false alarms occasioned by Larravaig warriors mistaking their own shadows or the Ardcoll milch-cows for Cormac MacColl in person, the night passed without event.

But in the morning, a patrol led by two of Sorley's men brought in a prisoner, one of three apparently, the others having escaped, who had been caught some distance inland, but still wet from the waters of Loch Coll. Obviously they had swum ashore from the castle during the night. A little pressure brought to bear had drawn from their captive the information that he was bound for the area of Ardtarff and Duligarry, with urgent instructions to the lairds thereof to muster at once, repair to Iain Cam's remote township of the Cairn, there to await further orders.

Cormac had passed the night more profitably than had his brother, perhaps.

Colin sent out a scouting-party to keep an eye on this rallying-place of the Cairn, and had another long-range though this time short-lived conversation with Cormac—it being essential, amongst other things, that Cormac himself should not slip out of Duncolin overnight without his absence being noted. Deeming it unnecessary to go into details, Colin merely informed that messengers of the opposition had been intercepted and their errands discovered. Hopes of the clan rallying to the support of a tyrant and usurper, he had ascertained, were entirely groundless; contrariwise, support for himself as the legitimate heir was widespread. Consequently, he advised his brother to come to terms forthwith, or to select such number of champions as he cared, to decide the issue in suitable and traditional fashion.

To none of which did Cormac make response other than mockery.

Two days, and more important, two nights, passed thus, without decision or any major activity. Patrols caught another of Cormac's unfortunate messengers, a boatload of supplies was intercepted as it sought to reach the castle in the darkness, a large proportion of the galley slaves elected to serve as an armed company under Colin Og—though their physical condition was on the whole so poor as to make them of little value. The scouts, also, watching the township of the Cairn, reported the muster of only a handful of men. One or two other groups had been noted, here and there, but none were large and none appeared to be actively converging on Ardcoll.

There, similarly, the internal situation remained on the face of it favourable. Morale still was good. Food, and those other services which men released from the restrictions of home life tend to find so necessary, had not yet run out. Marsala was back in her uncomplaining shell—which, cold and disappointing as it might be for Colin, did not upset things in the same way as did her outbursts.

Despite all this, however, Colin Og was uneasy, frustrated, and fretful. This situation, ultimately, meant defeat for him. This was not what he had crossed Scotland twice to achieve. But what more could he do than he had done?

And then, on the fourth morning of the siege, Cormac it was who initiated the daily exchange of shouted pleasantries. His horn, that still awakened such of Ardcoll as had achieved any sleep, with the news that An Colin Mor had slept well, etcetera, was on this occasion used to summon the said somewhat nebulous potentate's elder son to parley. Cormac had elected to change his tune. He had decided, he said, to accept the challenge of the champions. He would put the issue to the test of battle. How many were to make that test was now the matter for decision.

Colin had to think quickly. What was behind this sudden change of face? Did this mean that Cormac saw a way out? Had his spies perhaps advised him that the Larravaig contingent was raw to a degree? Was this switch in tactics a trick—or had he merely come to the conclusion that he was going to get little help from the clan at large, and therefore some limited commitment was desirable?

Colin indicated wary attention.

His brother declared that he had given the matter much thought, and had come to the conclusion that, in view of the large numbers of imported warriors from Badenoch and his not unnatural suspicions thereof, it would be wise to set the numbers of the token forces high enough to reassure him—

and, of course, the clan council. Accordingly, and after due consideration, he had decided on the figure of five hundred per side.

To say that Colin was shaken by this announcement would be an understatement. Five hundred! This was something quite beyond his remotest anticipation. Five hundred made a farce of the entire token idea, and Cormac undoubtedly was well aware of the fact. His protest was spontaneous rather than reasoned and coherent. Where would be the saving in bloodshed, he demanded, with a thousand men doing battle?

The other urged him to be less precipitate, in the irritating fashion that he had. The entire five hundred need not fight, unless they so desired. Let them meet, fully armed, select whatever equal numbers they decided upon to fight it out, and let the remainder as it were hold the lists. In this way, fair play might be assured.

Cormac was living up to his reputation for cunning. Colin was put into a serious dilemma. Despite the talk of a thousand Badenoch broadswords, he had in fact less than two hundred and fifty, all told—and not all of them very lusty brands, at that. Even with the armed galley slaves, doubtful reinforcements as they made, he could muster little more than three hundred. Cormac's spies probably had discovered as much. Where were the other two hundred to come from? To raise them from the most evidently reluctant ranks of Clan Colin was going to be a task of some magnitude that would take considerable time. And yet . . . he could not refuse outright. To do so would be as good as to admit that he could be out-manned and out-manoeuvred, to admit eventual defeat.

Summoning such nonchalance as he could discover, Colin announced that the numbers involved mattered little to him, save in his desire to avoid any unnecessary decimation of their people. But if Cormac must have a holocaust, let it be two hundred and fifty, or three hundred. Surely that was enough for anyone?

But Cormac would have none of it. Five hundred per side was his figure—five hundred or none at all.

Colin shrugged, and achieved a yawn. So be it, then. Five hundred let it be. Where, and how soon?

The other would require time, of course, to assemble his array from a wide area. A week . . . ten days, at least. It could not be done in less. And the wide haugh and water-meadows of Invercoll, where the river joined the sea-loch, would serve excellently—an arena for the combatants and the surrounding grassy banks for the watchers. Also, of course, his messengers to the clan must be allowed free passage to and from Duncolin.

Colin did not like this timetable, this postponement of a decision, this surrender of most of the advantages of surprise. But he was going to require time himself, to try to find two hundred more supporters. And if he accepted Cormac's five hundred, he could scarcely deny him the opportunity to try and collect them. With scant enthusiasm he agreed. In ten days, then—that would be Friday, twenty-second day of September— at twelve noon, they would meet in the haugh at Invercoll, to settle once and for all who was to rule Clan Colin . . . in the name of An Colin Mor, of course.

The loyal shout of acclaim, from both sides, though dutiful, was tending towards raggedness.

If Cormac had seemed to seek too long a period for his mobilization, in the event the days that followed appeared all too short for Colin Og. Never had he imagined that Highland gentlemen would be so loth to draw sword in the cause of justice and honour, nor MacColl clansmen so thirled to their shielings and their cabins. Never were harvests more slow to be ingathered, despite the weather, sheep more difficult to shepherd and clip, domestic affairs so pressing. And the number of babies about to be born, and urgently demanding the presence of the fathers, was phenomenal. That these circumstances apparently applied equally to Cormac's recruiters was only partial comfort. Two hundred fighting men were going to be as difficult to find as two thousand. The old days, when honour came first and a Highlandman's sword kept his conscience, were passing, it seemed.

Colin, who did most of his canvassing personally, achieved some small successes, of course. Here and there a young lairdling or a handful of birkies would rally to his cause. Even one or two fairly substantial tacksmen were brought to the point of promising aid, but such promises tended to be vague as to time with numbers unspecified. Colin's five hundred remained nebulous, whatever was the situation with his brother.

There were one or two amusing interludes, when rival embassies happened to arrive at the same establishment simultaneously, and out of such encounters Colin, naturally, always came off best; Cormac evidently did not trust his person outside Duncolin meantime. But these were infrequent occasions, and by and large the tendency was not towards hilarity. Ten days shrank to six, to four.

Thereafter Colin did not proceed on any more visits. He did not trust Cormac to wait for the tenth day. If he could muster sufficient men before that, he was entirely capable of sallying forth and attacking his brother's people without warning. Besides there was nothing more that Colin could usefully do. Only to wait, now, and watch, if not to pray.

One precaution did occur to him. Marsala might well be got rid of, so that, if the day indeed went ill for him, at least she would not fall straight into Cormac's hands. Much as he would like her to see him in his triumph, she would be better out of the way. But it would have to be carefully done, for he must on no account lose his grip on her. He would have to have a word with her—but alone. Not with that Tormaid hanging about; he seemed to haunt the woman now, and Colin suspected that he could no longer be relied upon always to take the correct side in any argument with the lady, a deplorable state of affairs indeed for a clansman, and a churchman moreover.

Accordingly, Tormaid was dispatched on a not very hopeful errand to a distant MacColl laird whose support had not yet been solicited, and Colin sought out the girl, dismissing the guard whose duty it was to keep an eye on her.

He found her picking berries in the priest's garden, for their midday meal. It was the first occasion on which he had been alone with her, save momentarily, for many a long day. Judiciously, he stooped to assist her at her task, a bush or two distant, before he spoke his mind. She barely looked up to acknowledge his greeting.

At length, he sighed, and said, "You will be wearying, *a graidh*, for a sight of your father? To be so near . . ."

"Yes," the girl said.

"It will be some time since you have seen him, I think?"

"Seven months and two weeks," she answered into her bush.

"That is a long time," the man acceded. "Too long. Cormac is a harsh man. . . ."

"Half of that time yourself it is that has kept me from my father's house!" she reminded him.

Colin frowned. "That was quite otherwise . . ." he began, and stopped. Such argument would not serve his cause. Assiduously he pulled raspberries, dropping them into his befeathered bonnet.

Presently, patience in every intonation, he tried again. "It may be possible for you to see Torquil Macleod," he said.

She did not speak.

He glanced up at her. "Well . . . ? You *wish* to see him, do you not?"

"I have asked you before, Colin—do *my* wishes matter?"

"They do. I swear they do. Have I not all along considered you, sought your comfort? Is not your least desire my concern?"

She raised her head to look at him, level-eyed, wordless.

He found that gaze offputting. "Do you wish that I make it possible for you to see your father?" he asked, heavily.

"It requires nothing from you to make it possible, Colin," Marsala told him. "It is possible now. Four hours' ride up yonder glen will bring me to my father's house. Only you it is that makes it *im*possible."

"You are unjust," the man cried, stung to righteous indignation. "Am I not offering that you *shall* see your father?"

"And for that, after so long, I am to thank you?"

"It is not your thanks that I seek," the other declared, gruffly.

"Only your well-being."

There was silence in that garden for a time, and painstaking industry.

Unreasonably, but woman-like, it was Marsala who reverted to the topic that she had decried. "What is it that you desire me to do for you, with my father?" she asked presently, selecting her berries with care.

Her companion looked at her out of the corner of a wary eye. "I . . . er . . . ummm," he said. "I want nothing from your father. I . . ."

The girl brushed that aside. "If you want him to fight with you against my . . . against Cormac, you can spare yourself the asking. He will not fight, for you or for Cormac. He is a man of peace, is Torquil Macleod . . . and a stronger one than your Nicol MacColl of Larravaig!"

"That was not my intention," Colin replied, stiffly, reproachfully. "Quite otherwise." His indignation was thoroughly sincere—though, of course, it had not failed to occur to him that a hundred or so of Eynart's Macleods would make a highly satisfactory solution to his present difficulties. "My intention was that you should go to your father's house until Friday's affair is over and the issue settled."

She raised her scimitar eyebrows. "And the price that I have to pay for this, this privilege?"

Pained, Colin shook his head. "You are unkind," he reproved. "You should not speak so. All that I ask is that you give me your word that you will come back to me, without complaint, when I send for you."

"And that word, I assure you, I will *not* give!"

"You . . . you will not, Marsala?"

"No."

The man ate practically all the raspberries that he had gathered, in rapid succession, his brows down-drawn. "Surely you are over-hasty, inconsiderate . . . ?"

"Have I not had ample opportunity to discover my own mind?"

"Perhaps. I do not know how works a woman's mind. But—

see you, if you will not give me your word, I cannot let you go."

"Then, to my sorrow, I may not yet see my father."

"But . . ." Colin paused, and shook his head. "You are hard, Marsala," he declared, "unfeeling. You have changed, beyond all recognition—why, I cannot tell. But, for your own sake, I beg you to reconsider this matter. There are the two days left for you to change your mind. Two days . . ." He raised a smile of a sort, the first that had been forthcoming during that conversation. ". . . time enough for a woman to change her mind many times! Is that not so, *a graidh*?"

He received no reply. Whether thereby he also achieved the last word is open to question. He left that garden with considerable dignity, but with little satisfaction in matters either strategic, emotional, or horticultural.

However brief the period in which a woman can be expected to change her mind, two days, in the event, were not allowed to Marsala Macleod, nor to any of them. That same evening, one of Sorley Dam's scouts, on a foam-lathered pony, rode hotfoot into Ardcoll with the panted word that a horde, an army, not far off a thousand strong, was approaching from the south-east and now entering the valleys at the root of the peninsula. At its head rode Mackenzie of Kintail himself, and at his side the crooked figure of Iain Cam of the Cairn.

Cormac MacColl had baited and set his trap, and done the unforgivable thing—he had called in the hated Mackenzies to spring it.

XVII

COLIN OG, after an initial and epic outburst, wasted no time on fruitless lamentation. Summoning all that he had as leaders—Tormaid, of course, was not available—he hurled his orders at them. The fiery cross was to go out at once, into every glen of the MacColls, charging them to rally to the defence of their homes against invasion by the Mackenzies, in the name of An Colin Mor. Cormac's infamy was to be shouted aloud in every haunt of men—save to Cormac himself, who, if possible, must be kept in ignorance that his secret was known. The strictest watch was to be maintained on the castle, and no further messengers allowed in or out. And Sorley's veterans, with the toughest of the other levies, to the total of fifty, were to assemble at once for immediate action.

They set out as soon as darkness gave them cover from view from the castle, and rode all that remained of the night up Glen Coll, with scouts well forward against surprise. By dawn, they were close to the high pass of the Lairig Garve where the infant Coll River, spilling itself out of its watershed, had cut a deep cleft for itself through harsh rock and bare scree, down into the more open valley. Through or near here the Mackenzies would have to come if they were going to approach Ardcoll with any directness—and to bring an army otherwise would be next to impossible. Two or three men could skip and clamber like deer amongst the tops, as Colin knew, none better; but a large body had to keep to more beaten tracks. It would be the merest justice to ambush Iain Cam of the Cairn in such a place.

But it was inconceivable that the Mackenzies would not have their own scouts out in advance; the Wryface, of all people, would be alive to the dangers of such passes. They had, however, already passed through many similar, unmolested, and unless the invaders had reason to believe that their approach was discovered, there was no cause why this particular pass should be suspect. Colin based such hopes as he had on this line of reasoning.

Some two miles short of the Lairig, he turned his company off the drove road and climbed them up a tapering side corrie, through the misty dew-drenched morning, to a gap in the ridge above. In a corresponding corrie beyond, facing north, he left the horses, hidden and under guard, and then led his silent following eastwards along the high ground till they were above the pass. Cautious and scrupulous scrutiny revealed no trace of scouts or army, nor any hint of man's presence, in all that wilderness—in fact, the only sign of life, a small herd of stags feeding quietly on the hillside opposite, was the surest indication that the vicinity was undisturbed. Satisfied, Colin, with Sorley and Angus Macdougall, slipped down into the gut of the pass to make his dispositions.

A brief examination sufficed, for he had known this territory since boyhood. Sorley Dam, who was no tyro in the matter of ambuscades, agreed with his findings, and they returned to the main party.

The company was split into two, about one-third of it, under Angus Macdougall and Alan the Stutterer, being sent down the steep side of the ravine to cross the rushing river, and to climb to the opposite heights beyond. Their instructions were definite. After surveying the rock formation at the head of their slope, and loosening such of it as they could, they were to lie well back and very low, and were to do nothing until signalled from this side. Colin set his own party to judicious rock-loosening, whilst a sharp lookout was kept from nearby eminences.

The work went well, and undisturbed. Though here and there odd boulders went plunging abortively down into the chasm below, they managed to prepare and maintain in suspended equilibrium a considerable weight of seamed and fissured stone. Also they were able to insert, in a deep crevice of the rock-face, the single small keg of gunpowder that Colin had been able to find in the barrack-bothy at Ardcoll. A fuse of sorts attached thereto, and their preparations were fairly complete. By mid-forenoon, Colin was moderately satisfied.

But when midday came and went, and the afternoon sun smiled over all that upheaved land, his modified satisfaction had commenced to fade. The lookouts reported no sign of life nor movement. The Mackenzies should surely have put in an appearance by this time. Could they have changed their route? Could it be that they had missed them? Not a thousand of them, surely, nor half that. Questioning closely the man who had originally brought the news, he confirmed that the invaders had been a bare ten miles farther east twenty-four hours ago, and moving along the drove road. By no means could such an array have changed direction suddenly, other than by going back whence they had come.

It being hardly likely that they had precipitately retreated only the one alternative seemed to remain—that they had stayed stationary. There might be sense in that, Colin decided. If their arrival at Ardcoll was timed for Friday, or just prior, then Kintail might well have elected to hold back a space in unpopulated country, in order to make his appearance, unheralded, at the arranged moment. If this was the case, the watchers might have still longer to wait. At least, he ought to have information on the subject. He sent the former scout, with one companion, to gain it.

In the meantime, no harm would be done by a little more stonemasonry.

Before dusk, one of the spies was back, with the word that the Mackenzies were indeed still in front, camped in the great wooded hollow of Laggan am Fasach, about six miles to the east, and displaying no signs of movement that night. The second scout remained to keep an eye on them.

It was the mention of that wooded hollow of Am Fasach, that set Colin furiously to think, and abruptly, as his people were settling themselves down for the night in their high and comfortless quarters, to change all his plans. With typical and decisive energy, he roused his company and bade them prepare to march, had the keg of gunpowder recovered, and sent an urgent message to the party across the valley. They were to move at once, and forward. He would meet them on the drove road, ahead. There might be better ways of dealing with a thousand Mackenzies than rolling stones atop of them.

To term Laggan am Fasach a hollow is perhaps to give a wrong impression, though that is what its name means—the Hollow of the Forest. It was a wide open space in that constricted land of towering hills and steep valleys, caused by the convergence of three glens, one large and two small, and the morainic floor of it, of sand and rubble and therefore less waterlogged than was usual, was carpeted with tall heather and fading bracken out of which grew ancient twisted pines and slender green birches, a haunt of roe-deer and capercailzie. The trees were scattered, not dense, and there were open patches amongst them, an excellent place to shelter and hide a large body of men over a short period.

On foot, and silently, through the mirk, Colin led his reunited company. Two hours' march, over the watershed and down into the glen beyond, and they neared the edge of the great wood. Their scout warned that there was a Mackenzie picket camped about a mile this side of it, in the glen floor, and this they carefully circumnavigated. At the dark rim of the hollow of Am Fasach, the far-flung shadowy trees of which whispered and sighed in the night breeze, Colin halted and addressed his people, whispering likewise, even if he did not sigh.

Flint and steel and a handful of dead bracken would serve them as weapons now, he told them. The shape of the hollow, and the unfailing south-westerly wind that funnelled up the glen, would, he trusted, do the rest. They were to spread out, on either hand, fifty paces between each man, and to light as many fires as were necessary to ensure that each sector was ablaze, with no gaps in it. Fifty of them should cover almost the entire western arc of the hollow. When each man's portion was well alight, he was to run round farther to his flank and light more fires until himself and Sorley Dam, who would be at the extreme horns of their crescent, told them it was enough. Then they were to hasten on, farther round still, to the mouths of the three incoming glens, north and east, and to stop these bolt-holes. Ten men under Alan Liogach to the northernmost glen, ten under Angus Macdougall to the southernmost, and the remainder with himself and Sorley in the main central glen. Was that understood? It would have to be fast work . . . but there ought to be noble killing in the mouths of those glens before the night was much older. They would singe the Mackenzies' shanks for them!

A murmur, a shudder almost, of appreciation came from his hearers.

Colin Og spoke, low but tense, then. "Sons of the Eagle— cook your meat!" he said. "Go, you!"

It was almost too easy. The bracken was dying, and below it last year's crop lay dead, the knee-high old heather was fading, more stem than bloom, and the summer had been at least drier than many. The fires started without difficulty, and once started, fanned by the breeze, few tended to die out. Within a few minutes of Colin's final word, scores of pinpricks of fire were gleaming against the black curtain of the trees and the night, a minute or two more and the number was doubled, and then, swiftly, the actual numbers fell, as individual fires ran together and merged. Soon, in little more time than it takes to tell, there were no single fires any more, only a wall of flame, unbroken and growing mightily, curving in an ever-widening arc around the doomed hollow of Am Fasach.

The place was roughly circular, and perhaps three-quarters of a mile across at its widest. Colin, having seen the conflagration well started, hurried round the perimeter on the southern side, making for a point approximately two-thirds of the way round, where, if he remembered rightly, a shoulder of the enclosing braeside thrust inwards, just before the opening of the southernmost glen. Whether fires lit so far round as this would be effective, owing to the direction of the wind, remained to be seen; his object was to create a great horseshoe of flame, driving inwards, that would force the luckless men within to flee before it, eastwards, for the only gaps available, the narrow mouths of the three glens. If the prongs of the horseshoe did not reach far enough round, it was possible that certain of the hoped-for fugitives might elect to try to bolt straight up the hill-face, there, instead of into the traps in the valleys. But without men to line these slopes, that must be accepted. The proportion that might seek to do so was unlikely to be large.

Climbing a little way up the shoulder, Colin obtained an excellent view of the situation, above the treetops. The fire was going admirably—better than he could have hoped for. A wide belt of licking, darting orange flame was sweeping forward and inward, like a racing tide, out of which the scattered pines thrust up like flaring torches, crackling in their resinous fury, and showering sparks and flaming embers far into the billowing clouds of dense smoke that rolled onwards ominously, red-tinged, into the gloom. The belt of fire was, at a guess, perhaps fifty yards in depth—wide enough for no man to penetrate, at any rate—and behind it was a black and crimson inferno, that glowed and sank and glowed again amidst a myriad wriggling snakes of fire. Already, the incendiaries were nearing the foot of his knoll, but these latest-lit fires were not doing so well, blowing straight in front of them, not trending inwards, nor were they linking up as farther back. This was inevitable. Colin, with the heat already reaching him, even up here, and the ruddy acrid smoke-rack stinging eyes and nostrils, decided that probably he should be satisfied. What it would be like in the centre of Am Fasach beggared imagination; he could not conceive that there would be any attempt at fire-fighting. Running down his hill towards the latest fires, he yelled his orders, above the crackle and roar, to leave it, and to get round to the glens' mouths at once.

It was not before time, either. As, running, stumbling, in the eerie evil glow, and panting in the throbbing smoke-laden air, they came to the entrance of the first glen, already shadowy figures were hurrying thereinto. Shouting to Angus Macdougall to take charge, Colin felled a lurching person whom he hoped was a Mackenzie, with a backhanded blow of his broadsword, and ran on, followed by at least a proportion of what were probably his MacColls.

They made their unsteady way round the stone-littered base of the steep and rocky pinnacle of hill that separated the two valleys, and as they turned in at the jaws of this glen also they found themselves in a stream of men going the same way. From the cries and thuds that sounded from ahead, just discernible above the rumble of the fire, it seemed that Sorley and his people had got there first, via the northern flank, and were dutifully engaged in stemming the rush. There followed considerable shouting, slogan-crying, argument, and miscellaneous head-cracking, before the identity of everybody was satisfactorily established, and the survivors could turn a united front upon the demoralized minions of Clan Kenneth. More or less united, that is; Colin suspected, almost to the point of conviction, that the lusty individual who plied a Lochaber-axe to such good purpose, immediately on his left, was a Mackenzie, no less. The fog of war, which can be very thick on the clearest day, as any old soldier can vouch, is by no means likely to be dispersed by flickering flame-lit darkness and streaming, enveloping smoke.

It was warm work, there in the constriction of the steep valley. The heat from the fire, sucked into this channel, met them like recurrent blasting, and the numbers of customers for their active attention was unfailing and monotonous. It was no sword and dirk work, Colin soon perceived—indeed there was little or no fighting in it, with the oncoming refugees looking for nothing in front of them save sanctuary from the terror behind. The business merely developed into a wearisome cracking of heads, for which purpose Colin found a stout thorn club, dropped conveniently at his feet by somebody whom he had cut down, much more suitable than his cherished steel. He stood actually in the middle of the drove road, which ran through this central glen, with supporters so close on either hand as to considerably restrict good arm-work, right across the narrow floor of the valley to its steep and rock-ribbed sides. Like a stopper in a bottle, they were, and just as tightly uncomfortable.

This unedifying situation had continued long enough for all concerned to be breathless, perspiring, and limp with heat and effort, and for bodies to have piled around them inconveniently, when there was an interlude. The press of oncoming hurrying Mackenzies was just getting too great for a score or so of conscientious men to cope with, when a curious sustained screaming sound, from Am Fasach, pierced the general uproar. An unpleasant noise, it was difficult to account for. Then through it, and the rest of the clamour, a drumming sound penetrated and grew louder. The tortured air, already vibrant with heat and sound, appeared to throb to a different beat. The very ground seemed to tremble to it.

Sorley Dam it was who shouted the answer to their question. "The garrons!" he bawled. "Their beasts, it is!"

He was right. It took only a few moments to confirm. Fleeing in frantic neighing terror from the flames, the Mackenzie horse-flesh, hundreds of ponies, broken loose, came stampeding into the glen, mowing down all before them.

Immediately all was confusion. To get out of the way of that trampling horde became the sole objective of every man. Friend and foe alike fled side by side, right and left, to clamber and scrabble up the screes and loose rock of the glensides. Some were more fortunate than others. None who remained in the floor of the valley had the faintest chance. The screams of men mingled with the neighing of maddened horses, with the thunder of hooves and the roar and crackle of the flames. Hell itself, Colin decided, even as described by Tormaid the Priest, could scarcely be more daunting.

The garrons streamed past, below them, in a solid steaming mass, no individual outlines being discernible, but hundreds of red gleaming eyes reflecting the fire. How many there were it was impossible to calculate—but it was fairly obvious that, hereafter, whatever was left of the Mackenzies would travel, either backwards or forwards, on their own feet.

When it seemed that the last of the brutes had gone, the men began to straggle down to the road again, just a trifle sheepishly. Perhaps the Ardcoll contingent was not entirely unaffected, thus—even Colin Og himself. It is difficult, a little, having all passed together through a sudden and universal peril, to immediately revert to a methodical breaking of heads, as though nothing had happened. There could be something undignified about it. Somewhat put out, Colin scratched his head for a suitable gesture with which to appropriately restart hostilities, and could think of none. He was tired, of course—they all were tired. And it was getting unbearably hot and smoky.

It is to be feared that quite a lot of Mackenzies were permitted to drift away, with the smoke, up that glen, before the sight of a single eagle's feather silhouetted against the leaping background of flame, now coming very near, jerked Colin Og into action. It waved above the press of heads, and Colin thrust towards it, cleaving a passage with his club.

"Sirrah!" he addressed the anonymous person underneath. "Stand you, and fight! I am Colin Og mhic Colin of Ardcoll. Out with your sword!" And he flung down his club, approximately at the other's feet, and reached for his own steel.

"Sorrow is me!" came from under the feathered bonnet, distressfully. "I have no sword—lost, it is! And I could not fight you, sir, if I had it—I can see nothing for this thrice-damned smoke. My eyes are running like a spate. And I have burned my hand, too . . ."

"Mother of God, pity us!" Colin cried peevishly. "What lily-livered creature is this . . . ?"

"I am Kenneth Ruadh Mackenzie of Berrisdale, sir," the other declared, with some dignity. "And I will fight you some other where and time, with pleasure. Indeed, yes. Good night to you."

"Damnation!" Colin spluttered. "And there's a Mackenzie for you!" Angrily, disgustedly, he stooped for his down-thrown club, to knock this wretched degenerate on the head with it—which was obviously all that he deserved. But unfortunately, it had got kicked aside in the press, and he could not find it. He straightened up. "Where is your chief, craven?" he demanded, then. But the other had moved on. "Berrisdale!" he raised his

207

voice hotly. "Where is Kintail, tell me?"

The man's weary words came back to him, thinly. "Kintail is well in front," he said. "Himself travels with the van, see you."

"By all the Artillery of Heaven . . . !"

A coarser voice, close at hand, spoke fleeringly. "Kintail should be half-roads back to Kintail by this, my mannie," it said. "Our chief has the long legs to him, I tell you. I doubt if his garron will ever make up with him!" That was followed by a single hoot of derisive laughter.

Colin frowned blackly. "That is no way to speak of your chief, fellow," he cried. "Shame on you!" And he stooped once more for that club, for he thought that he could feel it roll under his brogan—and this presumptuous cateran badly needed it.

And the uncouth Mackenzie raised the stick that he himself was grasping, and brought it down promptly, heavily, on the back of the stooping man's head, eagle's feathers and all, before passing on.

Colin Og sank into peace and quiet.

When he eventually regained consciousness, it was to find one of Sorley's heroes in the act of searching his person, presumably for valuables. The subsequent outburst, whatever effect it had on the recipient, all but split his own damaged head wide open. With tears of mixed origin, indignation, pain, sorrow for himself, and smoke in his eyes, Colin raised himself unsteadily on one elbow, to survey the scene.

It was darker than ever. The Mackenzies—such as were able—seemed all to have gone. The fire still burned, but it obviously had passed its zenith and was now producing considerably more smoke than flame, in particularly obnoxious choking black clouds, the majority of which most evidently were blowing directly into their glen. The heat was stifling. Of Sorley Dam himself, and the rest of his people—apart from one or two shadowy corpse-searchers—there was no sign; whether they were all hewn down, were fallen exhausted, or were off up the glen pursuing the Mackenzies, was not to be known. Actually, at the moment, Colin did not greatly care. He felt sick. He looked on all that he saw with a jaundiced and resentful eye, decided that he had been much better off when unconscious, pulled a corner of his plaid up over his aching, splitting head, and went to sleep.

He awoke to a new day, and a less disenchanted outlook—though his head still throbbed damnably. Laggan am Fasach was a black desolation over which a pall of smoke hung broodingly, but the rest of the landscape was bright under the morning sun. It was the arrival of Alan the Stutterer and his people from the northern glen that had awakened Colin—and not only Colin; all around, men were sitting up, yawning and rubbing bleary eyes, Sorley Dam included. What at first glance had appeared to be the serried ranks of the slain proved to be largely sleepers. Some corpses there were, lying around, of course, but not nearly so many as had appeared to be the case in the night. Undoubtedly, the majority of those knocked on the head had come to themselves during the early hours—as had Colin—and had wisely and quietly betaken themselves off, in the wake of their uninjured colleagues and clansmen. The casualty rate, accordingly, did not look like being high, and the worst of it could probably be blamed on the stampeding ponies. Of Colin's company, no single man was dead—though there were a few miscellaneously damaged. Nevertheless, all agreed on assessment that it had been an excellent battle, and worthy of the best that the sennachies, in time to come, could find to say and sing about it.

After a scratch meal of raw oatmeal from their pouches, and cold burn water, Colin insisted on following up the Mackenzie rout for some distance at least, to ensure that they were not regrouping for any sort of counter-attack, or for a resumption of their onward march. Unfortunately the MacColl garrons were still six miles back, at the Lairig Garve, so it meant pressing on up the drove road on foot. This was an unpopular move, for tired men, but Colin was adamant. Putting out a couple of scouts well in front, they started off eastwards into the early slanting sunshine.

Though signs of the rout were evident all along that trail, no word came back from the scouts that they were in contact with the enemy. A couple of hours of this, and they were out of MacColl territory, out of the Eorsary peninsula, and into the no-man's-land of peat-pocked wilderness beyond. Near the edge of this grim expanse, a single isolated hill rose, like a sleeping monster out of its wallow, and around the base of which the drove road curved. Here a scout waited for them, with the word that his companion was up above, spying the land. Colin followed him up.

At the top, with its wide and extensive view, they learned what they wanted to know. The drove road forked, not far ahead, the main track leading away across the desolation, south by east, towards Ullapool, Gairloch, and ultimately Kintail; the other branched off to the south-west, to Eynart of the Macleods. And scattered and strung out along the former, as far as eye could see, were men, singly, in pairs and groups and parties; nowhere was there any sign of a halt or rallying-place. Obviously, the Mackenzies, after their chief, were for home. Wise men.

The MacColls might now, with equal profit, do likewise.

It was a long road to Ardcoll. Nearly fourteen miles on foot before even they reached their garrons at the Lairig. Weary but satisfied, they turned their faces to the north-west.

It was evening before Colin's company rode into Ardcoll. Tormaid met them before ever they reached the township, and though he asked dutifully for news of their doings, and praised God for a mighty deliverance, his mind seemed to be less than wholly engaged. And just as soon as his praise was delivered, he drew Colin aside, and spoke urgently.

"Marsala Macleod is gone," he informed.

"Gone?" Colin stared. "Gone where? What folly is this, man?"

"Where, the saints alone know. But she is gone—run away." His priestly fingers lifted to quell the rising storm. "She was gone before I returned—back from the errand you sent me, to Lochure." There might have been just a hint of reproach there. "I found all here disorganized, you and Sorley and Angus away—and Marsala gone. I thought at first that she was with you. And then I learned differently. She was here, at Ardcoll, up till nearly noon this day. She has not been seen since."

"And her gear—her clothes?"

"I looked to that my own self. Some are gone—what she carried when first we took her. The rest remain."

"Mary of Mercy! She will be gone to her father at Eynart. And yet . . . we saw no sign of her on the road. She must have kept to the hill. There is nowhere else that she could have gone. She would not take a boat, surely . . . ?"

"Not from Loch Coll, no. That I enquired into. Unless, as ourselves did one time, she crossed the hill to yonder place of the women. . . ."

Colin muttered something indistinct.

"*Forsan et haec olim meminisse juvabit,*" said the priest. And then, "She might be more fortunate than were we, and prevail upon the fishermen to put her across."

Colin snapped out an oath. "Get me food, drink, and a fresh garron," he commanded. "I ride at once."

"But . . . but . . ." Tormaid swallowed. "Colin, my heart— you cannot do that! Tomorrow, at noon, is the time for the contest, the fight. Cormac will . . ."

"Cormac can wait for me!"

"Cormac will not wait. Cormac will fall upon us. There were near two hundred men assembled up at the Cairn yesterday, Rob Molach says—they will be on their way down, now. And there are other parties about, they say—I saw one myself. Cormac will have them timed to be here by noon, for certain. If he finds you amissing, he will not wait. . . ."

"He will wait for his Mackenzie friends awhile, at any rate," the other returned grimly. "But I will be back ere that, I think. Now, go—and quickly."

"But . . . these men, these from Larravaig—they will not fight if you are not there. You are their champion, their

211

backbone. They will break, and scatter. All that you have worked for may be lost. . . ."

"Then *you* must save it, foster-brother. You must hold the fort, till I return. *Marsala* is lost, see you, and must be found. Marsala I must have. . . ."

"Are you mad, Colin!" the priest demanded. "Does Marsala Macleod mean more to you than Clan Colin?"

For a long moment Colin stared at him, unseeing, unspeaking. Then he drew as long a breath. "Who knows," he said, slowly. "Perhaps she does." He jerked his head up, then, sharply, finally. "At any rate, I go to find her. Fetch me what I ask— and at once."

Tormaid, who knew that tone of old, turned, head ashake, to do as he was bidden.

XVIII

COLIN rode alone. On a sure-footed broad-backed garron
that picked its own wise way up the long side of the hog's
back that separated Glen Coll from the great Bay of Eynart,
he pondered and questioned the circumstances, and himself.
And if, by his frequent frowning and sombre mien, much of
his thinking gave him no pleasure, at least he worked out in
his mind the girl's probable movements, and therefore his own
immediate advisable course of action. What would follow
thereafter, he left to the future.

Firstly, he could think of no other likely destination for her
than her father's house of Eynart. Where else could she go?
Even if, ultimately, she sought other sanctuary, first surely she
would visit her home, her father. That accepted, since they
had seen no sign of her on the road, which was the straightforward route thereto, it seemed obvious that she had taken to
the hills. But if it was a weary journey, on foot, by road—well
over thirty miles—it was infinitely worse by the hills, especially
for a woman, and alone. It seemed almost certain that she
would seek to shorten her ordeal by cutting across the Bay in
a boat. She had not obtained one from Loch Coll, Tormaid
asserted—therefore this harsh and rock-bound southern
coastline of Eorsary could provide her only opportunities. And
since it was so largely uninhabited, her route was narrowed
down further. Indeed, there were only the three points on its
long and barren shore where a boat could be sought. Had not
himself and Tormaid had the same problem, one time? The
salmon-fishers' bothies at Drumbain, and at Urinish—scene of
their adventures with the ladies and the leaking boat—or, lastly,
the small township of Aranbeg, far down near the root of the
peninsula. One or more of these Marsala must visit, if she
sought a boat. It was to Drumbain, most westerly and nearest
to Ardcoll, that Colin was heading now.

The shadows of night were welling deep in all the valleys as he climbed, but the last traces of the sunset were staining the western sea as he crested the ridge and started to slant downhill. Scan that level expanse as he would, he could see no sign of boat or sail upon it. Far below him, he traced the faint blue drift of peat-smoke that rose from the bothy fire at Drumbain, smoored against the night.

But by the time that he had worked his careful way down that unchancy slope, the sunset and the light were gone, and the cottage crouched dark and silent in the gloaming. Colin had to bang loudly on the door to gain an answer, and that only a grudging one shouted gruffly from within.

In the name of An Colin Mor, he bade them good evening and good fishing. Had a woman come this way, today—a woman, alone?

There was some muttering at that, and a lack of clarity about the answer.

Peremptorily Colin repeated his demand, reinforcing his words with the hilt of his broadsword on the door.

The response was more suitable. Yes, there had been a woman.

And had she asked for a boat—asked to be rowed across the Bay?

Yes, she had done just that.

And had they done as she asked?

There was a moment's pause, and then two voices began to speak simultaneously. Unfortunately, they had been just home from the fishing. They had been tired. One of them had a bad hand, nipped by a lobster . . .

Colin cut short the excuses. They had not taken her, then?

No. They were sorry, but . . .

When had this been? How long ago?

Debate was required to establish it as three hours, or maybe four, back. They had sent her on to Urinish. Two boats they had, there. . . .

Illogically, Colin cursed them for surly dogs, and proceeded on his way.

There was no consistent track along that stretch of empty coast, with the hillside falling almost straight to the tide's edge, and the man would have been better without his mount, having to lead it most of the way. Stumbling and tripping and swearing, he yet spared a thought for the young woman who had come this way before him. She would be a footsore lass this night, wherever she was.

It was no more than four miles to the bothy at Urinish, yet it took Colin more than two hours to cover it, over the fallen rocks and the legion of the tumbling burns, and with the mirk thickening about him. No light nor sign of life showed here, either—though the man noted that two cobles were drawn up on that stretch of shingly beach that he had reason to remember only too well. For all that, he approached the house with considerably more confidence and authority than he had done on the previous occasion. Undoubtedly, clothing has a lot of the making of a man.

His rapping on the door evoked considerable disturbance and discussion within, in which women's voices were foremost. He was thankful, nevertheless, that it was a man who eventually opened the door, however suspiciously.

Colin put the same question to this shadowy individual— and met with anything but a shadowy reply. Indeed yes, a young woman had been at them, two-three hours back— wanting them to put her across to Eynart that same night, no less! The foolishness of the creature! There were too many of these loose and broken folk about—the country was full of them, these days. Not that long ago, himself had had a boat stolen and his women put in fear of their lives and honour by two such desperate characters. Wicked times they were. And what for was a young woman the likes of her stravaiging about alone, and at night, too? There was no good in it, whatever. They had sent her packing—whoever she was. Honest folk had to look after their own. These scoundrels that had assaulted the women . . .

With an effort Colin managed, not to stem the tide, but to very temporarily interrupt the flow. She had gone on, then, this ill-advised young woman—gone on towards Aranbeg?

She had, yes, the shameless minx—where else was there to go, at all? It could be, of course, that she was not alone, at that. It could be that she had a pack of rascally caterans at her back, somewhere, waiting to fall on them. The times were as bad as that. But they kept the oars inside the house, now—there would be no more stealing of boats, whatever the tale she might have to her. They had watched her walk along towards the cliffs—but, och, it was dark getting, and they have been waiting for her, any place.

Dark getting, Colin cried. And they had turned a young woman away, to face the night and the hills, with no house nearer than Aranbeg! By the Holy Mother of God, that was an ill deed!

The fisherman was reiterating the probability of wicked and rascally customers using the hussy as a decoy, when his protests were submerged and swept aside in a torrent of female indignation from behind. Colin caught just a glimpse, in the dull red glow from the peats, of at least one large figure advancing to the fray, and decided forthwith that nothing was to be gained by further parley. Over his shoulder he said an abrupt goodnight, as he hurried off.

Aranbeg was another six or so miles off, around a sizeable bend in the coastline, but it was impossible to reach it by the shore. The hills here met the sea in great and jagged cliffs, culminating in a frowning headland, around or below which there was no passage for man nor beast. The only route—and no path, at that—lay inland through the jumble of foothills. An unpleasant course to take by night—but less unpleasant for himself than for Marsala Macleod. That could be accepted. Leading his pony, Colin turned his face to climb inland.

Once away from the coast, the night seemed to grow vastly more dark. The sea appeared to retain some cold memory of the light that was gone, some glimmer that the land rejected. Into the blackness of hill and valley, Colin picked an uncertain and halting course. He had been this way before, of course, but long ago, and never at night. His pony was no use to him—only a drag, indeed. Also, his progress was not helped by the fact that he kept nodding as he walked, all but asleep on his feet. He had slept only for a few hours in the last forty-eight, and even then had been unconscious more than asleep. His head throbbed vilely. He might have been wiser to lie up, and let himself rest for a while; but so long as Marsala was somewhere ahead, there, he could not consider such a course. He stumbled on.

At some time in the night he came to a valley junction which he believed that he could recognize by the waterfall just below it. If this was where he thought, he was more than halfway to Aranbeg. His onward route, however, lay practically along the bed of the same stream, and by no means could the man contemplate dragging the horse thither. He could get another beast at Aranbeg, if need be. He tethered the garron to a stunted birch, and took to the river bed.

He had no idea of the time at which he reached the sleeping township at the head of its narrow bay. There were perhaps a dozen houses in all, small scattered cabins in the main, and each of them Colin knocked up in turn. Had a young woman come to their door this night, he asked, in the name of An Colin Mor? And in each case the answer, helpful or otherwise, was in the negative. Who and why, in the name of the good God? No strange woman had come to Aranbeg that night.

Weary, anxious, dispirited, Colin sat down outside the last cottage. She had not reached here. He must have passed her in the dark. Perhaps she was lost in the hills. . . . She might be in trouble, in danger, desperate. He could not just wait for her, here. He would have to go back. . . .

Stiffly, unsteadily, he got to his feet, and started to return whence he had come.

Perhaps an hour thereafter, he commenced his calling, calling, "Ma-a-a-arsala! Ma-a-a-arsala!" into all the night-shrouded hills. And all those unseen hills answered him back, "Ma-a-a-arsala-a-a! Ma-a-a-arsala-a-aa!" That was all the answer that he got, for all his shouting.

At some stage during that unhappy night, the man realized

217

that he himself was lost. He found himself in deep peat-hags surrounding a lochan, that he did not recognize. Stumbling on, he came to the base of a steep, a precipitous, hill that he knew not. It was almost with relief that he conceded the situation. No use going on farther. Nothing to be done, now, save to wait . . . and to sleep. Sleep. . . .

Colin sought and found a clump of old heather, and sank down into it. He slept exactly in the position in which he met the earth.

It was the sun in his eyes that awoke him, a slanting yellow beam that reached him through a gap in low hills to the east. Cramped and stiff and a little sick, Colin rubbed his eyes, staring about him. He was in a wide and boggy valley amongst jumbled rugged hillocks, all bare stone ledges and rust-tinged deer-hair grass, and before him a steep escarpment rose, high and barren. Without being able to say exactly where he was, he knew to within a mile or so where he must be. He had come too far to the north, from Aranbeg. But it was difficult, confusing country. Small wonder if Marsala had lost herself in it, likewise.

He still had a handful or so of oatmeal in his pouch to serve for breakfast, and a ducking of his head in a nearby burn made up his toilet and refreshment. Then he started out to climb the soaring face of that hill, with the stiffness to lift out of his limbs.

In twenty minutes Colin was on the crest, and his own man again. The view from here only emphasized how little he need blame himself for losing his way in the darkness. Though the distant prospects were wide and far-flung, indeed breathtaking in their immensity, closer at hand the scene was one of constriction and enigma. All around his high ridge stretched the sea of small featureless hills and shallow boggy valleys, identical, without pattern. No general direction gave coherence to those valleys, no individuality served to differentiate one of those hillocks from another. Only the fact that he had followed the river down through them on his outward journey must have brought him safely to Aranbeg in the dark. And he had not thought to cling to that kindly river on his return.

For long Colin scanned that immediate prospect, quartering all the southern and western arc of it, where Marsala Macleod might have strayed. There was much of it, inevitably, that escaped his scrutiny, hidden by higher land intervening. But over it all nothing moved save the cloud shadows, and a pair of wheeling buzzards. A briefer glance north and east revealed a similar emptiness, right to the barrier of the great mountains of Ross. Perplexed and disappointed, the man turned to retrace his steps downhill, to make for the river that had been his last night's guide, and his tethered garron. He might find some trace of her on his way thither, or farther back still. Surely she would not have attempted to work her way round by the coast and the cliffs . . . ?

He was perhaps a third of the way down, when, out of the corner of his right eye, he glimpsed movement. It was away north-westwards, and a couple of miles off at least. Only sheep, he decided, after a narrow-eyed stare, but moving with the abrupt and flouncing gait that indicated that they had been disturbed. More things than wandering young women could disturb the three-parts wild sheep, of course, but . . .

Then he saw the darker figure, tiny, unidentifiable, but obviously human, emerge from a hollow in the land behind the sheep. It was not necessarily Marsala; it might be a shepherd—though the man was inclined to think not, at that hour of the morning in that place. Yet the figure was moving in the wrong direction, for Marsala—north by east. . . . If only he had brought Tormaid's telescope.

There was no question but that he must make a closer inspection. Tracing his approximate route, and memorizing such landmarks as were available to guide him, Colin plunged down into the valley.

There was no eminence tall enough to permit the man to see over the multitude of similar hillocks. Many he climbed, panting, but from none could be seen the area in which he was interested. He could only hasten on, circling the bogs, plowtering through the peat-hags, leaping the burns, in what he trusted was the right direction.

It was well over an hour, then, and after much casting about and searching, before he discovered a set of footmarks on the black lip of a peat bog. And they were small footprints, woman's footprints. His heart leaping to the sight, almost choking him indeed, he hurried on.

It was a simple task, once found, to follow those wavering pathetic tracks; there was ample of peat-broth and mud and sand in that waterlogged terrain. She could not be more than a mile or so ahead.

And yet, in the event, the meeting was a surprise. Rounding a knowe, glance largely down-bent, Colin was beginning to cross a scattering of grey lichened outcrops of granite, when movement on one of them drew him up, suddenly. The young woman, who had been crouching on one of the rocks, head down between her hands, sat up, startled. At sight of the man, she rose to her feet, turning, eyes wide.

"Colin!" she gasped. "Oh, Colin . . . !"

In a series of enormous strides the man was at her side, and caught her to him. "My heart!" he cried. "My dear! Marsala— my delight, my pigeon, my little trout!"

She buried her face in his broad chest, and clutching him, sobbed convulsively.

For how long they stood still, thus, was not to be known; it could be, that time for them stood still likewise. At any rate, it was long enough for the young woman's sobs to sink and dwindle, and her tense and trembling grip of the man's arms to slacken. But still she did not raise her head from his breast. For his part, Colin did not complain. If occasionally his lips brushed her windblown raven hair, that was excusable, almost inevitable.

At length, she drew away. And even yet she did not lift her eyes to his face. "So you . . . you followed me, Colin," she said, and her voice was not level, at all.

"Yes," he nodded. "I missed you, in the night. . . ."

"In the night, yes." She shivered, involuntarily.

"It was bad, was it, *a graidh*? You were frightened?"

"Yes. When I knew that I was lost. . . ."

"Poor Marsala. But it was easy for you to lose yourself. My own self, when I came back from Aranbeg, I was lost." He smiled, "I was frightened too . . . and me shouting all night, just to be keeping myself company! You did not hear me?"

"No," she said. "No—I wish that I had. I heard nothing, I think, save my own heart beating!" The girl shook a rueful head, though still her eyes were averted. "Never did I think that I would be frightened in my own heather."

"But this is not your own heather, see you—this is the ill and enchanted land of Domdaniel, where left is right, and back is front, and up is down. It is not a place for young women, at all, and I have come to take you out of it."

Despite the heedful soothing of his voice, the other looked away. "To take me back to Ardcoll," she asserted.

"To take you where you may wish to go, *a graidh*," he corrected, mildly.

Marsala risked a glance at him, there. "Where I *wish* to go . . . ? That is a changed tune surely, Colin?"

"Perhaps it is," the man admitted. "Perhaps more than just yourself has been lost and found, Marsala Macleod, since last night!"

She stared at him, now. "I do not understand," she said, uncertainly. "You . . . you came after me, seeking me, just to let me go again?"

"I came after you, to find you. It was a thing that I had to do. And now, I must take you where you wish to go."

"But . . . I have not agreed that I would come back to you when you called me. You said . . ."

"I have said many things, not all of them wise nor kindly, Marsala," Colin declared, slowly. "But when I came back to Ardcoll last night, and found you gone, I knew what I must do. Just as I know what I must do, now. It may be that I had myself to find, as well as you."

Marsala shook her head helplessly. "You will take me to my father?"

"If that is your wish, yes."

"You are not angry that I ran away from you? You do not blame me?"

"The night that swallowed us, I think, swallowed any anger or blame with it. First, I learned what it meant that you should be lost to me, and then, that you should be lost altogether, possibly to everyone. And I learned that the first was more supportable than the second. I have been learning a lot, you see. I learned what you meant to me. But more than that, I learned that your well-being, your happiness, meant more to me than anything else. So—whether it is to your father, or to Cormac, that you would go, I will take you there."

"To . . . to Cormac, even, Colin?"

"If that is your wish, *a graidh.*"

The girl drew a long breath. "I will not ask you to do that, I think," she said.

"I thank God for that word, then," her companion returned, simply.

For a few moments there was silence between them, but no empty silence. Then Marsala looked up, suddenly, a catch in her voice. "But, Colin . . . !" she cried. "Today it is that Cormac . . . today, at noon, your people are to meet Cormac's! This contest, this terrible fight—it is today!"

"That is so, yes."

"Then why are you here? Surely you should be with your men?"

Colin shrugged. "A man may not be in two places at the one time, *a graidh.* And I had to find you."

The young woman bit her lip, her cherished composure sadly upset. "I am responsible, then! I may be responsible for the deaths of men, of many men! These men that you have brought from Larravaig—they are no warriors. You know it. Without you, they will be as sheep before the shearers. Cormac and his ruffians will mow them down like corn. And it will be my doing!"

222

The other shook his head. "It is not just so bad as that, I think, Marsala. Cormac will not find all just as he planned it. The Mackenzies are gone back to Kintail. Cormac's legions have melted like snow in the sun—in the fire! The heroes of Nicol Spliugach will not have to work miracles, at all."

"But they still will have to fight Cormac's own people. They will break, without you."

"I am honoured, my dear," Colin said, with a hint of a smile. "And gratified that you are so concerned for our cause."

Impatiently the girl brushed that aside. "You must go, Colin—at once. I will not be responsible for more trouble, more bloodshed, than I have been already. I do not know what hour it is—but you cannot be back at Ardcoll in time, as it is. Not by noon. You must make haste—the lives of men depend on it."

"The lives of men depend on their own stout hearts and their own right arms," Colin asserted. "It is not for . . ."

"But the responsibility is yours and mine!" the other insisted, and her interruption was the measure of her urgency. "Yours, because you brought them here, to fight in your cause. Mine, because . . . because by my action, apparently, I have left them leaderless in the hour of their peril. . . ."

"They have Tormaid and Sorley Dam," the man pointed out.

"Tormaid is an amiable windbag—and the other no more than a hireling, and a scoundrel at that!"

Colin blinked. This was a new Marsala indeed, and very sure of herself for a young woman lost in the wilderness. "And my own self?" he enquired, mildly.

"You . . . you are an obstinate and foolish man, who has raised the Devil, and now must lay him!" she returned spiritedly. "Come, you." And grasping his sleeve, she started off.

Smiling and sighing in one, the man came. "And where would we be going, at all, Marsala?" he wondered.

"To Aranbeg, to get a boat."

"Very well so," he agreed. "Only, in that case, we would be better, I think, to be going the other road!" And disengaging his arm, he took hers in turn, and drew her round. "This way, *a graidh*," he said, and led her in exactly the opposite direction, approximately whence they had come.

In time, of course, and out of much casting about and reconnoitring, they found their way to Aranbeg. It would be strange country indeed that could have wandered Colin Og MacColl for long in broad daylight. After a deal of bog-hopping, burnfollowing, and peering from the tops of identical hillocks, they managed to find that broader stream that had conducted Colin to Aranbeg during the night, his footsteps still visible here and there along its banks.

At the township, dishevelled and mud-spattered, Colin asserted his authority. A boat he must have, in the name of An Colin Mor, with four stout rowers, to row this lady to Eynart, and to deliver her safely to her father's house. The tacksman of the place must see to it.

The tacksman was not so foolish as to object.

The girl protested that the urgency lay with Colin. The boat should be to take him to Ardcoll. It was late forenoon already. He must make haste.

Colin shook his head. With the wind westerly, they would be hours pulling along the peninsula to Ardcoll. Let him have, instead, the fleetest-footed garron in Aranbeg, and he would do the journey in half the time.

The tacksman, glad to be rid of him, found him a pony of his own, and agreed to send a boy to fetch in Colin's own tethered beast from the hills. And since it takes less time to produce a pony than four rowers in a boat, Colin Og was ready to leave Aranbeg sooner than was Marsala. She would not hear of him waiting to see her embarked.

Under the interested regard of the tacksman and most of the inhabitants of the township, their distinguished and unexpected visitors took leave of each other.

"You will convey to your father my duty and my respects," Colin said gravely. "And it is my hope that you will speak as well of me to him, Marsala, as your charity will allow."

The girl inclined her head. "Yes," she said.

"And you may, in time, I hope, in your own mind, come to think less ill of—of an obstinate and foolish man, I think it was . . . ?"

"Yes," she repeated, to the toes of her shoes. Then she looked up, quickly. "Colin," she said, "you will be careful . . . ?"

"Careful? Careful of what, *a graidh*? Of the Larravaigach? Of Cormac? Of my honour—or just of my skin?"

"Of . . . of yourself, just, Colin. Do not be doing the foolish thing, the unnecessary thing. Do not be pushing yourself into danger . . ."

"But . . . Sweet Mary—is that not what you are rushing me back for? To lead these cattle-dealers—in the forefront of the battle! I am to hurry to their aid, to save them from defeat— but to be careful!"

Marsala shook her head. "It is difficult, I know . . . But try, please. Oh, why must this fighting be necessary, at all?"

"As well ask why the good God had to drive Lucifer and his angels out of Heaven," Colin answered modestly.

The young woman's eyes widened at that, as well they might. "Oh," she said. Somewhere between laughter and tears, she gulped, "Colin—you are . . . you are . . ." Helplessly her head wagged. "You are just . . . Colin!"

Surprised, he raised his brows. "Yourself it was that wanted to know," he pointed out.

"Yes. Yes. Myself, indeed. There was something else that I wanted to know, too. Something that you said." She gestured a hand towards the hills behind them. "Back there. This morning. I . . . ." The girl glanced at the faces of the tacksman and the other interested watchers, and sighed. "But not now. I cannot ask you now. Go you, Colin—before I tell you *not* to go, at all!"

For a moment their eyes met, and held fast. Above them, the screaming gulls made their plaint, and below them the making tide sighed deeply. Then, as by a physical effort, Colin lowered his glance, and nodded briefly.

"Yes. Time it is that I was gone," he said, and his voice had a harshness to it. "God be with us both. Goodbye." Vaulting on to the garron's broad back, he slapped its rump, and was off. And over his shoulder, he threw back at the young woman. "And if it is Cormac that comes, one day, seeking you at the door of Eynart House, say you a prayer for my soul—and for your own!"

He did not look back, again.

XIX

THE man did not ride back as he had come, but headed his beast northwards and even east a little, inland, following a well-defined track. This was Aranbeg's only landward link with the rest of the world, and eventually, after four or five miles, it joined the drove road down the centre of the peninsula, not far above the Lairig Garve. Colin reckoned that he would be quicker to take this dog-legged route rather than the shorter, more direct, course across country. Considering the terrain, no doubt but he was right.

Keeping the pony at a steady if uncomfortably stiff-legged canter, he made good time until the steepening ascent reduced the garron to a trot, to a walk. The long lift to the watershed was a trial to man and beast. But this was the worst of the journey, and Colin drew on such patience as he could summon. Crossing the high peatlands thereafter, by an only sketchy track, offered little opportunity for making up time, but when at length the path started to dip towards the main axial valley of Eorsary, he could give his mount its head. He was not finished with his climbing yet, of course, for he was still on the wrong side of the Lairig pass, but once on the drove road both the gradients and the surface were easier, and the ascent to the pass no more than a mile in length.

By the time that the man finally reached the summit of the Lairig, the sun, he perceived, was past its zenith. Past noon— and he was still fifteen miles from Ardcoll. Slapping his pony into a canter again, he drove on downhill, the gravel flying.

It was a gallant beast that Aranbeg had found for him, and Colin drove it unmercifully. In a lather of sweat and foam they ate up the miles of that long twisting glen, beside the no-less-urgent and foaming Coll River. Not once did the pace fall below a trot.

With three or four miles still to go, the brute was foundered.

The stocky Highland garron is not built for speed. He was coming into populated country now, fortunately. Clattering up to the first farmstead that he came to, Colin flung himself off his steaming, heaving mount, demanded the best animal that the alarmed tenant possessed, and in less than five minutes was off again.

This beast was a heavier lumbering smoke-grey, ungainly but tough and long-winded. It would serve.

He had covered perhaps another two miles when he began to hear the noise, above the hoofbeats and the refrain of the river. It was a confused sound, that rose and fell and rose again, a sound that that man knew of old, and only liked in certain circumstances. And since it seemed to be growing in intensity, coming nearer, he did not like it now. A running fight has a sound of its own.

A running fight was perhaps an overambitious description of what confronted Colin Og as he rounded the last great bend on the glen before it began to open out towards the head of the loch. A mob of men, some mounted but more afoot, was streaming towards him, strung out along the road in the valley floor, and it would only be fair and accurate to say that a great many more were running than were fighting. In fact, any fighting that was going on, not unnaturally, was taking place at the rear of that straggling company, very far to the rear. Colin's brows were black as he lashed his beast onwards. No special perspicacity was demanded to identify the runners.

As the first of the headlong pack, horsemen as was only to be expected, came up with him, Colin Og reined his garron across the road, and whipped out his broadsword.

"Fools!" he cried. "Dolts! Cravens! Is this how you prove yourselves? Think you that you can run all the way back to Larravaig? Stand, you! You are in a narrow place, and can hold it. Stand, I say!"

At sight of Colin, and more particularly at sight of his flashing sword, the firstcomers might conceivably have been prepared to halt. But they were pushed on by the press behind so that their retreat was only slowed a little.

Furiously Colin gestured with his sword-tip. "Back, scum!" he roared. "Hold, I tell you! I skewer any man that tries to pass!"

A medley of shouts greeted that, protests, contumely, threats. If the foremost escapers were impressed by his commands, those a little farther back were less so—being farther from his naked steel. There was considerable pressure from the rear, physical and vocal. One big fellow on a black horse, in especial, was vehement for progress, decrying the waverers in front, and pushing forward himself. He waved a heavy cutlass above his head in highly menacing fashion, shouting his opinion of chiefs who deserted their clansmen in the hour of battle.

Colin did not wait for this bold Badenocher. Digging his mount with his knees, he plunged to meet him. The cutlass came down, but slashed only empty air, and the point of Colin's broadsword ran through the fellow's thigh. But not too far through. Even as the man's scream shrilled high, the blade was whipped out, and without pause it flickered sideways and down to slash the upraised arm of an individual who was taking the opportunity to slip by on foot on the other flank. A second screech rose to mingle with the first.

Colin's shout lifted, likewise. "The next gets it through his yellow heart!" he yelled. "No man passes here. MacColls you are—remember it! Turn you, and fight."

It was probably the screaming, and the sight of the red-stained questing blade, that held them, rather than his exhortations. At all events, there was a noticeable cessation of forward movement, a considerable physical if not moral confusion, and then much pushing, jostling, and pressing back.

Colin took full advantage of it, driving his garron in amongst the struggling throng, and laying about him with the flat of his sword, heartily. "Back!" he bawled. "Turn and fight, damn you! Up MacColl! Eat meat, Son of Colin!"

It would be too much to say, perhaps, that he actually turned the tide. But certainly he checked the onward flow, and set at least some proportion of the flood into a vaguely reverse movement. He came across the somewhat shamefaced Laird of

Lochinch amongst the press, forbore just in time to belabour him with his sword, and ordered him instead, fiercely, to collect this disgraceful rabble and bring it along in some order behind him. Without waiting for discussion, or even to see his instructions carried out, he pressed disdainfully on.

Thus he rode down that half-mile of choken glen, flailing, smiting, reviling, commanding. And he had his effect; at least, all men knew that Colin Og MacColl was now returned.

The actual fighting, when he came to it, was a minor and comparatively tame affair. No more than fifty or so men were involved, all told—less than a score of Sorley's veterans, retiring shoulder to shoulder in the face of twice their number of Cormac's people. So tightly packed were they, on their garrons, between the river and the hillside, that, precious little of elbow-room being available to either side, no great deal of fighting was going on at all, most of the shrewdest thrusts being verbal, apparently. In this wordy warfare, Father Tormaid, centrally placed, was very prominent, as, his robes kilted up around his waist, and using his sword more to beat time to his sonorous periods than anything else, his great voice boomed and echoed in declamation, vilification, and prophetic utterance generally. Undoubtedly, the principal target for this eloquence was the notably crooked person of Iain Cam MacColl of the Cairn, who seemed to be in command of the attacking party, and whose angry rejoinders did no more than punctuate the priest's rhetoric. Similar contests appeared to be in progress on either hand. There was a most obvious lack of powder and shot about the entire scene.

Colin changed all that, changed it with remarkable rapidity. Without waiting for challenges, greetings, or explanations, he dashed in amongst Sorley's horsemen, dashed through them, tight-pressed as they were. Shouting his scorn and fury, he forced his way on past the stalwart rearguard, past the mouthing Tormaid, and drove on, straight for Iain Cam.

"Blackguard!" he cried. "Miscreant! Stone-roller! Crooked soul in a crooked body! Your sword . . . ! Colin Og will honour you with his steel!"

Iain Wryface was a professional swordsman, and other things besides—but he was no fool. Honour troubled him nothing, and he knew that single combat was not to his side's advantage. Whatever the outcome, it would give time to the sore-pressed rearward and to the fleeing rabble, possibly give heart as well. And while he might well dispose of the arrogant Colin Og himself, most certainly he could be disposed of more efficaciously by a concerted assault. And once he was suitably brought low, the opposition would collapse entirely, without a doubt. So, instead of spurring forward to meet the most personal challenge, he gestured right and left to his supporters, in clearest urgency, his import plain.

He reckoned, however, without two factors, or three. Colin's reputation, the clansmen's inborn respect for the idea of individual champions—and, not least, the precipitancy of Colin Og's approach. Even whilst the issues thus jostled for decision, the challenger was upon them. With one accord the warriors drew their beasts in, and allowed their leader the full honour of the situation.

Colin struck out with his sword even as he same up with his chosen opponent. But he was dealing with no cattleman, no clumsy novice, this time. Iain Cam had learned his swording in the foreign wars, and at little over forty was spry enough to make excellent use of what he knew. He gave an admirable indication of his agility, now. As he perceived the blow that was coming, he hurled himself bodily sideways, off his horse, to fall on all fours on the far side of it, while the sweeping stroke that could have ended the fight before it began came down on his unfortunate garron's haunch, laying it open. As the brute reared, Iain Cam scrambled away from its lashing hooves, to crouch, sword in one hand, dirk in the other. And even as Colin slewed round his own beast to face him, the older man, with a remarkable exhibition of sleight-of-hand, appropriate only to an expert card-player, switched weapons from one fist to the other, and in almost the same movement threw up the right hand and hurled that dagger. Colin glimpsed

231

the gleam of it in the sunlight, and twisted away violently. But barely in time. The dirk took him in his left shoulder, pinning his plaid to him. Gasping, Colin dropped his left hand to his side, his own dirk falling from nerveless fingers.

"You fight . . . like the rest of you—crooked!" he panted. Then, jerking his head round, he gripped the black haft of the other's knife in his teeth, and dragged it out of his shoulder and the folds of his plaid, shuddering convulsively. And as Iain Cam stooped to draw his *sgian dubh* from his hose-top, Colin threw himself from his garron and launched himself directly at the other, sword flickering.

Wryface had his blade up to meet him, though he gave ground a couple of paces. Their points met, and shrilled.

"Dastard!" Colin said, with force to make up for his lack of clarity—for he still held the other's dirk between his clenched teeth. "Hangman—prepare . . . to die!"

His opponent said nothing, though his jaws worked.

But while their mutual hatred and lethal purpose was thus emphatically displayed, the two men were wary now. Each had a measure of the other's calibre and agility. Their blades crossing and darting and weaving, they sparred for an opening. The blood ran down and dripped from the fingers of Colin's left hand.

Iain Cam saw an opening, and lunged. The other leapt back, parried the stroke, and thrust in turn. Wryface sidestepped, feinted for Colin's throat, abruptly ducked down, and drove upwards with a vicious left-handed thrust of his dagger. With a lightning-swift kick that all but overbalanced him, the younger man brought his foot up against the other's wrist, with a force that drew a yelp from the man's lips, and sent the little knife spinning away in a glittering arc. Odds were more even, now.

Panting, the contestants circled each other, both drooping their left shoulders somewhat. On either side, the ranks of their supporters stared tensely. More and more of the Larravaigers were drifting back down the glen to join the watchers. The screak of cold steel, whistled breathing, and the stamp of feet were all the sounds to be heard above the rush of the river.

Colin perceived only the one weakness in his opponent's swordplay. His recovery from the fully extended thrust tended to be a little slow—possibly the result of one of the many old wounds with which his person was disfigured. To play on that weakness must be his cue. . . .

And then the unexpected happened. Wryface's pony, wounded and held by one of his troop, suddenly took fright. It reared, broke loose, and cannoned into Colin's back, sending him staggering sideways. Losing his balance, he involuntarily thrust out his hand to save himself—his sword hand, since the other was incapacitated. The weapon's point drove into the ground, struck stone, and, as Colin's toppling weight bore down on it, the blade bent, arched, and snapped like a musket shot. He fell, clutching in his hand the hilt and three inches of his sword.

The quivering sigh that arose from the ranked watchers was pierced by a strident shout, Tormaid's shout. Part warning, part encouragement, part diversion it was. Colin did not require the warning; he could see Iain Cam coming at him with a rush, point lowered. But the encouragement and the diversion were more than moral or merely vocal. Tormaid was waving his own sword around his head, and as his foster-brother looked up, he tossed it, hilt-first, through the air. Spinning, it missed the advancing Wryface by inches, and clattered to the ground beside the only half-risen Colin. That man grabbed it in mid-blade, lurched back a staggering pace or two, and with an explosive jerk of the wrist launched it, javelin-like, at his assailant. Iain Cam, almost upon him, arm outstretched to run him through, took Tormaid's sword through his middle, yittered his agony, and cringing, fell forward with his own impetus, driving the point right through him, and collapsed transfixed.

The entire abrupt incident took only a matter of brief moments—less time than it takes to tell. Fewer than thirty seconds after his pony's rearing, Iain Cam MacColl of the Cairn was little better than a twitching corpse.

Colin Og raised an open hand. "So fall all . . ." He stopped,

233

and removed his victim's *sgian dubh*, which he found to be still between his teeth. "So fall all who would raise their hands against the great and noble Colin Mor!" he declaimed, if a little breathlessly. And in a different voice. "My thanks, Tormaid." He handed the dirk to Sorley Dam to mercifully put Iain Cam out of his misery, and turned to face the latter's supporters, with further good advice.

But only their backs and their horses' tails, he saw. Discreetly and unanimously the chase had decided that in a new and transformed situation, further instructions were required from higher authority. They dutifully and at speed proceeded to seek it.

Shrugging, and swaying a little, Colin sat down rather suddenly, a hand vaguely to his head. But his voice was still authoritative. "Tormaid, man—come you and look to this shoulder of mine," he directed. "And you can tell me, at the same time, what for you were running up Glen Coll, and where you were going, at all!"

So while the priest poured some whisky into the wound and then bandaged it up in rough-and-ready fashion, his foster-brother was told, with only a modicum of implied reproach, how MacColl clansmen had been arriving at Ardcoll all morning, a little uncertain as to whose side they were going to support, but with judicious eyes as to comparative chances; how Cormac, with a solid phalanx of about four score had issued from Duncolin at prompt noon, with considerable display and circumstance; how the ranks of Larravaig had waited and waited for their leader, and how the word had gone round, eventually, that Colin Og was dead and the cause lost. Cormac had apparently got word of this, and decided to strike at once. Without warning, he had led his cohort to the attack, whilst the assembled MacColl clansmen had to a man stood aside to watch, and the unhappy ranks of Larravaig had broken and crumbled and fled. Only the score of Sorley's veterans had put up a fight, and retired in good order. Curiously, Cormac himself had ceased to pursue them very soon, leaving this Iain Cam and his two score bravoes to follow them up, while he fell back on Ardcoll. It was Tormaid's opinion that Cormac suspected that Colin's absence portended a trap of some sort, and he was taking no risks. Also, he probably still was unaware of the Mackenzie rout, and imagined that the fleeing Larravaigach would fall straight into Kintail's hands. But it had been a bad business, for all that, and a sore disappointment. If Marsala Macleod was . . .

Colin Og, getting to his wide-planted feet, indicated that Marsala Macleod could be left out of it. He took Iain Cam's sword in distasteful lieu of his own, and lurched over to his smoke-grey pony. "What are we waiting for?" he wanted to know, and throwing his long leg over its back, he set the brute into its heavy canter once more. Behind him his henchmen looked at each other, shrugged, and turned their beasts to follow him whence they had so lately and stubbornly come.

Emerging from the constriction of the glen into the open amphitheatre of the hills that cradled Loch Coll, it was to perceive across the marshy flats at the head of the loch, that Cormac had indeed withdrawn his people to Ardcoll itself, whereinto the last of Wryface's riders were now streaming.

Colin paused, to summon up Rob Molach. "If Cormac expects a trap, then we must encourage him," he declared. "Go you, Rob man, up to the top of yonder knoll, and light a fire, a smoky fire. More smoke signals, see you. Light two. And, Sorley—send you two of your ruffians to ride right round the rear of Ardcoll, there and into the small glens beyond, to the north. Let them ride not over-far out—they are to be seen, mark you. They can start waving as they enter the glens. We can ill spare them, but Cormac may well take it that we are communicating with forces behind him, and that he is threatened from the north. Off with them, now. Away! Tormaid—you said that Cormac had but four score or so of his hirelings, and that our MacColl clansfolk were hanging back? We have less than one score of good men—but some of these Larravaig heroes may rediscover their manhood. Where is Alan the Stutterer?"

"The good God knows! I have not seen him since the fighting commenced. And many another. But some of our own MacColls may decide to fight, when they see that yourself is here."

"And the galley slaves? Where are they?"

"That also is a secret of the Most High. I have not smelt so much as the stink of them," Tormaid admitted. "Nor many of these Larravaigach. They are not all behind us in the glen, there. . . ."

Colin shook his head. "You are a better priest than a general, brother," he mentioned briefly. "On with us, then, with God's help!"

"Amen—and us requiring it all!" the other agreed fervently.

"Faith! Faith is what you require," Colin reproved. "You for a churchman! Is Cormac MacColl less easy to remove than a mountain?"

So they rode on, in full view of Ardcoll. Twenty staunch men, with behind them, a fair distance behind them, a scattering of perhaps a hundred very doubtful Larravaigers, who looked backwards as much as they looked forwards. And at their backs two columns of brown smoke arose from a birch-clad knoll, whilst away to the right a pair of horsemen galloped headlong around the flank.

Cormac, in Ardcoll, might well be puzzled.

As they neared the township they could see the black mass of people watching, waiting. But there was more than waiting afoot. To the rear, there was commotion, and presently it was clear that half a dozen mounted men had been dispatched to try to intercept the two messengers.

"Six less to deal with, anyhow," Colin commented grimly.

But there were more detachments than this. A compact body of horsemen was seen to be leaving Ardcoll from the opposite side, heading north by east towards the small glens that opened on that side. The actual number was difficult to count, but Colin assessed it as a score at least. Cormac, obviously, was nervous about his rear. For the expenditure of two men and a little flint and tinder, the results were excellent. But so much

236

more was required. . . .

They rode on, unspeaking. Less than half a mile separated the opposing companies.

Then, there was an unlooked-for diversion. From up on the hill that rose due east of the township, that same Beinn Buie whereon Rob Molach had once signalled the departure of Cormac's galley on its wild-goose chase—a long halloo came down to them, followed by a prodigious hailing. Up there, from scrub woodland, men were emerging, many men, all waving and apparently all shouting.

Tormaid it was who first perceived the implications of the situation. "The Stutterer, it is! And the galley slaves . . . and the rest of the Larravaigach! They have been hiding up there. And is not that Angus Macdougall's bellow? They have recognized you . . . And, see you—they are coming down to us!"

It was true. Out from the wood they streamed, to come running and leaping downhill, in no sort of order but in a great hurry, a thudding undisciplined loud-voiced rabble. And there was a great lot of them, none mounted.

Colin stared. "There are hundreds!" he said.

"Fifty galley slaves," Tormaid told him. "Perhaps half of the Badenochers, a score or more of loose men, the mariners from the ship . . ."

But Colin was not listening. He had switched his gaze to the front again, to Ardcoll. They were near enough to see the effect of this on the watching throng. People were hurrying away from that end of the township nearest to this avalanche of humanity. Mainly, these would be the indwellers there, and the assembled clansmen. But they obviously thought that this was a charge, a concerted attack. They would see their mistake, presently, no doubt—discover that this noisy horde was not plunging down in assault upon Ardcoll, but was merely hastening to get back to comparative safety behind the shield of their leader and his bodyguard. But Cormac's fighting-men, even perhaps Cormac himself, might be making the same mistake. . . .

Colin swung round, slapping his bare knee, his laughter a

237

bark. "Mary Mother—it is worth a trial!" he cried. "Tormaid—there is faith for you! There is the mountain moving—moving down to us! Did I not tell you? Look you— these fools here only want to shelter behind us, but those fools there think that they are for attacking them! It may be that they think that these are new allies. We will strike now, before they discover otherwise!" He raised his voice, and his sword above his head, "Come you, my children! On with us! Follow me!" and kicked his garron into a gallop.

Behind him, even if they did not quite rise to a gallop, the valiant twenty followed obediently. Their hoofbeats drummed impressively on the ground, a confident and self-encouraging sound. All the same, Colin Og drew rather noticeably ahead. It was as well, perhaps, that they had no great distance to cover.

However, the waiting warriors in Ardcoll apparently were sufficiently impressed. There was considerable shouting, hub-bub, and running hither and thither. But in the general commotion, one more coherent trend, one positive movement, was discernible. It was the more disciplined body of Cormac's hirelings moving from the comparative constriction of the township down to the open space before the castle. Seeing it, Colin cursed, and swung his mount's head a little to the left, thitherwards. If Cormac was going to ground, in Duncolin . . . !

Though, eventually, his brother's minions paused, wheeled, and drew up in a solid phalanx a few hundred yards from the castle drawbridge, it was obvious that Cormac was taking no chances. He was no coward, but like many another commander before him, he suffered a certain restriction of manoeuvre out of preoccupation with his own personal irreplaceability. And no doubt he considered that the present situation merited caution. His wretched brother seemed to be very confident; and it looked as though he had reinforcements to the north, as well as this host that was hurtling down on them from Beinn Buie; there was no sign of the looked-for Mackenzies; and he himself had lost his lieutenant Iain Cam, with consequent loss of morale amongst the men whom that man had led. Also, the assembled MacColl clansmen seemed much more disposed to be interested spectators of events than to draw sword on his behalf. Cormac's cause being Cormac's person, and Duncolin his trump card, it behoved him to play his hand judiciously.

Colin held no trump card, but a fairly strong conviction that in war as in love, victory very often went to the bold. In token of which, he rode straight for the ranks of Cormac's bodyguard before the castle, straight for Cormac himself, signing to his supporters to form themselves into a tight wedge behind him. Thus, grimly, in compact formation, driving like a spear-point, they thundered across the sea turf to the waiting ranks of the enemy, Colin's sword waving.

The clash of that meeting was sensationally impressive— especially upon the front ranks of the defenders, which would have been wiser to open out and let the assault through, and to close in thereafter as the charge spent itself. Men and horses went down like ninepins, in screaming, lashing confusion. Swordplay, other than a wild hacking and slashing, was impossible. That Colin himself was not unhorsed was largely due to the fact that, as point of the wedge, he and his mount were held up by the very press into which they drove, as well as by the pressure from behind. His sword was like a flail about him, and his shouting rang like a pealing bell.

Cormac's fifty-odd came ill out of that wild trampling onslaught, being trained for shipboard fighting and individual thuggery rather than for cavalry tactics. They gave ground, many went down, while more got in the way of their fellows, so that fully half of the total were unable to engage the enemy. Inevitably they broke in the centre, and the attackers were through. Immediately, Colin swung round, right-handed, waving his cohort behind him, to concentrate on that portion that contained Cormac. His eye never off his brother, he bored in like an arrowhead, and at his back Sorley's ruffians, perceiving the strategy, kept tight company, and had only their flanks to look to. Precisely in the midst of them, Tormaid, with a growing and welcome sense of security, raised his great voice in resonant exhortation.

This performance had a very similar result to its predecessor. Once again the band round Cormac was split in twain, and Colin wheeled his close-knit formation relentlessly on the section that held his brother. Only a dozen or so men it contained, now, and anxious men at that. Tormaid mentioned afterwards, modestly, that it had just been as easy as chopping sticks, whatever. And of the lopped-off segments of Cormac's troop, only a few were assailing the attackers' rear, the others, leaderless and lacking enthusiasm, tending to become preoccupied by the clamorous rabble that was now coming up in the rear, led by Angus Macdougall and Alan Liogach.

Even on the third drive into his brother's reduced escort, Colin did not let his wedge break up, though they now outnumbered the men around Cormac. Balefully, doggedly, his eye was fixed on his target, not to be diverted nor deflected. And his target knew it. As his last dozen wilted and disintegrated around him, Cormac recognized the inadvisability of allowing this process to develop further. With his brother only separated from him by a yard or so and a single devoted horseman, he pulled his only too ready mount's head around, drove in his heels, and plunged off in the direction of Duncolin's drawbridge. Colin, ignoring the intervening warrior, at the cost of a glancing blow that laid open his sword arm from shoulder to elbow, spurred on after his brother, leaving the fellow for Sorley's attention. And as he rode, gasping with exertion and with pain, he cried:

"Stand, Cormac! Wait, you! Stop, I say!" Desperately he urged on his garron, and desperately he hurled his appeals at the other's back. "Stand . . . for the clan's sake! For your own honour's sake—for the honour of our father's name . . . !"

But Cormac was shouting too, shouting to the door-ward of Duncolin to get the drawbridge moving. His mind, clear as to the vital issue, even in the red confusion of battle, was not to be bemused by any fool's talk about honour and suchlike. His honour would undoubtedly be much more secure within Duncolin's thick walls. And there was only a bare three hundred yards to go.

Colin's spurring was no more efficacious than was his shouting. His brother's horse was entirely fresh, and a better beast into the bargain. Indeed, another of Cormac's henchmen actually passed Colin, at an angle, imbued with similar ambitions to those of his master. The door-ward, with prompt obedience, had his drawbridge rising slowly as Cormac thundered up. He put his horse to the widening gap, leapt it, the beast's hooves slithering as it landed on the slanting timbers of the bridge, but managed to retain his seat as they slid down on to the safety of the castle rock. His minion was less fortunate. Arriving three or four seconds later, with the drawbridge steadily lifting, his garron balked at the difficult upward jump, and the rider, leaping off, ran and flung himself bodily across the yawning gap. He reached the edge of the bridge, but only with his chest and arms. The thing checked its rising, but at Cormac's yelled order to continue, rose again, the angle steepening. The man could not pull himself up. His grip slipped and slipped, and with the now inexorably lifting bridge two-thirds of the way to the perpendicular, his arms could hold him no longer. With a despairing scream, the wretch fell down and down, to boiling surf and rocks below.

And on the lip of rock, Colin pulled up his sweating pony to its haunches, and burst into impotent and furious inco-herencies. He shook his blood-dripping fist, sword and all, at those frowning walls, and knew the bitter salt anguish of frustration and failure. And from Duncolin's rock his brother's hateful laughter echoed, shaky but clear.

"Give me but five minutes, Colin my heart," he called, "and I will send you to hell with a culverin ball, and all the pleasure in the world!"

XX

"H'R'R'MMM," said Tormaid, at his foster-brother's angry back. "I know just how you are feeling, see you, and you with the rights of it. But with a lady present . . ."

Colin completed what he was saying with emphasis and increasing eloquence. He was starting afresh, when his voice faltered. "A lady . . . ?" he wondered, and swung round. "By the Holy Mother—Marsala!" he cried.

"Yes, Colin," the girl said, almost apologetically.

He stared at her, seeking for words. "But, how . . . ? Where . . . ? Why are you not at your father's house?"

"I changed my mind," she declared, small-voiced.

"You . . . you changed your mind! The saints have mercy! But how came you here . . . ?"

"By boat to Drumbain, and then on foot and by pony."

"You did! And why, in Ninian's name, did those scoundrels at Aranbeg not do as I told them, and row you to Eynart? I . . ."

"Because I am afraid, Colin, that I countermanded your orders . . . in the name of An Colin Mor," she informed, eyes downcast. "In the same way that I got the pony at Coul . . ."

"Well, may I be damned!" the man requested. "You tell me . . . ?" He shook his head—but quickly desisted, with the pain of it. For some reason or other, he had a headache. "And why?" he demanded. "*Why* did you do all this? *Why* did you change your mind?"

"Because . . . well, I had something to ask you, you see."

"You had something to ask me!" As a man to a man, Colin turned to Tormaid. "She had something to ask me! So she, she . . ." He raised his right hand to push the bonnet back from his brow, helplessly—and thereupon revealed the unsightly gash that ran from shoulder to elbow, that had been hidden hitherto in the folds of his plaid.

"Colin!" The young woman's voice changed, heightened. "You are hurt! Your arm, your hand . . ." And she started forward.

He glanced at it, for the first time, and shrugged. "A mischance," he commented. "Just an accident." But he let her take and examine his arm.

"One of Cormac's bullyrooks was more ambitious with his sword than was his master . . ." Tormaid was explaining, when he was interrupted.

"It was an accident," Colin repeated, with asperity. "An Colin Og does not cross swords with such as that!" Perhaps involuntarily, he drew himself up.

"Hold your arm still," the young woman directed, evidently unimpressed. "This is a wicked wound."

"A mere scratch," the sufferer protested.

"He has another in his left shoulder," Tormaid mentioned. "If you . . ."

"Quiet, windbag!" Colin growled.

"You must come over to the priest's house, and have this dressed," Marsala announced. "At once. There is no . . ."

"What was it that you came to ask me?" the man intervened.

She shook her head. "That can wait. This wound cannot. You must come, at once."

As though to reinforce her command, a hail came to them from the castle rock. "A pretty scene, 'pon my soul! A pity to spoil it with a cannon ball! Go you, brother, and take that camp-following trull with you, or I shall be brotherless and widowed both before I am much older, I promise you! I go up, now—and I can lay a culverin as well as any cannoneer!"

"Does that jackal still yelp!" Colin demanded. He raised his voice. "You are more ready with your threats than with your sword, Cormac!" he shouted. "But you will pay for that ill word against Marsala Macleod, I swear to you. It will be the last thing that you eat before you die. . . ."

But Cormac had disappeared through the door of Duncolin, that clanged shut behind him. Colin turned to Tormaid.

"His hirelings . . . ?" he questioned, with the merest glance

243

backwards. "They are being attended to?"

"Sorley has the matter in hand," the priest assured. "No trouble at all, they are, and most of them racing the Mackenzies to Kintail! Cormac is going to be the lonely man in Duncolin, this night. He cannot have more than the old door-ward and the shameless priest, and maybe Alan Glas the cook, left to him, I think."

"It is enough," Colin almost snarled. "He has escaped us—that is the kernel of it. So long as that fox is earthed up in Duncolin, we have failed in our task. And I nearly had him . . ."

"Better come to the priest's house, Colin," Marsala interposed. "I will look to your arm."

"I will not run from Cormac's culverin," her patient declared, stubbornly. "But you go. Tormaid, take you Marsala. She will be safe there."

"I did not come here to be safe . . ." she began.

"No—you came to ask me something! What was it, Marsala?"

"I . . . it is not important," the girl said.

"Important enough to keep you from going to your father's house—that you ran away from me to do!"

"Yes, but . . . well, the situation is not suitable."

"Why not? What ails you, woman?"

She glanced around her. "It is . . . we are not alone. It is for your ear, only."

"Tormaid," Colin mentioned, "be off. Away with you. And these others, too." And he resumed possession of his damaged arm sufficiently to wave away the circle of interested watchers, much as though they had been domestic poultry. "Shoo!" he said. "Your question, Marsala?"

Frowning, she considered first the rather prominent point of his chin, very bristly, and then the muddy toes of her shoes. "You are extremely, wickedly, obstinate," she asserted.

"Yes," he acceded, patiently. "What was it that you wished to ask me?"

Marsala sighed, helplessly. "It was . . . it was about something that you said when you found me this morning. When I was lost."

"Yes?" he prompted.

"When you came to me, you said . . . you said things that you had never said before. You said . . . well, I wanted to know what you meant by what you said."

He wrinkled his brows at her. "What I say, I mean, *a graidh*—to you, especially. What did I say?"

The girl looked away. "Do you not remember, then? If you do not, then perhaps my question is answered, already!" Her voice levelled again.

Inexorably, he put it to her. "What did I say, Marsala?"

"You said . . . oh, foolish things, it may be. You said that I was your, your pigeon, your little trout, even. Foolish things, indeed. . . ."

"I said more than that, I think," the man added, quietly now.

His changed tone caused her to look up, quickly. "You said that I was your heart, your delight," she agreed, strain evident in every word.

"And why not, at all?" Colin demanded, simply. "The truth it is—and less than the truth."

He heard her breath catch, but she said nothing.

The man's brows puckered a little. "But what was it that you wanted to ask me?" he wondered.

Almost she sobbed. "Can it be that you do not know?" the young woman cried. "Surely it is obvious! I wanted to know if you meant what you said, when you said . . . those things!"

"You did not come all this long road to ask me *that*?" he questioned, incredulously.

"Why not? It may mean much to me, you see. I had to know. . . ."

"But surely you did not need to ask that? Always it has been that way, with me. Always you have been my heart's delight. Always *my* feelings have never been in doubt."

"But never have you said so!" Marsala exclaimed.

He stared. "Have not I proved it, every day in these last months?" he charged. "Has not my every action shouted it aloud? Does not all the world know that An Colin Og wants to make you his wife!"

"His wife, yes. All the world knows that, indeed! But that is Macleod of Eynart's daughter that is to be wed—by yourself or by Cormac, or by whosoever rules Clan Colin. It is the Eynart Macleods that you are for wedding, not myself, Marsala! Myself, I am just a pawn in your game, something to be married so that the MacColls' rear may be secure. . . ." Impassioned at last, breathless with the violent release of her long pent-up hurt and distress and resentment, the young woman trembled, her knuckles white. "I am to be bargained for, fought over, dragged about the country, threatened, and—and harried—but not for myself, not for anything that is *me*—only because I am Torquil Macleod's only child and heiress! This has been my fate, my life . . ." She tossed her head and the hair from her white brow. "Oh," she cried, "I . . . I hate you—hate you all, hate the very name of MacColl!"

But Colin Og was not listening; he was looking, instead. "My beloved," he said, "my dark hind of the hills—you are lovely! You are beautiful. Never have I seen you, nor any woman, so beautiful. You are like a storm about a forest pool. You are like the birches tossing in the wind. You are like summer lightning amongst the corries. You are beautiful, I tell you, and I love you with all my heart, with all that is in me! And one day, Marsala Macleod, I will make you love me. I will so. One day, when all this folly is but a bad dream past, and you are your own woman again, I will come to you, and . . ."

"Oh, Colin, you fool, you *fool*!" she interrupted him, and grabbed his arm, that damaged arm, in her extremity. "Can you not see—anyone but a fool would have seen long ago, that I love you now, that I have loved you always! I will never be my own woman again, because I have been yours always—even when I was Cormac's wife! Always yours—if you had held out your hand for me . . . instead of your fist! I . . ."

But she could say no more—she was not permitted to say more. Damaged arm, wounded shoulder, or none, the man held out more than his hand for her, grasped her, and crushed

246

her to him, his lips on her hair, her brow, her eyes, her mouth. They had had enough of words, anyway.

But words came to them, just the same, urgent shouted words, Tormaid the Priest's words. "Colin, man—look you!" he cried. "See—the parapet!"

Colin looked indeed, if reluctantly, to see the semicircle of the interested spectators that he had banished withdrawn only to a hundred yards or so, and as interested as ever. But Tormaid, in its centre, was pointing, and past his foster-brother, to the castle. Colin turned.

Up on Duncolin's parapet-walk, Cormac had appeared, hastening. But he did not seem to be making towards the big culverin—indeed, he was hurrying around the other side of the tower-head altogether. And he was not alone. Staggering after him came another figure, a strange, ungainly and improbable figure, huge, but bent and shambling, and shouting. And its shouting was as extraordinary and alarming as its appearance, a wild and incoherent skirling babble, crazy but menacing. Half-naked but wielding a great sword, this mouthing and gangling giant chased the hurrying Cormac, and his screeching gibberish was the fearsome evidence of his intention. Nemesis was in process of catching up with Cormac MacColl.

Colin's grip on the girl had tightened, and though he said no word the beginnings of a groan escaped from between his tight lips. The corporate shudder that ran through the watching throng almost could be heard as well as felt. But no man, not even Tormaid the Priest, raised the loyal and dutiful cry of An Colin Mor.

Round the parapet-walk of Duncolin the old man chased the young, his yelping laughter and gabbled threats interspersed with strangled sobs, his gaunt and emaciated frame slithering and tripping, his tangled grey hair and long beard streaming wildly in the breeze, a madman for all to behold. But if demented, he was none the less dangerous and determined. And Cormac seemed to be less able, less agile, than was his usual; perhaps he had already suffered something from that avenging brand. He stumbled as he ran and backed and dodged, and he had no weapons in his hands.

Round a crow-stepped gable-end Cormac scurried, his father's sword only two or three yards behind. But as he disappeared, the wreck that was An Colin Mor paused. Then, in an amazing series of convulsions, it somehow flung itself up on to the great stone flags of the roof, clawing and scrambling, balanced for a moment precariously, sword waving, on the ridge, an all but comical picture of malevolent frenzy, and then launched itself downward, beyond.

For a few moments both figures were lost to the view of the watchers, though the unearthly shouting faded nothing. Then Cormac reappeared alone on that part of the parapet-walk that topped the wing of the L-shaped tower, and a quiver of intensified excitement ran through that section of the watching throng that knew Duncolin. This stretch of the battlements, though enhanced with the flagstaff and also the gallows, culminated in a dead end, caused by the projection of the caphouse that covered the stairhead. There was no way out of that lofty cul-de-sac.

That Cormac recognized the fact was clear in every desperate line of him. Darting behind the flagstaff, he sought to keep its bulk between himself and his assailant. Beneath the proud eagle banner of An Colin Mor, fluttering in the breeze, son and father faced each other. But only for a moment. The older man hurled himself forward, sword high. Cormac stooped swiftly, and when he rose something glittered evilly in his hand—obviously a *sgian dubh* whipped from his hose-top. Leaping a couple of paces backward, to avoid the down-drive of that great sword, he flung his dirk. It struck home—it could scarcely do other, at such range—but wherever it struck, it was insufficient to halt the berserk figure of his father. Only, the shrieking rose to a higher pitch, as An Colin Mor lurched on, round the flagstaff.

Cormac had only two or three paces farther to retire, and he was leaning against the parapet itself, the rocks and surging waters far below. But there was one last brief line of retreat, one slender straw at which to clutch. The great boom that thrust out from the wall-head, and acted as gallows-tree for

Duncolin. Frantically, the young man turned, threw himself over the parapet, and began to creep on hands and knees out along that dizzy perch. It was a stout beam, nine or ten inches in thickness, designed to carry a heavy load on occasion, but it made only the most inadequate gallery for a man, even on all fours. Cormac precariously changed his position to a straddling seat, and sought to hitch himself along, over the encircling chains that hung therefrom, some burdened with their rotting fruit, some from which the crop had dropped.

But An Colin Mor apparently cared nothing for danger nor for vertigo. Out on to the boom he clambered, and came reeling drunkenly, every step seeming as though it must be his last, his sword weaving arcs and parabolas above his head. Cormac, staring back over his shoulder, saw that his father, so much swifter, would be upon him in a second or two, and despairingly struggled to his feet again. Swaying horribly, his arms outstretched for balance, he took two or three hurried steps forward. Probably he intended, in this last extremity, to dive off the end of the beam, clear of the rocks below, into deep water. But his foot caught on the second last of the chains looped round the beam, he staggered, and fell forward. His body struck the wood, and madly he scrabbled and clasped to save himself. He would have been better to have let himself fall; he might have cleared the rock and plunged into the water. But his grasping, clutching hands, unable to get a grip on the massive boom, caught on to the chain below as he fell. Down its rusty length they slithered as, feet foremost, he dropped, until with a sickening jolt and a single stabbing scream, he was brought up short. The great hook on the end of that chain had stopped his fall, driving up under his chin, up and up into his brain, and so held. The thing that he had displaced on that hook fell away in pieces to the sea below.

Above, An Colin Mor shouted his baffled maniacal fury, stooped even as he toppled, to lunge at his son beneath, with the sword that had been the terror of the West, and pitched headlong, downwards. Curiously, his anger changed to laughter as he fell. He did not quite avoid the rocks, nor tried to.

A long sigh from the staring company, and a sob in the throat from Colin, was interrupted by Tormaid the Priest's sonorous voice. "An Colin Mor, the mighty and gracious prince, is dead! *Reqiescat in pace!* Terrible in life, he was no less terrible in death, ridding his people of a tyrant and a traitor. May he sleep in honour with a thousand generations of his fathers. God, and the blessed saints, receive his soul!"

Like the sough of waves on shingle came the murmur of agreement from the watchers. "Amen," Colin said, into the hair of the young woman, whose face these last moments had been buried in his chest.

Sorley Dam's bull-like bellow rose above the rest. "An Colin Mor is not dead!" he cried. "An Colin Mor is never dead. There stands Himself—Colin mhic Colin, An Colin Mor, Lord of Ardcoll, Eorsary, Ardtarff, Calinish, the Hundred Glens, and all the Islands of the Sea, Chief of MacColl and all its kindred Septs, Knight of the Holy Manger . . . and the good friend of Sorley mhic Seumas, my God! Long live An Colin Mor!"

"Long live Colin of my heart!" Marsala Macleod whispered, into the storm of acclaim.

Colin MacColl swallowed, and had nothing to say at all.

From somewhere in the rear, an inspired piper said it for him.